SHE OVERHEARD MURDER
A Nic and Nora Mystery

Jean Sheldon

Bast Press

SHE OVERHEARD MURDER
Jean Sheldon

A Nic and Nora Mystery

She Overheard Murder is a work of fiction. Characters, places and events exist only in the author's imagination or are improvised for the story. Resemblances to real occurrences, locations or people, living or dead, are unintended.

Copyright © 2013 by Jean Sheldon. All rights reserved. No part of this book may be reproduced in any form without permission in writing from the publisher except for brief quotations for articles or reviews.

ISBN 13: 978-0-9838136-2-0

Library of Congress Control Number: 2013912339

Published by
Bast Press
an imprint of Wellworth Publishing

www.wellworthpublishing.com
Oregon USA

A Note from the Author

One of the most rewarding aspects of writing historical mysteries for me was the discovery that researching was nearly as fulfilling as writing. In a television interview after the release of my book *The Woman in the Wing,* also set in the 1940s, the host asked if I was a history buff. My response—"I am now." Prior to writing that book, I had a passing interest in history. After studying Rosie the Riveters and Women Airforce Service Pilots, and the work they performed, the interest became a passion. I wanted to know the details.

My desire to share those details took hold when I discovered that at the end of the WASP program, documents and files were sealed and put into storage in the Pentagon. For thirty years, people wrote about WWII without that information and the stories of the women who ferried military planes went unreported. Women's achievements are often under-reported or ignored. Without role models, young girls grow up believing there are things they can't do. Limiting choices and the ability to learn and grow of half the population weakens a society and hurts us all.

I write mysteries, but the stories focus on the strength, resilience, and wisdom of women and men—gay and straight. In *She Overheard Murder,* you will meet the characters of the Nic and Nora Mystery series, a series that, I hope, will entertain, enlighten, and remind you that in all of us, there are more similarities than differences.

Jean

I can only note that the past is beautiful because one never realises an emotion at the time. It expands later, and thus we don't have complete emotions about the present, only about the past.
Virginia Woolf

Chapter 1

"Boy, that was sure close, Inez. If you didn't break that window before we went in, we never would have made it out of the warehouse alive. How did you know?"

"Woman's intuition is highly underrated, Jeff. Let's call it a day. I'm ready to soak in a tub of Modern Woman Bath Oil."

CUE ANNOUNCER

"And so, Inez and Jeff thwart the thieves and keep Chicago safe. Join us next time for another thrill-packed adventure featuring Inez Ingalls, Private Eye. Until then, don't forget. If you're a modern woman, Modern Woman Soaps and Oils are made with you in mind."

CUE BAND

On October 29, 1945, fading notes from WBAC's studio orchestra signaled an end to the premier episode of radio detective *Inez Ingalls, Private Eye*. The "on the air" sign flickered and went dark, sending Nic Owen to a nearby chair to relax her tense muscles and take a few deep breaths. The relief left her only faintly aware of a compliment from studio manager Frank Myers as he hurried by. "You were great, Nic. Really great."

When the praise had a chance to sink in, Nic reflected on her new career as Inez Ingalls, star of a radio detective show.

Only eight months earlier, the twenty-seven-year-old was working at an airplane factory west of the city. For most of her two years at the plant, she had popped rivets into fuselages of Douglas C-54 transport planes. When an agent from the War Department discovered she had a voice well-suited for broadcasting, she took on an added duty—reading war bond commercials. The Allied victory brought not only an end to her riveting and recording careers, but a great deal of uncertainty about what to do with her life.

Nic's aunt had spotted the newspaper advertisement for a female to read ads and suggested she audition for the job. While standing in line with hundreds of other women, Nic doubted that she had the voice or the talent, but like the War Department, Frank Myers found her a perfect fit for radio. He hired her on the spot to read commercials and work as understudy to other female cast members, including the star, Carolyn Park. Frank told her she was learning the part 'just in case.' He had not suggested it was just in case someone shot Mrs. Park two days before the first episode aired. Nic's new career began, quite literally, with a bang.

Ten minutes after the closing notes faded, Nic remained unable to stand, or pry her fingers from the script. She felt exhausted and guessed it was her body's response to suddenly relaxed muscles. Instead of trying to stand, she slumped further into her chair and used the script as a fan, waving it slowly so as not to deplete precious remaining energy.

"Carolyn never used a script."

"I know. She was amazing." Nic turned to a dark-haired woman that she remembered seeing at the back of the studio during the show. Her expression suggested she was not there to strike up a friendship.

"I hope you don't consider yourself the next Carolyn Park. On your best day, it would take more of a woman than you to fill her shoes."

The offensive words dissolved any ailments, real or imagined. Nic shot to her feet and directly into the path of two piercing dark eyes. "I barely knew Carolyn Park, and I'm not trying to fill anyone's shoes. Who are you?"

Her critic looked about to respond, but instead, a blank gaze replaced her defiant stare, and in keeping with her abrupt arrival, her high heels clattered on the floorboards as she hurried off the stage.

The encounter gave Nic another opportunity to examine her list of pros and cons for working in radio. As she returned to the chair, she found it more relaxing to examine the surrounding architecture than her unsteady thoughts.

The Merchandise Mart, a massive twenty-five-story, four-million-square-foot, Art Deco-style building, spanned two full city blocks and overlooked the Chicago River. Although no stranger to the building, Nic's visits never took her to the two floors that housed WBAC radio station. She recalled her astonished first look at Studio A, one of the three largest spaces. Designers had removed the ceilings from studios A, E, and D, allowing them to span the nineteenth and twentieth floors. Their towering twenty-six-foot high walls gave them the look and feel of a cathedral rather than a sound stage.

While marveling at her surroundings that first morning, Nic unintentionally blocked the doorway that Greg Devens was attempting to enter with his acoustic bass. Greg, a member of the studio orchestra, had been her first friend at the station. The memory of that meeting sent her in search of the tall blonde musician for information, and perhaps a little sympathy.

"Hey, great show, Nic. Very cool." Greg spoke the often-cryptic language shared by jazz musicians and their supporters. He spent every free minute away from the studio practicing with the Torrance Trio, a local jazz band of which he was one-third.

"Thanks, Greg. It was a little scary, but I had fun. I have a question. Do you have a minute?"

"I do."

"Who is that thin woman in the black trousers? The one smoking a cigarette by the back wall." Nic gazed in her direction, but rather than point, used the rising finger to wrap a strand of shoulder-length brown hair behind her ear.

"That's Nora Hahn. She and Carolyn Park were close friends. I think they started at the station around the same time. Carolyn worked here in the studio and Nora is one of the writers. Their offices are up on twenty."

"Why do you suppose she was hanging around during the show?"

Greg shrugged as he moved the bass from the stand to its case. Even with his ample height, maneuvering the instrument was a challenge. Once he had it safely tucked away, Greg put his hands on his lower back and bent backward until something cracked. Nic guessed by his satisfied grin that he had achieved the desired result. "Ah. Much better. I should learn to grind a smaller axe." The blank look on Nic's non-jazz-speaking face said she needed a translation, which he supplied. "Play a smaller instrument. Maybe Nora wanted to see how you did playing Inez. Why are you interested in her?"

"She came on stage after the show and told me that I wasn't Carolyn Park, and shouldn't think I could fill her shoes." He studied the lone figure. "Maybe for her, you can't." Nic sensed an invisible wall around Nora, but decided that rather than allow the harsh words to scare her away, she would engage the woman in a conversation. Unfortunately, Frank chose that moment to call her to the stage. "Miss Owen, you were great." His enthusiastic hug increased her embarrassment. "You were. In spite of finding yourself center stage on such short notice."

People nearby clapped and Nic blushed. The rose in her cheeks was a mix of embarrassment and pleasure, but the warm fuzzy feeling dissolved when she saw Nora's dark eyes staring, and two now-familiar Chicago Police Detectives, O'Brian and Jones, glowering from the engineer's booth.

The cleaning crew discovered Mrs. Park on the Studio A stage the previous Saturday morning. In Detective O'Brian's mind, the fastest way to find a killer was to harass everyone remotely involved. He and Jones spent the weekend interviewing members of the cast and crew at their homes. Nic, to her chagrin, had earned a top spot on the suspect list.

There was no need for O'Brian to slam the booth door to announce his entrance into Studio E. Nor was a microphone required for amplification. When his grating voice boomed through the acoustically superb room, conversations stopped mid-sentence. "Nobody leaves until we finish our interviews." Had the staff expected their collective groans and boos to influence the detective's plans, they were disappointed. "I hope none of youse mistook that for a request. Keep your noises to yourself and let's get started."

She Overheard Murder

Before joining the force, O'Brian spent a few years as a heavyweight boxer. Twenty years at a desk instead of a gym had taken its toll. When he wrapped his arms over his chest and smirked at the irritated group, it was not muscle stretching the seams of his jacket.

"You've already interviewed everyone," Frank yelled. "These people have put in a long and difficult day and should be allowed to go home."

"They go home when we say they go home. Why don't we start with you?" The person close enough to receive a poke from O'Brian's stubby finger was Barney Mills, one of the sound effects men. Barney gulped. "You and me are gonna have a nice chat in here." O'Brian waved the engineers, Harold and Stanley, from the booth and escorted Barney inside.

While their discussion took place, Detective Jones left to gather employees from the offices and other parts of the station. Jones did not have O'Brian's excess weight, but when he returned and leaned against the wall next to the studio door, no one tried to leave. His broad frame deterred some, but the exposed firearm beneath his partially open jacket held the rest in check.

Minutes into Barney's interview, Nic noticed that Frank and her fellow performers had left the stage. She returned to the band area where Greg stood with another member, Belia Malecek. Belia, a gifted violinist, would soon audition for a chair with the Chicago Symphony Orchestra. If she knew what a huge feather that was in her cap, it did not show.

Nic arrived to see Belia placing her violin in its case with the tenderness of a mother laying her newborn in a cradle. Belia had immigrated to the United States from Czechoslovakia six years earlier, but struggled with English. That effort, and a heavy accent, often discouraged her from joining conversations.

It was not her words, or the soft rolls of blue-black hair that framed her face and highlighted her rose petal skin that intrigued Nic. It was the glow in her eyes—a glow that ignited when she played her violin.

"How long do you think they'll keep us?" Nic faced the engineer's booth as she spoke, leaving Greg and Belia unsure who should reply.

Belia spoke, her tone as ghostly as the tremolo of a single note on her violin. "I do not know. They come to my apartment on Saturday and act as if I kill her." She and her father were the only family members to escape the Nazi invasion of Czechoslovakia in 1939. The rest disappeared, and Belia lived in a perpetual state of fear. O'Brian and Jones did little to lessen her anxiety.

"Why would they think you killed her, Belia?" Nic could not imagine the tiny woman killing Carolyn Park, who had been an inch taller than her own five-foot-six inches. Of course, a gun removed any size advantage.

"I am one of the last people to go from the studio that night. It was after eight o'clock." Belia glared at the engineer's booth. "The Detective O'Brian ask me if I am in this country legally. I am," she assured Nic. "But I know this does not make a difference to police."

"I left right after you, Nic." Greg joined the conversation. "I grabbed dinner and went to the club to jam. O'Brian asked if anyone saw me, and I told him that I had my bass and figured a number of people could vouch for me. He grunted."

One by one, members of the troupe entered the booth and returned to the studio as limp as a towel put too often through the wringer. Everyone except Nora. Nic watched her lean back in boredom while O'Brian pushed his finger in her face. If she cared what the detective said, she hid it well, and he appeared less than pleased with her attitude. When she left the booth, Nora strolled past Jones and exited the studio without looking back.

By five o'clock, Nic and Frank sat alone on the stage while his assistant, Alice Redding, had her turn in the inquisition booth. Nic did not want to talk to O'Brian, but since she had no choice, she wanted it over as quickly as possible. She held her coat in her arms and her purse in her lap, ready to leave when they finished.

Frank had clearly run out of patience with the investigation but he did not take it out on his star. "Tell me, Miss Owen, is radio everything you thought it would be?"

"And more." She was about to add a more inspired response but the door to the engineer's booth opened and Detective O'Brian waved her over. Nic wanted nothing more than to finish the interview and go home, which was why she found it extremely irritating that he stood in the doorway blocking her entrance.

"I hear your first show went real well, Miss Owen. It's a shame Mrs. Park never had a chance to do the part. Your coworkers tell me she was damn good. Put your coat on. We're going to the station."

"What do you mean we're going to the station?" Had she heard him right? "Why are you taking me to the police station?"

"If you know what's good for you, lady, you'll shut your trap."

The detective's warning did not make it past her outrage. She repeated her question. "Why are you taking me to the police station? You can ask me anything you want right here. Am I under arrest? Is that why you saved my interview until last, because you planned to arrest me?"

O'Brian pulled her coat from her arms and tossed it back. "Put that on and shut up. Didn't anyone ever tell you it ain't smart to argue with an officer of the law?" A pair of handcuffs appeared and as soon as Nic secured the last button on her coat, O'Brian turned her around, put her hands together, and snapped them on her wrists. "You can wear these until you learn to keep your mouth shut. Don't make me gag you, Miss Owen."

Nic stopped talking. She offered no resistance when O'Brian shoved her purse into the fingers of her coupled hands, or as she followed him to the elevator. She tried to smile at Sam, the operator, but as the reality of the situation sank in, various body parts failed to respond.

Shock and disbelief kept her silent in the back seat of the police car. She struggled to slow her racing thoughts. Four hours earlier, she starred in her first live radio show. Now, she was frightened, confused, and a murder suspect, and it was only Monday.

CHAPTER 2

Nic identified the source of one unpleasant smell in the room where O'Brian and Jones left her. An inverted lid from a coffee can serving as an ashtray overflowed with discarded matches, ashes, and cigar and cigarette butts. Those that had not made it to the receptacle, cluttered the table's light wood top, itself a patchwork of stains, scratches, and burns. Nic studied a barely legible carving that belonged to a previous occupant named Bill.

The table filled much of the space, and two chairs, which matched only in that they too were wood, and greatly abused, occupied the remaining area. Nic found the stillness surprising. She imagined a police station would be at least as noisy as the sound effects that Barney and George created for her office on the show, complete with ringing telephones, wailing sirens, clicking typewriters, and multiple conversations. The knot in her stomach reminded her that the present situation was not a show. She had no script and no idea of what the next scene would bring.

When the detectives first deposited her in the room, Nic remained on her feet. After it became clear that they were not coming right back, she backed up, still in handcuffs, and dropped her purse on the table. She chose the cleaner of the two chairs and sat, but the handcuffs made it difficult to find a position comfortable enough to hold for an extended period. For more than an hour, she alternated between pacing and sitting. She had just risen to ease a cramp in her shoulder when O'Brian and Jones returned. Her anger grew when she saw toothpicks protruding from their smirking mouths. They had gone to eat.

"Sit down," O'Brian roared. She sat and clenched her jaw as he dropped into the opposite chair and slid it back to accommodate his bulk. With effort, he hoisted his feet to the table. "And keep your mouth shut, Miss Owen, except to answer my questions. Maybe you'd rather I should call you Detective Ingalls. Hey, Jonesy, this lady's a detective like us."

Nic winced at 'like us,' but Jones did not respond. She couldn't see the second detective, but sensed him behind her chair. What she could see, too well, was the man across the table. Uncombed, greasy brown hair barely covered O'Brian's shiny head. If he had shaved, it was much earlier and without the benefit of a mirror. Nic tried to ignore his stomach, which, encouraged by the recent meal, tested a number of small, yellowed buttons struggling to hold his shirt closed. She released a weary breath and a question. "Is that why you brought me here, Detective, to make fun of my job?"

"You haven't learned much, have you, girlie? I told you to watch how you talk to me." Dried ink on the tip of the fountain pen O'Brian uncapped matched the stain on his jacket pocket. He flipped open a small notebook and locked his dull gray eyes on Nic, but spoke to his partner. "Cuff her to the table leg, Jonesy. I don't want her jumping across to attack me."

Nic was not a small person, but Jones lifted her from the chair like a rag doll. He opened the cuff on her left wrist and gave her right arm a yank until he could wrap the restraint around the table leg and snap it closed. He returned to his position behind her without a word. Nic interpreted the silence as an invitation to sit, and dragged the chair closer to the leg. When she raised her head, she saw the filthy soles of O'Brian's shoes, which he moved to expose an equally scruffy sneer. "Where were you last Friday between six and midnight?"

"I already told you where I was."

"Tell me again."

Pain in her right arm and wrist increased, as did her discomfort. The temperature in the room rose significantly after the arrival of the two detectives and Nic still wore her coat. She slid the left side from her shoulder, but nearly flew off the chair when O'Brian removed his feet from the table and shoved it at her.

"Did I tell you to take off your coat? You don't do nothin' unless I tell you. Got it?" She pulled the coat over her shoulder. "Tell me again where you were on Friday."

"I went to a movie with my aunt and my neighbor."

"What movie?"

"*The Lost Weekend.*"

"What time did it end?"

"Around nine-thirty."

He scribbled in his notebook. "Where did you go after the movie?"

"We were home by ten o'clock. I didn't go out after that."

"Here's the problem, Miss Owen. If your aunt and neighbor are your alibi, how do we know they ain't lying for you? You said your neighbor is an old friend. Maybe now that you're the leading lady, you promised her a job. I'll bet your aunt's happy about your new career, too. Happy enough to cover for you."

"How dare you." Nic leapt from the chair. At least she tried to leap. The handcuff had slipped down the leg and after catapulting upward, she leaned awkwardly with her knees bent and her wrist in pain. "How dare you call my aunt a liar?" The uncomfortable stance lessened the impact of her angry glare, and when a large hand grasped her shoulder, she returned to the chair.

"You don't want to talk about your aunt? Okay. Why don't we go on before you hurt yourself? What year were you born?"

She didn't have the energy to question why he needed to know, and she didn't care.

"Nineteen-eighteen."

"That makes you, what…?"

"Twenty-seven." A week ago, she felt closer to twenty. At that moment, she felt over fifty.

"You told me your name was Nic, but your birth certificate says it's Nicole. Is Nic an alias?"

"Alias?" She choked on the word. "Nic is short for Nicole. It's a nickname, not an alias." Exhaustion and self-control silenced the response she intended, "Are you insane?"

"How long have you worked at the radio station?"

"Three weeks."

"See, that's another problem, Miss Owen. You've only been there three weeks and already you're the star. Don't you think that makes you a good suspect?"

"Yes. I'm sure it makes me a good suspect, but I didn't do it. I never spoke to Carolyn Park except to say hello."

"You don't need to talk to a person to put a bullet in their head."

"Detective O'Brian, I didn't shoot her." She said the words slowly, one at a time, and punctuated them with an annoyed sigh.

"You wouldn't believe how often we hear that." O'Brian doubled his chin with a nod.

All Nic could think about was going home and sinking into a hot bath, but O'Brian was in no hurry. He pulled a black cigar stub from his jacket pocket and added another nauseating smell to the space. The whiff of sulfur from a wooden matchstick he dragged across the table was not as repulsive, but his action added another scar. He held the match and puffed until the cigar end glowed. Nic drew back.

"Don't like the smoke, eh?" After an approving nod at the cigar, he released a puff in her direction. "Nora Hahn was a special friend to Mrs. Park. You know her?"

"I met her today for the first time." Compared to her present situation, the meeting with Nora was a minor event.

"Do you think she killed Mrs. Park?"

The question surprised her. "I have no idea. I told you, I just met her." As she said the words, Nic realized there had been an undercurrent to her exchange with Nora that made her think she had not killed Carolyn Park. She wasn't sure what caused her doubt, but she felt no urge to share the exchange or the revelation with O'Brian.

Whether from the warm temperature, the detective's cigar, or maybe the detective, Nic felt ill. O'Brian took no notice of her discomfort. He stood and dragged the table to its original location, pulling her along and pointing the soggy end of the cigar in her face. "Here's how I see it, Miss Owen. You had the most to gain by Mrs. Park's death, you're the newest member of the cast, and you ain't got what I'd call an airtight alibi. That gives us a damn good case."

He closed his notebook and dropped it and the pen in his pocket as he lumbered to the door. Before pulling it open, he extinguished the cigar with his shoe and issued a warning. "I'm sure I don't need to tell you to stick around, do I, Miss Owen?"

Nic jumped when Jones followed his partner out and slammed the door, but two things pleased her. They were gone, and O'Brian forgot to put the cap on his pen before putting it in his pocket. Her relief over their departure was short lived as questions formed in rapid succession. What would happen next? Had they finished? Would they let her go home? Would she go to jail? Would she spend the rest of her life hooked to the table in that smelly room?

Her mind buzzed with images of horrible scenarios until a piece of advice from her Aunt Anna surfaced. She told Nic that it made little sense to worry about imagined future events. The more you thought about possible dreadful outcomes, the scarier the present moment became, and the more frightening the present became, the more horrifying the future looked. Nic recognized the dangers of such circular thinking. She slid the handcuff up the table leg, straightened in the chair, and tried not to visualize what the future might hold.

After what seemed hours, but had been closer to twenty minutes, an officer came in. He removed the handcuff from the table leg, and helped her stand, an act she appreciated. Unlike the solid wooden legs under the table, her shaky flesh and bone pair were not much support.

"O'Brian wants your fingerprints."

His young voice surprised her. After taking a closer look, she guessed he was a few years younger than she was. That seemed reason enough to demand answers. "Why does he want my fingerprints? Am I under arrest? Why didn't he tell me when he was here?"

His uniform-clad shoulders lifted slightly as he cuffed her hands, took her purse from the table, and tilted his head. She assumed that meant they were leaving and wondered if police went through special training to communicate using only nods, grunts, and shrugs.

The corridor smelled much like the stale room. Luckily, dim lighting forced her to focus on the officer's back and where she was stepping rather than her surroundings. She was congratulating herself for remaining calm when they turned a corner and walked toward a row of cells. Her heartbeat grew faster with each step, and although their pace never slowed, it was only when they reached the end of the hall and he ushered her through the door of another small room that she exhaled.

The handcuffs came off and the officer directed her to a counter where she watched with interest as he rolled her fingers on an inkpad and pressed them and her thumbs on a piece of paper. The entire process took only minutes. When finished, he handed her a towel and her purse and told her she could go. Unfortunately, he left without showing her the exit.

It took several minutes to make her way through the maze of corridors, a process slowed by her effort to avoid another confrontation with O'Brian. She found the front desk and saw the policeman in charge had his hands full with a crowd of unhappy teenagers and their unhappier parents. Nic closed her coat and hurried outside.

A streetcar arrived and she decided that between the ten-minute ride and the short walk to her apartment in the cold night air, her nerves would settle and she would smell less like an old cigar. A sniff of her coat sleeve raised doubt about the latter, and a look at her trembling fingers suggested she might need additional time for the former as well.

In May of 1918, Charlie Owen, Nicole's father, left for France, leaving his wife and unborn daughter behind. Two months later, at the Battle of Château-Thierry, he became one of the 119,000 American casualties of World War I. In 1928, Nic's mother, Grace, died of pneumonia, and Anna Owen, Charlie's sister, took her in. Anna was one of the few people who, after her mother's death, Nic allowed to call her Nicole.

As Nic stepped into the apartment she shared with her aunt, the darkened room was a surprise and a disappointment. Time with Anna would go a long way in soothing her battered person. "Aunt Anna, are you home?" Hearing nothing, she closed the heavy oak door with her hip and reached for the light switch, but before she found it, lights came on and two familiar voices yelled, "Congratulations."

Anna, and Nic's friend and neighbor, Millie, stood in front of the dining room table. It was set for a feast. "What's this?"

"We listened to the show this afternoon, Nicole. You were wonderful. The show was, too." She kissed her cheek and stepped back frowning. "You smell terrible, dear."

Nic realized that, with all that had happened since the show, her debut performance felt more like a dream than a real experience. It was time to focus on one of the more enjoyable parts of her long day.

Millie hugged her excitedly. "If I didn't know that was you on the radio I'd have thought it was a big star. But that's what you are, isn't it?" Millie beamed with pride, until, like Anna, she backed away. "Anna's right. You do smell bad."

"I could take a bath and change before we eat if it's that bad," Nic offered.

"We can handle it, Nicole. It's not that bad, and I want to hear about the show. Don't you agree, Millie?"

Millie applied her thumb and forefinger to the bridge of her diminutive nose and gave a nasal response. "I'b sure be cad." Anna's scowl quickly cleared Millie's blocked passages. "I mean, I'm sure we can handle it. I want to hear about the show, too, and about your new cologne. I hope it's not one of your sponsor's products."

The war in Europe had officially ended in May, and the war with Japan in August, but some products, sugar, meat, cheese, fats, and a few others, still faced rationing. Those limitations had not prevented Anna from creating an enticing spread of roasted chicken, mashed potatoes, green beans, and homemade biscuits.

Since few things had the power to dampen Nic's appetite, her curious tablemates waited for her to fill a plate and enjoy a few mouthfuls before she shared the day's events. The police station segment, Nic decided, would wait until after the meal. "I wasn't nervous. I'm not sure if it makes sense, but I was too scared to be nervous." After a momentary lull to enjoy a forkful of mashed potatoes, she continued. "I pictured Carolyn Park performing the scenes at earlier rehearsals. I tried to remember as much as I could about how she played Inez. She was perfect for the part. I'd never have known what to do if it weren't for that."

Anna had more faith in her niece than her niece had in herself. "I'm sure you would have been fine, Nicole. The station must have believed you could do it or they wouldn't have hired you."

"The station didn't expect me to play such an important part this soon. I think seeing Carolyn perform Inez is what saved me. It wasn't just her acting talent. It was everything about her. She was confident and completely relaxed, but you knew she was there to work. I pictured Carolyn, read my lines, and tried not to think."

"I do that last part a lot." Millie laughed.

"Well, that's what I did, Millie, but as soon as the 'On the Air' light went out I collapsed into a chair. There I sat thinking I could relax when this woman, Nora, showed up and told me I shouldn't think I could replace Carolyn. She seemed angry, and I guessed it was at me. I have no idea what I could have done to upset her."

"Who is she?" Anna had an appetite, too, but she could not compete, fork to fork, with her niece, and abandoned her efforts. "I mean what does she do at the station?"

"Greg told me she's one of the writers. I hadn't noticed her before today, but since the writers' offices are on the twentieth floor, that's not surprising. Besides, in the few weeks I've been there, I've been too focused on learning to make many friends."

"Why was she in the studio during the show? Do people hang around and watch?" Millie asked.

"Greg suggested she might have been there to see how I did playing Inez." As Nic reached for her coffee, she dipped a sleeve in the mashed potatoes. Further examination revealed dirt and grime stains on the cuffs. She was wondering how bad her coat sleeves looked when she saw Millie's expectant face and remembered their conversation. "Oh. You asked me why she was there. I have no idea why she was in the studio. I was a little surprised to find out she was a writer. I just figured she was an actress because she has a beautiful deep voice. I suppose it might be considered appealing if it isn't yelling at you."

Millie's raised eyebrow meant she was about to ask another question, but Nic thought it was time to discuss matters other than Nora and the broadcast. She patted her satisfied stomach. "Aunt Anna, this was wonderful. I think it's time I learn how to cook." Nic had made similar vows over the years, and neither Anna nor Millie looked convinced. "I mean it."

Anna's brown and grey striped feline, Alley, strolled into the room and stared at her owner. "Oh, no," Anna said with conviction. "I'm not giving you anything from this table." Her announcement met with the same disbelief as Nic's cooking comment, especially from the feline. As Anna dropped a small piece of chicken to the floor, she noticed the stains on Nic's sleeves. "So, Nicole, are you ready to tell us why you're scuffed up and fragrant? Even Alley is interested."

Nic knew that the only thing of interest to Alley was chicken, but rejuvenated by the meal she was ready to talk about her strange evening. "Sure, I'll tell you. After my debut as Inez Ingalls, I went to jail."

Chapter 3

The news of Nic's trip to jail startled unflappable Anna Owen, but the petite sixty-two-year-old needed only a second to recover. "Why did you go to jail?"

"Do you remember the detectives O'Brian and Jones that were here on Saturday?" Anna nodded. "They came to the studio today. After interviewing the entire cast and crew, they took me to the police station for questioning. Detective O'Brian seems even more convinced that I'm a good suspect." Nic showed them her stained fingers, dirty sleeves, and the red ring around her wrists. The irritation was barely visible on the left wrist, but more pronounced on the one that had struggled with the table leg.

"The ink stain is because they took your fingerprints, but why is your wrist red, Nicole?"

Before Nic could respond to Anna, Millie made a comment that, judging by her laughter, she meant to be funny. "Oh, I know what happened. They cuffed you, right?"

When Nic didn't respond, Anna's shocked look returned. "Nicole, I can understand why they'd want to interview you, and maybe even why they thought it necessary to take you to the station, but why would they put you in handcuffs? They don't usually do that unless a person is uncooperative or threatening."

The prospect of discussing her lack of self-control made Nic uncomfortable. She took a minute to admire the napkins Anna had chosen for their celebration and used the green linen to wipe her mouth while formulating her response. She decided it was best to be honest, but wanted Millie and Anna to understand the reason for her behavior. "Well it certainly wasn't because I was threatening. I might have been a little more vocal than the detectives liked. When O'Brian said I had to go to the police station, it caught me by surprise and I asked a few questions. That seemed to irritate him." Her cheeks flushed. "Maybe more than a few questions, but as soon as I felt the handcuffs, I kept my thoughts to myself."

"I'm sure I'd have behaved the same way, dear. Tell us what happened at the police station." A determined wail from the feline interrupted, and Anna, never taking her eyes from Nicole, dropped another small piece of chicken to the floor.

Good food and familiar friendly company made recounting the incident less of a struggle than Nic thought. When she finished, Anna patted her hand. "Nicole, I know it doesn't make your experience any less horrifying, but if they believed you were guilty, you wouldn't be sitting here. They wanted to scare you."

"If that's what they wanted to do, it worked. What's strange is that my brain won't accept that I'm a murder suspect. I mean, I'm scared, but it doesn't feel real. Does that make sense?"

"It makes perfect sense. That was an awful ordeal. I'm sorry."

Nic heard Anna's sincere concern, but she also detected that her aunt was slightly distracted, a sure sign her brain had shifted to another avenue of thought.

Anna confirmed the assumption. "Maybe we should do a little investigating on our own. It couldn't hurt, and Nicole, you have a personal interest in finding a quick solution."

Anna Owen looked law-abiding enough. At an even five feet, with a gray braid nearly half that length, most people would not suspect that she had an interest in solving crimes. She did. Her passion for mysteries had begun in 1898, when at fifteen she'd read an Anna Katharine Green mystery in which a spinster sleuth named Amelia Butterworth investigated a murder. Since most books focused on women as wives and mothers, the female detective was welcome and inspiring.

Eventually Anna grew less drawn to a career as a detective, but her passion for books remained. She completed her studies in English Literature and following a decade of teaching in Chicago public schools, landed a position at the University of Illinois Chicago Campus. Eighteen years on the job with only one promotion convinced her that, like most women in her position, she would not advance beyond Assistant Professor. Without a chance at tenure, Anna saw little reason to put up with the oppressive patriarchal system. She decided to work with students one-on-one and retired to do private coaching and tutoring.

The only complaint Nic had about her aunt was that because of her business, or perhaps her personality, she knew half the population in the city of Chicago. Her students, those from her university days and those she tutored, stayed in contact and became part of an information and resource network that spread citywide. A network Anna used whenever she found her own personal cause to investigate.

"Aunt Anna, I recognize that look. What are you planning?" The 'look' came as no surprise to Nic or Millie. It meant that very soon, Anna would poke her long straight nose into places it was not invited, and was probably not welcomed. "I assume you're not waiting for an invitation from O'Brian and Jones."

"They're busy with other things. Besides, I've noticed that the police don't jump at the offer when a citizen volunteers their services, no matter how valuable they may be. Nicole, you might want to talk with your co-workers. Ask questions to see if they saw or heard anything unusual or strange, but be discreet and keep your eyes and ears open."

"I'll do what I can if it will help end this, but I've only been with WBAC for a few weeks and strange and unusual occurrences seem commonplace. Maybe the worst is over. I mean, what could be more out of the ordinary than murder?"

*

Nic gave a firm push on the handrail and set the polished metal and glass revolving door in motion, propelling her into the lobby. Three weeks after the start of her new career, she still felt a sense of excitement entering the Merchandise Mart. In fact, except for her uncomfortable position as a suspect in a murder, she was quite pleased with her life.

Her eyes made the adjustment from sunlight to the subdued incandescent light of wall sconces and she saw there were only a few people in line at the newsstand. Until recently, she'd rarely bought a paper, but personal involvement in a murder investigation gave her a greater interest in current events. Once in the line that paralleled a row of phone booths, she overheard bits and pieces of a conversation. "We gotta see what the cops plan to do." His words, audible because of his anger, and because he held the wood and glass booth door open with his foot, continued. "If pinning it on the girlfriend don't work, we'll think of something else. Stop worrying. She's dead. The hard part's done."

"Hey, lady. Did you want a paper?" Another voice, this time from in front of Nic, interrupted her eavesdropping. She saw that the paperboy, who stayed in business because his customers paid their three cents and stepped out of the way, was encouraging her to do that.

"Sorry." She paid and turned to the now-empty phone booth. Had the caller really said what she thought he said? The noise from people hurrying through made it impossible to be certain. She headed toward the elevator and replayed the last sentence with a shiver. "She's dead. The hard part's done."

Sam held the elevator door open with one hand and tipped his cap with the other. "I see you were O'Brian's guest last night, Nic. I felt bad for you. He's such an irritating man. How did it go at the station?"

"It wasn't much fun, Sam. Have you talked to him?"

"He's questioned me twice, and I didn't know any more the second time than I did the first. I left at five on Friday and didn't have a clue what happened after that. O'Brian told me that since us Colored folks were more familiar with violent crime, I'd have an easier time recognizing the killer if I saw him."

"He didn't say that, did he?" Nic had mistakenly thought she couldn't feel more disgust for the detective.

"He did. I told him he was right. If the killer had come up on my elevator, I surely would have known, so I didn't think he had." Sam winked.

As others boarded and the car filled, Nic moved to the back and leaned on the wall. Her mind, which had started the day processing thoughts slowly, with the lazy sway of a front porch

She Overheard Murder

swing in a light summer breeze, now spun like a pinwheel in March. Had she overheard someone talking about a murder? It seemed more like a plot for a radio show than real life. She must have been mistaken. Maybe her experience at the police station the previous night had affected her more than she realized. No one would talk so casually about murder.

As the arrow made its way around the arc and dutifully stop at nineteen, Nic decided she had been mistaken about what she thought he said. When the door opened, she said goodbye to Sam and stepped off the elevator ready to focus on the crimes Inez Ingalls had to solve. The blonde head of the receptionist rose. "Hi, Marcy. I hope the quiet surroundings are a good sign."

"So far, Nic. Thank goodness. My nerves need a rest."

"Any news from the police?"

"They've had people here this morning doing a final whatever they're doing. Frank said to let everyone from the Ingalls show know that since the police are done in Studio A, you'll go back to working in there. Nic, the rumor mill said O'Brian took you to the police station last night. That must have been pretty scary."

"There was nothing pretty about it, Marcy, but hopefully they're finished with me." Nic departed for Studio A, refusing to let her thoughts return to O'Brian. The likely success of that goal dimmed when she heard Mr. Myers through the open studio door. "You have nothing to worry about, Barney. O'Brian asked the same questions of the entire cast and crew. He gave everyone a hard time."

"They came to my house last night and took me to the station, Frank. They fingerprinted me and I answered questions for two hours. O'Brian kept bringing up my discharge."

"How did he find out about your discharge?"

"I don't know."

Nic realized she was listening to a second conversation she did not want to hear. She couldn't remember another time in her life where she overheard such dramatic conversations. Had she always overheard them and not paid attention? Did her new job as a radio detective activate an unused part of her brain necessary for detecting? The sound of people coming her way from the reception area encouraged her to rattle the handle and enter the almost empty studio. "Good morning, Barney. Mr. Myers."

Myers gave Barney a pat on the back before turning. "Nic, two of the sponsors called this morning to tell me how pleased they were with the show, with you in particular."

"Thank you, Mr. Myers."

"Call me Frank."

"Thank you, Frank. And thanks for the chance. I'm glad to be with the station."

"We'll see how you feel about that when we're halfway through the season. How did it go at the police station last night?"

"It was awful, but it's over."

Before he could respond, Harold called him to the engineer's booth. Frank congratulated her again as he used both hands to push his black hair flat before hurrying to the booth. Nic wondered if his combed-back hairstyle was to cut wind resistance. Everything Frank Myers did was at top speed, which frequently left his not-very-tall-assistant, Alice, running in his wake.

Nic was chuckling when she turned and found herself nose to nose with Barney. "Oops." She took a step back. "Barney. How are you?"

"I'm good. Thanks, Nic. How about you?"

"Mostly good. It's still hard to believe I'm starring in a radio show, and even harder to believe why. You've been at the station a while, haven't you?"

"Six years before I left for the war. I've been back going on three months." Barney Mills, an experienced soundman, looked older than his thirty-five years. Grey hairs had made moderate gains in the mostly short brown crop, and his thin frame could have used a few additional pounds. Despite the unhealthy appearance, his warm smile made him welcome company.

"Nic, I promised to show you the sound effects we use for the show. Do you have a few minutes?"

Frank was still engaged in a conversation with Harold. "I do."

Next to the engineer's booth was an area filled with objects familiar and foreign to Nic. "How did you create the sound of the fire yesterday, Barney? It was so real I thought I smelled smoke."

"Close your eyes." Nic obeyed and in seconds, heard the sound of flames. Her eyes, forced open by curiosity, saw Barney rubbing a piece of cellophane in front of the microphone. The demonstration continued when he twisted a sheet of metal to create thunder and rapidly opened and closed a small umbrella to produce the sound of wings. He pointed to a large wooden box filled with cups, dishes, silverware, a telephone, finger cymbals, wooden blocks, an assortment of sticks, and many articles difficult to identify.

"It looks like a big toy box."

"That's pretty much what it is. All of those little gadgets have magic powers when placed in front of a microphone. They help your fans see you doing your job."

"You must have fun."

"I do, and this has been a great place to work. I'd never have thought what happened to Carolyn could happen here, especially to her."

Nic recognized the opportunity to do a little sleuthing. She leaned on the wall next to the box. "Did you know her well?"

"I met her the first day she started, which was a few months before I left for the war. I liked her right away." Barney leaned next to Nic. "She and Nora are good people. I mean are and were, I guess."

A question about Nora surfaced, but before Nic could ask, Frank left the engineers booth and called her to the stage. Thanking Barney for the tour, she grabbed her things, but stopped cold when her foot hit the stage. She had not been there since before the murder, and felt strange standing where Carolyn lost her life. She noticed a light stain in the wood near her feet.

"That's where they found her." Frank appeared at her side. "The cleaning crew tried everything to remove it. Carpenters will replace the boards next weekend. Are you all right?"

"Yes. I'm fine." Nic smoothed invisible wrinkles from her skirt and was barely aware of Alice handing her a script as they followed Frank across the stage.

Interviews and other interruptions from the continuing police investigation threw rehearsals off schedule. At three o'clock, Frank told the actors to stop for the day, allowing him to work with the soundmen and band. He added a warning that beginning the following day, there would be overtime for at least a week.

Nic felt bad that she had not had time to make more inquiries. She brightened when she noticed Daniel Newman, the announcer, was still at his microphone. Gathering her thoughts for a short conversation, Nic hoped he had time and energy to spare.

In April of 1945, Daniel, while stationed on recently reclaimed Iwo Jima, had received permanently disabling injuries to his right leg. Like Barney, he had worked at the station before the war and returned to his old job. Although the cast gathered center stage and stood during the performance, Daniel remained seated and read his lines into a separate microphone off to the side. Nic approached, mesmerized by the blurred crook handle of his ash walking stick as he rubbed the shaft between his palms. "Hey, Nic. How are you doing after your sudden leap into stardom?"

"It's strange to think of myself as a star, especially when I'm also a murder suspect."

"I heard you went to the station last night. You seem to be holding up okay."

"I am. My aunt keeps reassuring me that this will pass. Daniel, forgive my abruptness, but did you know Carolyn Park very well?"

"Not really. I was in the service most of the time after she started. Why?"

"I suppose because of my relationship with O'Brian. I'd like to see the killer caught."

"Wish I could help. O'Brian sure knows how to rattle people."

"All I have to do is hear his name and I'm rattled. Thanks anyway, Daniel. I'll see you tomorrow." As she walked toward the exit, Nic heard familiar hurried footsteps and turned in time to hook Frank's arm before he dashed past. "Is Barney all right?"

"Why do you ask?"

"I heard you talking when I came in this morning. What's going on with him?"

"He's all right, and if I have anything to say about it, he'll stay that way."

Nic wanted to know about Barney's discharge, but Frank left without further explanation. As she mused over her earlier eavesdropping, she noticed the band waiting for their session and joined Belia who was removing her violin from its velvet-lined case. It was the first time Nic had seen it up close, and although she knew nothing about musical instruments, she recognized its beauty. "What a stunning violin."

"Thank you. It belonged to my grandfather. When my father and I leave Czechoslovakia, it is the only belonging we can take. We hide it because the Nazis take what is of value. This," she held the instrument toward Nic, "is important for me for my memories, but it is also valuable."

"What do you mean?"

"It is made in 1650 by Nicolo Amati and my family has passed it down for all these years." She rocked the delicate instrument in her arms. "It is for me a way to be with them."

When Belia and her father escaped Czechoslovakia and came to Chicago, he worked tirelessly to make a good life. In less than four years, he went from working as a tailor to owning his own shop, but the loss of his family weighed greatly. A year earlier, in 1944, his heart, laden with pain, gave out. Belia sold the business and looked for work playing her violin. Allen Reed, musical director for the studio, recognized her imposing talent and gave her a job.

"Belia, maybe one of these days you can show it to my Aunt Anna. She's had season tickets to the symphony for as long as I can remember. She'd love to see it and meet you."

"I would enjoy to show your aunt, and perhaps play a piece if she would like." Her eyes sparkled.

"She would love." The news would thrill Anna, and Nic could not wait to share it. She might not have done enough interviews, but Belia and her violin would make up for that. To be safe, she asked Belia how well she knew Carolyn and watched a sudden and amazing transformation. The woman, who, seconds earlier, was delighted to talk about her violin, returned it to the case and backed toward the door.

"I must go to the ladies lounge before we practice. I am sorry, Nic. Goodbye." She hurried off, leaving a very confused radio performer waving weakly as the door swung closed.

Chapter 4

Voices floated from the back of the apartment telling Nic that Anna was with a student. She reached in and hung up her coat and purse before closing the door to climb to 2B and visit Millie. When she reached the second floor landing, Nic heard the click of Mrs. Murphy's door below. The octogenarian lived in 1B, across from Nic and Anna, and thought no one knew she kept current on the comings and goings in the building through her slightly open door.

The flat above Mrs. Murphy belonged to Millie Cicerio, Nic's friend since childhood. She and her husband, Joe, moved in after they married in 1943. A short two months later, Joe left for the Pacific and Millie took a job as a bucker at the Douglas Aircraft factory. She was one of twelve million women across the country, many who had never worked outside their homes, doing jobs once performed by men.

It took Millie only a few weeks to convince Nic to leave her sales job at Marshall Field's and join her. Both women wanted to help the war effort, and both enjoyed the better pay. Nic popped rivets while Millie held a bucking bar to resist the impact. You had to be small and strong to be a bucker. Millie fit the bill.

"Millie, it's me." Nic didn't hear a response and opened the door. "Are you home?" Looking down the hall to the kitchen, she saw Millie waving from under the table. "What're you doing?"

"I'm fixing the table. No, that's not right. I'm trying to fix the table. I'll be right up."

Nic arrived in the kitchen as Millie crawled forward on all fours. "So, how are things with you?"

"Before I answer that, why don't you tell me what you were doing down there."

The table Millie abandoned for her visitor matched four chrome chairs that were scattered around the room. She gripped the green vinyl seat of the one nearest and climbed to her feet. "Maybe I should've wiped up before I crawled under the table." Dust scattered as she brushed her trousers and confirmed her observation. "It's not a big deal. I'm tired of putting folded pieces of paper under the table legs to keep it level. I thought I could figure out how to fix it."

"Did you?"

Millie leaned on the green-flecked Formica top and sent coffee splashing from a cup. "No. I made it worse, but that could be progress. My tinkering had an effect. I'll just do the opposite, if I can remember what I did." She grabbed a dishrag and wiped the spill. "You're in a good mood. Were things a little calmer at the radio station today?"

"Calmer yes, but I do have a few tidbits to share with Aunt Anna. As strange as things have been, if the first three weeks are any indication, it will be an interesting place to work."

"You have a good outlook, Miss Owen. Except for the occasional murder, and your involvement in a police investigation, it's a great job." Millie missed the scowl Nic shot her because she had turned to watch the other Miss Owen open the back door. She waved the rag at her guest before tossing it to the sink. "It's our favorite mystery lover. Hi, Anna."

"Hi, ladies. Did I miss anything?" Without waiting for an invitation, Anna grabbed a chair and sat. If Nic or Millie were curious about her visit, her motives became clear with the next question. "Did you have a chance to talk to anyone, Nicole?" She was ready to work on the case.

"Yes, I did. I talked to Barney, one of the sound effects men." Nic told Millie and Anna how excited Barney was to show her his work, and how much he thought of Carolyn. She also shared what she could remember from the conversation between Frank and Barney.

"Why was he discharged?" Anna asked.

"I don't know. That's all I heard. I can't talk to Barney about it. I mean I wasn't intentionally eavesdropping, but I'm sure he didn't mean for me to hear. I also talked to Daniel Newman, the announcer."

"Daniel Newman? The one with the gorgeous voice?" Millie grew more attentive, ignoring the wobbly table as she propped her elbow on it to lean closer.

Nic ignored her swooning neighbor and directed her conversation to Anna. "He was in the service for most of the years Carolyn was at the station and didn't know much about her. Aunt Anna, what I need to tell you about happened before I went up to WBAC this morning, but after I thought about it, I wasn't completely sure I heard right. I mean, it's so busy in the lobby I just can't be positive."

"What did you hear, Nicole?"

"I was in line to buy a paper and heard a man talking in a phone booth. I couldn't hear everything, but the last thing

She Overheard Murder 37

I thought he said shocked me." She had Anna's undivided attention. "He said, 'She's dead, the hard part's done.'"

"Oh, my. Did you see his face?" Nic shook her head. "Nicole, it might be a good idea for you to write down as much as you can remember about that conversation."

"Yes, you're probably right. He mentioned pinning it on the girlfriend, but I didn't hear much more. I know there is no reason to think he was talking about Carolyn Park, but that was what popped into my head. I couldn't see him because with the door open, the light was off, but that's why I heard the conversation. I'll write it down." Nic did a quick review of the rest of her day and stopped at the image of Belia's violin. "Oh, I nearly forgot. I saw the most beautiful violin today. It belongs to Belia, a member of the band. She said a man named Amat, or Amati made it a long time ago in Italy."

Anna's excitement at the news nearly brought her to her feet, but when she leaned on the table and felt its shaky response, she stayed seated. That didn't lessen her enthusiasm. "She has a violin made by Nicolo Amati?"

"I think that's the name she said. I don't know anything about violins, but it is beautiful."

"I'm sure it is. Nicolo Amati was a great violinmaker. How did she come to own such an instrument?"

"She said it's been in her family since it was made in around 1650. Greg told me that Belia has an audition for a chair with the Chicago Symphony. I told her you had season tickets and she said she'd play for you some time if you're interested." Knowing the last three words were unnecessary, Nic smiled as Anna closed her eyes and sighed.

"Tell Belia I'd be honored."

Nic gave Anna a few seconds to enjoy the coming event before interrupting. "Shouldn't we get back to the case?"

Millie knew nothing about Nicolo Amati or violins, but she did know a way to contribute to the investigation. "I'll put on a pot of coffee. Who wants a cup?" Nic and Anna raised their hands.

"Good idea, Millie. Caffeine helps when I'm on a case." Anna told her.

She had been right about the power of caffeine. An hour-long discussion ensued. Nic described various cast and crewmembers at the station, Anna made a list of questions she thought Nic should ask, while Millie offered advice on how she should approach her coworkers.

"That's quite a bit for you to do Nicole. Maybe we should stop for now." When Millie and Nic agreed, Anna pushed on the table to stand and frowned at the teetering top. Luckily, their cups were empty and nothing spilled. "You should fix this."

*

Seconds after finding a seat on the elevated train, Nic fought the effects of its sedative rocking. She wanted to think, not sleep, and focused on the neighborhood rushing past her window.

Wooden porches tacked on the backsides of brick and stone buildings and connected by a web of clothesline and electrical wire dominated the view. On the topmost porch of one four-story brownstone, ropes and pulleys held starkly utilitarian denim and cotton garments, while across the alley, a collection of colorful fabrics with intricate woven designs danced in the breeze to an unheard drum. To Nic, the clothes waved like flags of the diverse nationalities that called the city home.

Hardship and loss were common during the depression and two world wars of the last thirty-five years. Many, on both sides, rich and poor, lost everything. When an image of Carolyn Park drifted into her thoughts, Nic wondered if poverty could push a person to cross a moral line. Could need, or greed, remove barriers and allow the murder of another human being?

Nic considered Anna the deep thinker in their family, while she went from day to day without questioning the whys or hows of things. This day, questions came and went at a dizzying speed, continuing as she left the train and walked to the Mart. Persisting as the elevator rose to its destination. Refusing dismissal even as the car doors opened and she said goodbye to Sam. It was no surprise then that she approached Marcy and fired off a question before the receptionist noticed her arrival. "Marcy, did you know Carolyn Park very well?"

Nic had no preconceived notion of how Marcy would respond, but the look she wore when she raised her head caught Nic off guard. It was hatred. "I knew her as well as anyone at the station. She was arrogant, conceited, and spiteful. She had things her way, or removed anyone or thing that prevented that." The hostile reaction continued. "Ask anyone. Carolyn thought her money gave her the right to treat everyone like dirt. I'm sorry, Nic. I know I'm not supposed to talk badly about the dead, but if anyone deserved to have a chip knocked off their shoulder, it was her."

Although surprised by the outburst, Nic responded calmly and from her heart. "Having a chip knocked off your shoulder is considerably different than having a bullet put in your head."

"I'm not glad she was shot, but I don't miss her, if that's what you want to know." Marcy dug around her desk for a pen and began writing, a clear signal the discussion had ended. Nic headed for Studio A, recalling her discussion with Barney, and tallied the votes. One person thought a great deal of Carolyn, and one, most assuredly, did not.

At first glance, the studio looked empty. Then she spotted Jimmy. The copy boy rarely spoke, but after the uncomfortable conversation with Marcy, Nic felt up to pulling a few teeth. "Hey, Jimmy. Are you delivering scripts?" Instead of answering, he handed her one and kept walking without as much as a nod. "Wait, I'll walk with you. Did you know Carolyn Park?" He shook his head. "Do you know why anyone would want to kill her?" His silence and the increased size and speed of his steps suggested that another conversation had reached an unsatisfactory end. "Okay. Bye."

Nic turned and noticed George, Barney's assistant, leaning on the wall a few feet away. She wondered if he had heard her questions to Jimmy. He was close enough. "Hi, George. I was just asking Jimmy if he knew why anyone would have wanted to kill Carolyn."

"Yeah? What'd he say?"

"He didn't answer. What about you? Do you know anyone who wanted to kill her?"

Like Jimmy, George was a man of few words, but unlike Jimmy's tall, blonde frame, George was near her height, broad across the chest, and muscular. He had thick curly red hair that extended beyond his shirt collar in back and sideburns that nearly reached his jaw. Nic had never had a conversation with him, and when he responded to her question with a shrug and walked away, she knew that was not about to change.

With her third failed attempt, Nic considered a visit to the twentieth floor to talk to Nora, but as others entered the studio, she decided it made more sense to concentrate on work. Had she known how little opportunity there would be for spying during the coming week, she might have chosen differently. Interruptions by the police, changes from one of the sponsors, and a generally gloomy mood in the studio, barely gave them time to prepare for the following Monday's show. Even after the live performance, things did not improve, and rehearsals for the next show started with the same grueling schedule.

Nic had seen Nora a few times during the busy week, but had no opportunity to talk. Despite her less-than-friendly introduction, Nic felt an interest in the writer that she could not identify. The reason for that interest and questions relating to the case went unasked and undisclosed as overtime and long rehearsals dragged on.

Not only cast members worked long hours. Most of the crew came in early and stayed late in their effort to get back on schedule. One writer seemed comfortable, perhaps even grateful, for the excessive overtime. It was nearly eight when Nora finished on Tuesday, long after the other writers had gone. By the time she departed, the streets were dark and sparsely populated. It was not difficult to see that her mood matched the gloom.

Heavy morning traffic had forced her to park on the other side of the river along Wacker Drive, which meant a hike over the bridge. Walking was not usually a problem for Nora, but the extra hours and not sleeping or eating well had taken a toll. She was a mess physically and emotionally, struggling to understand how in one instant, her life could change so completely.

When she arrived at the Chevy, instead of climbing in to drive home, she raised her collar against the chilly air and sat on a concrete wall that separated waters of the Chicago River from city streets. She usually enjoyed watching the lights dance on its slow moving black surface, but even they made her heart ache. Everything that once brought pleasure, now made her want to scream in pain. Her sigh, like other recent unconscious responses, only amplified the emptiness.

Focused on her despair, Nora failed at first to realize that the movement of someone in the shadows had disturbed her thoughts. When the primal internal warning of danger registered, it was too late. Three things happened at once. She felt an explosion in the back of her head, heard the sound of a splash, and felt icy hands pull her into a suffocating darkness.

Chapter 5

The week of overtime left many WBAC employees in a near stupor. On Tuesday evening, Nic finished the dinner dishes and sat in the living room staring out the large bay window, too tired to think. Anna watched her unconsciously wrap strands of hair behind her ears, an action she had repeated throughout her life.

Her father, Anna's brother, Charlie, died before she was born. His long angular face was the only feature he and Nicole had in common. It was her mother, Grace, who she most resembled. She had her height and slim build, and as much as Nic complained about her own, she had her mother's straight brown hair. To Anna, it was the liquid green eyes and loving, trusting hearts that mother and daughter shared completely.

Nic was ten when her mother died and Anna took her in. Angry and frightened, the child barely spoke for weeks. She refused to go to school and ate little. Millie, with the determined love and support found only in the heart of a best friend, helped her rejoin life. Neither Nic nor Anna would ever forget.

"Aunt Anna, have you talked to Millie today?" Nic sat sideways in the stuffed chair, her legs draped over the arm while she pinched the shell off a peanut.

"No, but if I'm not mistaken, she's on her way down."

Anna was right. After a brief knock, Millie opened the door. "My sister called. *And Then There Were None* opened at the Uptown today. Should we go?"

The movie, *And Then There Were None*, based on Agatha Christie's book *Ten Little Indians*, was a mystery, and all three women loved them. Anna had the greatest devotion and backed it with a large collection of books from which Nic and Millie borrowed liberally.

A ten-degree drop in temperature and the promise of snow convinced the three to bundle up for the mile-and-a-half walk to the Uptown Theater. When they arrived, Millie dropped three quarters into the metal basin and collected their tickets, distributing them as they entered the lobby. The ornately decorated vestibule was a sharp contrast to the flat grey sidewalk and street on the other side of the glass doors.

"I love this place," Nic whispered. Her hushed comment and wide eyes reflected the childlike wonder with which she often observed the world.

The Uptown offered the perfect place to marvel. When it opened in 1925, it was the second largest theater in the country, with four thousand seats and a ten-thousand-pipe Wurlitzer organ. The elaborate mezzanine boasted two hand-carved curved marble staircases, brass chandeliers, and a myriad of sconces, gargoyles, and exotic carvings.

Two hours later, the threesome began their leisurely walk home through a half inch of fresh snow. Temperatures had warmed a few degrees and the crisp white blanket made the city streets glisten. Anna and Millie walked ahead discussing the movie, while Nic peered in the many shops that lined Broadway.

"I don't understand why they changed the ending from the way it was in the book," Millie complained. "I liked it better the other way."

"I agree. The movie followed the play rather than the book, and I read that Miss Christie didn't want an empty stage at the end of the play. I suppose that makes sense, and maybe the people who made the film thought audiences would like the happier finish."

"If you don't mind, Anna, I'd like to borrow another Agatha Christie book. Now that Nic is working, I get lonely up there all day every day. Reading helps a little."

"Have you thought any more about looking for a job?"

"Yes. I've decided to do it. Besides being bored, we could use the money."

As they crossed Broadway, Anna noticed that Nic had fallen behind. "It's unusual for those long legs of hers to be trailing us."

Nic had stopped in front of a pawnshop to watch the slow-turning base of an anniversary clock. A vague memory of a similar glass-domed timepiece disappeared when she heard an engine rev and looked up. She didn't see a vehicle, but noticed that Millie and Anna were across the street and hurried to join them.

Anna heard the engine, too. When a black car raced down the street and turned recklessly onto Broadway, she looked across the street and screamed, "Nicole, look out."

Nic had just stepped off the curb when she heard Anna shout, but the sight of two quickly approaching yellow headlights froze her in place. As the car slid to the sidewalk, she felt something push her and fell backwards. Her suddenly airborne feet landed on wet snow and she was unable to maintain her balance. She crashed to the pavement. The engine roared, the tires squealed, and the car sped away, throwing a pile of slush on her unmoving form.

Millie and Anna ran across the street as the car disappeared. In seconds, Anna was on her knees checking for a pulse. "Nicole, can you hear me."

Millie noticed a cut on Nic's forehead. "There's a lot of blood, Anna."

"Help me turn her on her back."

The months since Millie retired her bucking bar had not diminished her strength. She quickly turned Nic on her back and placed her own rolled scarf under her head. Anna filled a handkerchief with snow and pressed it on the cut above her right eye. Her clothes were soaked and her hair bloody. Beneath the matted locks, her face was as pale as the surrounding snow. "Nicole, dear," Anna said softly. "Open your eyes."

Obediently, her unfocused eyes opened. Nic recognized Anna and Millie, but could not connect her brain to her mouth, or the rest of her body.

"Nicole, did the car hit you?"

Nic remembered two yellow eyes staring at her from the street, but it was a giant panther, not a car. She willed her head to shake and felt a sharp pain on the right side of her face. Her hand flew to the soggy handkerchief, causing additional agony when she pressed it against the cut. "What happened?" Her voice sounded strange, and at the sight of the bloody handkerchief, a knot formed in her stomach. "Aunt Anna, why am I bleeding?"

"You hit your head. Try and lie still." Anna filled the cloth with clean snow and put it on the cut. As she turned to ask Millie to find help, a police ambulance pulled to the curb and a sandy-haired medic jumped out and knelt by Nic.

"Did she slip on the ice?"

Millie jumped to her feet. Her voice rose in volume as she pointed to the tire tracks. "She fell on the ice trying to avoid a car driving on the sidewalk. He left her there and drove off."

The medic was young, but had enough experience with emergencies to assess and handle the situation. He looked kindly at Millie. "We'll take care of her. Are you friends?"

Anna squeezed Millie's hand and gave her a chance to calm down. "I'm her aunt and this is our neighbor. A car turned onto Broadway and slid toward her. We were across the street and couldn't see if he struck her or if she jumped out of the way."

The medic checked the cut under the handkerchief. "Head wounds bleed a lot, but it's under control. The snow was a good idea. Let's move her off this wet pavement. Can you stand, Miss?"

While the others were discussing the accident and her health, Nic tested various body parts. Except for a sore knee and throbbing head, she felt okay. "I think so." Her green eyes had not cleared completely and her brain struggled to digest what Millie told the officer about the car, but she could stand.

The medics escorted her to the back seat of the police car where she sat facing out while the sandy-haired medic checked her injuries. She stayed quiet as he moved a shiny object in front of her eyes and tapped a number of body parts, and she answered as best she could several seemingly silly questions. Once satisfied, he made a few notes while his partner cleaned and bandaged the cut on her head. Though his touch was light, the activity proved painful and tears over which Nic had no control, streamed down her face. Anna handed her tissue.

"You're okay," the medic told her. "Your pupils are normal, breathing is good, and your pulse is strong. You'll have a headache for a couple of days, and you may end up with a black eye. Do you have aspirin at home?" Nic looked to Anna, who assured her and the medic that they did. "Your knee is scraped, but there doesn't seem to be anything broken. If you feel worse, have your doctor drop by."

Rising from a crouched position in front of Nic, the medic spoke to Anna. "Does she live with you?"

"Yes."

"Wake her in the middle of the night to make sure she doesn't have a concussion or other complications. If she is nauseous or dizzy, call your doctor." He waited for Anna to nod in response. "Why don't you three crawl into the back of the car and we'll take you home. Sorry it's so crowded."

A lack of ambulances during and shortly after the war forced cities to find alternatives. The large black squad car attending to the rescue was one of a handful converted for emergency use and filled with equipment and medical supplies. It was not a comfort to Nic to see, for the second time in ten days, the interior of a police vehicle. She'd gone the previous twenty-seven years blissfully unaware of the experience.

During the cramped trip home, the officer informed them that there was a call to the station reporting the accident. The caller, like Anna and Millie, saw the car, but could not tell from where he was if it hit Nic before she fell. They did not see the license plate, and did not leave a name or number.

Anna and Millie noticed almost nothing about the car, except that it was black. Anna thought the driver might have been a man, but explained that she was far too worried for her niece to notice a license plate.

As they talked, Nic understood what happened. The black car was her panther, and the eyes that kept her frozen in place were round yellow headlights filtered by a long forgotten fairytale that allowed them to cast a spell.

When they arrived at the apartment, the women unwound their bodies and crawled from the back seat. The medic shared his doubt that they would find the car or driver, and his surprise that he left the scene since the icy roads probably caused the accident. Nic had no response except to give him the soiled blanket with her thanks as Millie helped her limp to the apartment. To her delight, Nic found Anna running a bath.

In minutes, her filthy wet clothes sat in a pile next to the tub as she soaked in Epsom salts and extremely hot water. She washed the dried blood from her hair as best she could around the bandage and kept her knee elevated. Although a good soak was one of her favorite things to do, bed and sleep sounded even better.

Wrapped in a flannel nightgown, she dried her hair with a towel and crawled into bed where Anna covered her with a blanket. "Here, Nicole, take this aspirin. We won't need to change the dressing until tomorrow. Are you feeling better?"

Nic poured the powder on the back of her tongue and drank the entire glass of water to wash it down. "Aunt Anna, I don't remember things clearly. Who pushed me out of the way of the car? I couldn't make myself move and suddenly I felt someone shove me to the side."

"I didn't see anyone." Anna sat on the edge of the bed. "You were standing alone. After the car left, Millie and I found you on the sidewalk, but there was no one else in the area. I thought the car knocked you to the ground."

"I didn't think it was the car. Who do you think called the police?"

"I don't know. There are apartments above the stores. Maybe a tenant saw what happened and called. I doubt it was the guy driving the car."

"I'm sure you're right." As exhausted as she was, Nic needed a little calm support before she tried to sleep. "Aunt Anna, you said you heard the car idling before it turned the corner. Are you sure it was the same car?"

"There were no other vehicles in the area."

"I wonder why the driver took off without checking to see if I was hurt. Of course, maybe he didn't know anyone was there." She realized immediately that was not likely. "No, he must have seen me in his headlights."

"I don't know if it was an accident. As I said, I thought that car was waiting around the corner. If it wasn't an accident, we need to consider if anyone would have reason to hurt you. When you're feeling better, it might be a good idea to think about the people you talked to at the station and try to remember if anyone seemed unusually nervous or upset." Anna leaned to kiss her forehead. "I'll change the bandage in the morning. Stay in bed."

Nic had no plans to leave. The weight of the blanket was enough to keep her from moving. That was, of course, if she had a desire to move, which she did not. She had no desire to reexamine the accident either, but not thinking proved more difficult than not moving.

Was it an accident or intentional? Did someone want to hurt her? Why? She considered recent conversations. As angry as Nora was, Nic did not think it was at her, and besides, Anna had said she thought it was a man driving. Barney had no reason to want to hurt her. What about George or Jimmy? The pounding in her head overtook her need to think and she fell asleep.

In what seemed like minutes, Nic felt a push on her shoulder and heard Anna. "Nicole, wake up."

"What is it, Aunt Anna." She tried to sit, but a sharp pain kept her still. "Is something wrong? How long have I been asleep?"

"No, dear. Nothing's wrong. You've been asleep for four hours. How do you feel?"

"I feel okay. Why?"

"Go back to sleep."

"Why did you wake me to tell me to go to sleep? Aunt Anna?" As she watched her aunt turn out the light and leave, Nic faintly recalled being in a police car. She decided she was dreaming and would wait until morning to figure it out.

Chapter 6

Nic thought it odd that she and Millie were working on a snowy street instead of inside the factory, and that they wore winter coats and gloves instead of coveralls. What she found most curious was that the propeller turned on the plane as they riveted the fuselage. She was about to ask Millie for an explanation when another plane approached the field, landing lights growing brighter as it headed toward them. "Millie, look out," she yelled, but before she could jump clear herself, the tip of the wing smacked against her forehead. "Ow."

"I'm sorry, Nicole. I wish I could do this without hurting you. Do you have a headache?"

Waking from a deep sleep requires little more than waiting for the brain to accept a shift to consciousness. Waking from an active dream can take longer as the brain struggles to determine which images are real and which are part of the unconscious adventure. Nic drew her hand from under the blanket and touched her forehead. "Ouch." The pain was real, but was it from an airplane? She took the packet of aspirin Anna handed her and emptied it, followed by a glass of water. Her head fell to the pillow as she returned the glass to her aunt. "How does it look, Aunt Anna? Will people notice?"

"Yes, dear, people will notice. The cut doesn't look too bad, but you have a nasty black eye. Do you want a cold compress?"

"No. I just want a little more sleep."

Nic closed her eyes and Anna stood. "I'm off to do a few chores. I'll be in and out most of the day. Are you going to work?"

Nic turned on her side and shrugged as she pulled the blanket over her shoulders, flipping immediately to the side without the bandage.

Her return to slumber land was brief. A persistent banging coaxed her from under the covers, but she rose too quickly and grabbed the dresser to keep from falling. When her head stabilized, she put on her robe and staggered to the kitchen where Millie waved through the window of the back door. She hardly noticed Nic's sleepy state, asking a question as she entered. "Have you been listening to the radio?"

"Do I look like I've been listening to the radio?"

Millie took a minute to examine the bruise before guiding Nic to the kitchen table. She poured them coffee from the pot Anna left and joined Nic who began sipping hers quietly as she waited for Millie's news.

"The police made an arrest in the Park murder."

If Nic had been wide-awake, she might have done damage to the coffee cup. Even in her semi-conscious state, she slammed it to the table with more force than necessary and sent a small brown tidal wave over the side. She ignored the mess. "Why didn't you say so? Did they say who it was? Is it someone from the station?"

"All the announcer said was the police made an arrest last night. They'll release more details later this morning. Do you have any idea who it is?"

"I know I shouldn't say this, Millie, but I'm just glad it's not me. I wonder what happened. Do you suppose they were able to match fingerprints?"

Millie wiped up the coffee and added more to their cups. "Match them to what, Nic?"

"I don't know. They could have found evidence in the studio and not told anyone. Maybe they have the gun that killed her, but don't want people to know. Who can guess what the police are doing." Nic rubbed her eyes and felt pain on the right side of her face.

"I don't know about the fingerprints, but it's not terrible to be glad you weren't arrested for a crime you didn't commit. I'm glad. Nic, have you looked in the mirror? You have a nasty black eye. Are you going to work?"

As she felt the tender area around her bandage and eye, Nic realized she was not looking forward to explaining her accident to the entire station. Maybe she would tell Marcy at the reception desk, WBAC gossip central. "I feel good enough to go in. If I feel worse at the station, I'll come home."

"Take care of yourself. What if the guy in the car was aiming at you?" Millie deposited her cup in the sink and grabbed the doorknob. "Stop by if you're up to it after work. I want to know what people are saying at the station."

"I will. Millie, wait a second. Last night, right before the car drove on the sidewalk, I couldn't move, but then I felt someone push me. Aunt Anna said I was alone. Did you notice another person?"

Millie shook her head, clearly interested in the incident. "I didn't see anyone. Are you sure you were pushed? Could it have been the car?"

"Last night I was sure, but I'm not convinced this morning. If you and Aunt Anna didn't see anyone, I must have imagined it. It felt real, and I thought I fell before the car reached me." She shrugged. "I don't know. Maybe that's where I bruised my knee, from the car running into me."

"Or maybe you had help from a spirit. You hear about that stuff all the time. At the last second, a hand reaches through from another dimension and pushes a person out of the way of danger. I can't wait to tell Momma and my sisters. They'll love it, and Momma will want you to come by so she can read your cards."

Millie and her Momma and sisters visited tea readers, palm readers, Ouija board sessions, and whoever and whatever else might have information 'from beyond.' When her energetic neighbor charged out the back door, Nic remained to finish her coffee in the comfortable silence. It lasted ten seconds.

Darlene Renfrow stood at the front door as Nic pulled it open. "Hi, Nic. Ow. What happened to your face? Is it as painful as it looks?"

Darlene lived in the apartment above. Laden with books and dressed in layers for the weather, she was on her way to the university library where she worked as a librarian. The previous year, while studying with Anna, she was looking for a place to live when the apartment upstairs became available.

"Hi, Darlene. Do you want to come in?"

"I can't. I have to go to work, but thanks. Would you let Anna know I found the information she wanted? She can drop by the library anytime today. What happened?"

"I fell on the way home from the Uptown last night and hit my head on the sidewalk."

"Is that why the police ambulance was here?"

"They gave us a ride."

"Did the fall cause your black eye?" Nic leaned on the door and nodded weakly. "You'll let Anna know?"

"Sure, Darlene. I'll write her a note as soon as I close the door." An action Nic wanted desperately to complete.

"Thanks. Congratulations on your job at the radio station. It must be exciting." When Darlene opened the outer door, a blast of cold air reminded Nic that a robe and nightgown were little protection against Chicago winds. She returned to her cold coffee and the clanking kitchen radiator. Although noisy, it made the air around her cozy and warm, almost cozy enough to consider going back to bed. With everything she had on her mind, Nic suspected that going to bed did not guarantee sleep.

She remembered Millie's remark. Maybe she was right, and an otherworldly person pushed her out of the way. Nic sometimes felt her mom around. She talked to her about her hopes and dreams and felt a sense of connection, but she suspected it was the memory of her mom, not a ghost. After briefly considering that a tarot card reading might be fun, Nic returned to earth. The last thing she needed to do was to start believing in spirits.

Nic left a note for Anna, and once washed and adequately attired, attempted to hide the bruise with makeup. The sight of an ugly black eye covered with badly applied makeup changed her mind. She scrubbed her face, brushed her teeth, and left, feeling not quite up to her exciting job as a radio star.

The bandage and black eye had turned a few heads on the train, but people looked away quickly. When she boarded the elevator, Sam asked her what had happened and offered a sympathetic nod as she explained. Nic used the remainder of the ride to prepare for possible reactions from coworkers, but as she left the car, the crowd in the reception area dissolved those concerns. Cast and crewmembers sat and stood reading the newspaper or discussing its content. Marcy spotted Nic and waved her to the desk. "Do you believe it? You've heard, haven't you?" She noticed the bruise and stopped. "Good heavens. What happened to you? That looks awful."

"I fell on the sidewalk last night." Nic removed her coat and responded to the first part of the question. "Do you mean that the police are holding a suspect? Yes, my neighbor told me this morning. Have they said who it is?"

"You don't know. Here's the late edition." Marcy pushed her newspaper at Nic, seemingly delighted to be the bearer of the news. On the front page was a picture of Nora. Nic found the nearest chair and joined in the morning's activity.

The further she read, the further her mouth dropped. The police held Nora Hahn, writer and longtime friend of Carolyn Park, pending charges in Park's murder. Park and Hahn were rumored to have been 'special friends,' and police said they had information from a reliable source indicating that Mrs. Park planned to end their relationship. They believed Hahn became enraged and killed her. Police found jewelry belonging to Hahn in a pocket of the jacket Mrs. Park wore and think she grabbed it while defending herself.

Stunned, but unable to stop reading, Nic learned that a fisherman pulled Nora from the Chicago River the previous night, where, out of remorse, she had attempted to take her own life. A note found in her nearby car said that she could not live with herself because she had murdered Mrs. Park.

Nic laid the paper on her lap, her eyes no longer able to focus on the fuzzy gray patches. 'Special friends' the article said. Carolyn and Nora were lesbians. That shed a little light on the anger Nora expressed at Nic for doing the part, and so soon after Carolyn died. Had Nora's loss been so great that she tried to take her own life? Nic took a deep breath.

"Hey, Nic. What do you think? I mean about Nora killing Carolyn." Marcy seemed almost pleased. Her excitement at the news made Nic uncomfortable.

"I don't know what to think. I had no idea she and Carolyn were, um, that close. Nevertheless, just because they arrested Nora, doesn't mean she did it. You've met O'Brian. Ten days ago, I was the most likely suspect. Thanks for letting me read your paper." She returned the copy to the reception desk.

"She confessed, Nic. That means she did it."

Nic had no response, but Marcy was enjoying herself and not ready to end the conversation. "You didn't know about them?" Nic shook her head faster than she should have. "I thought the only person that didn't know was her husband, Cecil."

Nic wondered at the excessive pleasure Marcy derived from the gossip about Nora. She wondered even more when, as Marcy spread the paper across her desk, she shared another observation. "Nora Hahn will get what she deserves. Bad people have bad lives."

Nic listened to nearby conversations, surprised and saddened by a number of cruel comments. The news, and lack of compassion for Nora, created enough pressure to rekindle the headache Nic had almost forgotten. She turned back to Marcy. "Do you know where I can find some aspirin?" Marcy opened a drawer and handed Nic a packet of powder. Wanting to avoid further conversation, she grabbed the offered medicine and turned away. "Thanks. I'm going to the lounge for a few minutes."

The door to the women's lounge closed, and Nic leaned back, remembering that Greg had implied a deeper connection between Nora and Carolyn. She had heard it, but with no understanding of homosexual relationships, and nowhere to file the information, she let it go. O'Brian had even used the expression 'special friends' when he mentioned Nora, but she had heard it as close friends, nothing more. "I am so far removed from the worldly Inez Ingalls, it's pathetic." She faced the mirror, touching her colorful bruise and feeling embarrassed and annoyed at her innocence.

Her irritation increased when she took a paper cup from the stack and four others fell to the sink. In the few short hours since she crawled from bed, she felt drained. She sat at the back of the lounge to take the aspirin and regroup, but when she closed her eyes, she saw Nora staring at her across the stage. She was angry, yes, but there was something other than rage.

When the aspirin had time to work, Nic rose, testing her balance and the strength of the throb. Given the circumstances, she felt reasonably steady.

She arrived at Studio A to find it populated by a good section of the crowd from the reception area, newspapers in hand. Nic spotted Greg and Belia. "Good morning, you two."

Her friendly greeting was met with a shocked look from Belia. "What has happened to you?"

"I fell on the sidewalk last night." Nic raised her hand and added, "It's not as painful as it looks."

Greg deposited his bass in the stand and joined them. "Welcome to the zoo. Ouch, Nic, that looks awful." His lips formed a silent O as he stared.

"It's not bad. I forgot about it when I heard the news about Carolyn and Nora."

"About Nora being accused of killing Carolyn, or that Nora and Carolyn had a relationship?" On a less fair and youthful face, the raised eyebrow and pursed lips might have appeared stern and inquisitive. Greg looked mildly curious.

"Both, I guess. I don't know much about homosexuals." The embarrassment Nic felt about her lack of experience returned, as did her one and only conversation with Nora Hahn. "I wasn't enthralled with Nora after the way she talked to me, but I can't believe she killed Carolyn."

"Why not, Nic?"

"I don't know, Belia. Partly because of how fiercely she defended her."

"That could have been an act to throw off suspicion," Greg suggested.

"I suppose, but it didn't feel like an act. I heard her rage, but it wasn't at Carolyn." She sighed and asked the musicians a question. "Did you two know about their relationship?"

"I heard rumors from when I start here." Belia tilted her head at Greg. "From him."

"Hey, hey, I'm not a gossip." Greg tried for a pout, but withdrew his extended lip to explain. "They came to see my band at a club once and were with a number of other couples. Friends of mine have seen them in bars and clubs frequented by homosexuals, and rumors have floated around here for as long as I've been with the orchestra. Besides, you know how it is. Musicians are more hip to what happens outside the mainstream. It did surprise me when I heard recently that they were breaking up. They've been together a long time."

Nic had more questions, but they would have to wait. Allen Reed called the band members for a rehearsal, leaving Nic to look elsewhere for conversation. Harold, Stanley, Frank, and Alice were on stage with their heads together, looking collectively unhappy. She guessed there was a problem and waited until the engineers left before climbing the steps to sit next to Frank.

"Hi." She saw Frank staring at her bruise. "I fell on the sidewalk last night. I'm fine."

"You don't need to tell me the details, but that's quite a shiner. You're lucky we're not doing television in here yet. We'd have to make you the woman behind the curtain." His brief smile gave way to more bad news. "I'm afraid there's another problem. The main wiring box in the engineer's booth has multiple shorts and will take all day to repair."

"What about one of the other studios?"

"I checked. Every studio has a show or rehearsal scheduled for the rest of the day. Of course this happens just as we were nearly back on track." He turned to Alice. "Would you check with Harold and see if he thinks we can work in here tomorrow? If not, let's take a look at the schedules."

Nic waited until Alice left before asking Frank a question. "Did you know Carolyn and Nora well?"

"I've known them both since we were students at the University of Chicago. After we graduated, I didn't see them for a while. Of course, her foundation kept Carolyn in the news, but I hadn't seen them in person. Two and a half years ago, I advertised for a writer and Nora showed up. I knew she'd written for a number of reputable radio shows and ad agencies, and how good she was, so I hired her."

"I thought they started together."

"Almost. Nora mentioned that Carolyn was looking to do something apart from her philanthropic undertakings. She wondered if we had any openings. I remembered she was a theater major in college, and as it happened we had two more seasons left on a drama series and the female lead was going to have a baby. She didn't want to return and hoped we could find a permanent replacement. I gave Carolyn an audition and she was terrific. When the Inez Ingalls script turned up, I knew she'd be perfect." Frank looked sheepishly at Nic. "Not that you're not perfect."

"Thanks, Frank. She was perfect for the part. So, Nora and Carolyn met at school?"

"Yes, and were together from then on. Nora didn't kill Carolyn, and I don't believe she would have tried to kill herself, but if she did, it was because someone else killed Carolyn, not because she did."

"You sound sure."

"I am sure. Our reporter that covers O'Brian's station called me last night when he heard about the arrest. I went down there, but he wouldn't let me see her. Nora has been through a lot. She doesn't need this."

His face, a mix of sadness and confidence, put Nic squarely in the corner of Nora Hahn. "Was Carolyn as wealthy as people say?"

"The short answer is yes."

"And the long answer?"

Frank released the hold on his suspenders and folded his hands. "Her family came from Germany in the mid 1800s and built one of the largest textile manufacturing companies in the Midwest. They were shrewd business people, and from what

Carolyn told me, ruthless. In 1910, one of their plants caught fire. They kept the doors locked to make sure the women stayed at their sewing machines. Over one hundred and fifty women died in fifteen minutes, many died jumping from windows."

"How awful."

"That event didn't strain her family financially. I don't know what it would have taken to do that, but Carolyn said that from that moment on, dark clouds became a permanent fixture. Their wealth grew, but the family dwindled. There were suicides, breakdowns, and occasionally an uncle or cousin simply disappeared. Her father was the end of the family line, except for Carolyn. No one knew how much money he had. Some he earned, but most he inherited from the deaths of the rest of his family members. After her mother died," Frank added sadly, "another suicide, Carolyn, at twelve, became her father's nursemaid. She did that for the next six years, until alcohol killed him and she inherited everything, including the darkness. She was close to the edge herself by then."

Nic shivered.

"Are you okay?" Frank asked.

"Yes. Please go on."

"Carolyn was ready to follow in her mother's footsteps and leave her money to charity, when it dawned on her that she didn't have to die to give the money away. She established her foundation." His voice, already soft, grew reflective. "She may have been the only good to come from that group, which makes it sadder that her life would end this tragically and this soon."

"How old was Carolyn?"

"Same as me, thirty-five."

Nic dug in her purse for a tissue and wiped her eyes as Frank waved for Alice to join him. "We won't accomplish much here today. I'm sending everyone home. Alice, would you let the crew on twenty know?" Frank stood and cupped his hands around his mouth. "Everyone, Miss Owen thinks we should take the rest of the day off." Nic received a round of applause and took a bow. "For those staring at her face, she fell on the ice last night. Now, go home and rest. Tomorrow we're back on overtime." Frank turned to Nic and winked. "That goes for you too."

"I'm okay with that. I'll work long days for the rest of the month to go home right now."

Chapter 7

Not long after Nic moved in with her aunt, Anna took her to the circus. She had hoped the color, clamor, and vibrancy of the parade and show would offer Nicole momentary relief from her despair. It did help, and Nic developed a fondness for the big top that remained, but as recent events paraded through her mind to an imagined calliope, she felt little enjoyment.

There were few passengers on the midmorning train, which made it easy to find a seat. The removal of unwanted thoughts took more effort. Nic closed her eyes and focused on the humming steel wheels. She wanted to empty her brain, so when an image appeared, she pictured it as a stone resting in her palm. One at a time, she hurled the frozen moments into Lake Michigan. Some, like her dinner with Anna and Millie, were smooth and flat. Pitched from the bank, they skipped over the water, barely disturbing its surface. Others, like her visit to the police station, were rough and jagged, baseball-size rocks that created a disruptive splash and sank immediately. When the image of a fisherman dragging Nora from the river appeared, Nic felt a boulder form in her stomach. Luckily, she had reached her stop.

The exercise cleared some of the confusion, but questions remained. Nic remembered Anna's remark that caffeine helped her work and thought a cup of coffee might be just the thing. She hoped the small diner on Irving, a half block from the elevated station and a half block from her apartment would be just the place.

Two people sat at the counter and one occupied a booth. All three hovered over newspapers and Nora peered out from under every pair of elbows. Nic took a seat at the counter and ordered coffee. The aroma as the server poured suggested the pot had been on the burner for some time. She was braced for the strong beverage, but not the accompanying comment. "That's some shiner, lady. Whadja do to get the old man mad?"

Nic rarely visited the restaurant, and because of that, the person working was a complete stranger. She thanked him for the coffee and felt no guilt ignoring the question he obviously found amusing. To discourage further conversation, she grabbed a nearby paper and focused on the article about Nora. Before long, her thoughts went to Carolyn, a woman who had survived overwhelming misfortune only to be murdered. Frank was right. It made her death that much more tragic.

What had it been like for her to lose her mother and take care of her father at that age? Nic had been devastated when her mom died, but she'd had no other responsibilities. Even with the fierce support of Aunt Anna and Millie, she had barely coped. How had Carolyn done it?

Looking back to the picture of Nora, other questions arose. When did Carolyn know she was a lesbian? What about Nora? Did they become lesbians when they met? Nic stopped her thoughts, unhappy that she was more concerned with their relationship than with the fact that one person had died and another tried to take her own life.

The coffee wasn't worth the dime she left on the counter, and as she walked around the corner to her apartment, Nic knew she had done little to soothe her restless mind and a considerable amount of damage to her taste buds.

When she entered the apartment and found Alley home alone, Nic deposited her coat and purse and scratched the feline behind the ear. As much as she adored the cat, she required human companionship and climbed to 2B where Millie dragged her to the kitchen and fired off questions. "What happened at the studio? Were the police there? Did they send you home because of Nora? Did she kill her? That is an ugly black eye."

Nic pressed an index finger to Millie's lips and stopped the assault, giving her a chance to answer. "The studio was wild. Everyone was shocked at Nora's arrest, and most were surprised that she might have tried to kill herself. No one however, was unaware of Nora and Carolyn's relationship. No one except me. I may have been the only person that didn't know they were a couple." Even with a friend as close as Millie, Nic felt embarrassed and averted her eyes as she fell into a chair. "Millie, you've known me my entire life. Have I always been this dumb?"

"You don't really want an answer, do you? Come on, Nic. I'm kidding." She gave her shoulder a squeeze. "After I read the story, I remembered a rumor about them at the factory. Georgia and Irene are lesbians and they told Francine about Carolyn and Nora. I didn't know who they were, or remember their names, which is why I didn't put it together when you told us about Nora at dinner the other night. But you know how gossipy the factory was." Millie took two glasses from the cabinet and filled them with water.

"There was gossip at the factory? And lesbians?" Nic did a better job playing Inez Ingalls than keeping the surprise from her voice.

"There was gossip. I only knew Georgia and Irene, but there were probably other lesbians." Millie rolled her eyes. "Nic, you're not dumb, but you can be totally oblivious to what's going on around you. How could you not know there was gossip with thousands of people in one building?"

Another wave of exhaustion hit. "I'm going to lie down for a while. I'll check back later."

"I'll be here. The mailman should be by anytime with a letter from Joe."

Nic sought refuge on the sofa, and within seconds, Alley curled on her stomach. The cat's soft purr, and a determined effort to keep her mind free of rumor and speculation, slowed the bombardment of thoughts. She slept undisturbed for nearly an hour, when a sudden pressure on her stomach forced her from a dream to semi-consciousness. She saw Anna coming in the front door.

Alley had seen her, too, and hopped off her comfortable perch to welcome mom home. "Nicole. What are you doing home so early? Are you not feeling well?"

Still a little groggy, Nic was slow to respond. "No, I'm fine. There was a wiring problem. Aunt Anna, did you find the note I left on the table?"

"I did. Thank you." Anna joined her on the sofa and examined her eye. "Are you in pain?" Nic assured her she wasn't. "Tell me what happened at the station. I'll bet it was interesting."

"I will in a second. I'm trying to remember the dream I was having. A blonde girl was extinguishing flames in a burning building and others showed up to help, but instead of throwing buckets of water, they threw money. The girl begged them to stop because they were making it worse, but they didn't listen and she started to cry." Anna remained quiet as Nic struggled to describe the quickly fading images. "You know how dreams are, Aunt Anna, like fairy tales, where ordinary actions have extraordinary effects. In the dream, her tears flooded the building and stopped the flames. Then she gathered the money in a burlap sack and took it to the bridge at the edge of the city and poured it on the shantytown below."

"Well, that is an interesting dream. Who was the little blonde girl, Nicole?"

"I think it was Carolyn Park. Frank told me a little about her life and family. I'll tell you about that later, but first let's talk about the murder. Did you hear that they arrested Nora?"

"I bought a newspaper when I saw the headline. Do you think she killed her?"

"My first reaction when I read it was no, and after I talked to Frank, I'm convinced she didn't."

"Frank doesn't believe it. Hmm. Did you know about their relationship?"

"No, and I was the only one who didn't." She repeated her conversations with Greg and Belia, and most recently, Millie. "I felt dumb, but I felt worse that I was more shocked by their relationship than I was by the murder and suicide attempt. I don't why, or what I expected a homosexual would be. Do you know much about it, Aunt Anna?"

"I'll make us coffee and we can talk." When she returned with the drinks, they sat on the sofa, and after a few thoughtful sips of coffee, Anna spoke. "Nicole, life is full of things I don't understand. I'm amazed to be this old and continually finding more to learn. You're a good and kind person, and you shouldn't be harsh on yourself for your reaction. You've probably heard nothing but people making fun of homosexuals, or saying negative hurtful things. What's important is not your reaction to what others tell you as much as it is what you do after the reaction. It would be easy to say that since a large number of people feel that homosexuality is wrong, I'll go along with that. What's difficult is to know if what you're agreeing to is truth or someone's opinion. To me, it makes sense to learn what I can. If after I've investigated, I feel an idea is wrong, fine, but I have found that learning usually replaces ignorance with understanding. Do you see what I mean?"

"I think so. The only knowledge I have about homosexuals is what I've heard from other people—just hearsay. You've taught me that it's never a good idea to make big decisions with too little information." Nic could see that Anna had more on her mind. "What is it, Aunt Anna?"

Anna Owen rarely lacked opinions, or the words to present them. She took a deep breath and found her voice. "Nicole, my brother, Johnny, your uncle, was a homosexual. Our family learned first-hand the effect of hate and bigotry. Johnny was the oldest of the three of us by a number of years. Your father and I still lived at home when he moved out. He and his friend, Peter, worked in the office of a meatpacker at the stockyards. They'd been together for four years. One night, as they were leaving the building, a group of thugs dragged them to the alley and beat them. Peter didn't make it to the hospital, and

Johnny never regained consciousness. Your dad and I were at his side when he died."

Nic stared until she could make a nearly coherent sentence. "Uncle Johnny was.... They beat him to death because he was.... What happened to the men who killed them?"

"Nothing." Anna said softly. "We tried to have them arrested. We wanted to press charges, but the police said they didn't have time to pursue an investigation."

The response, though soft, was bitter. It, and the sadness on Anna's face, crushed Nic. Her heart hurt, her eyes flooded with tears, and she pulled her aunt into her arms. Unlike the dream, her tears did not flood the room and extinguish the pain. Nic leaned back and asked gently, "Why didn't you tell me?"

"I wanted to, and I almost did dozens of times." Anna wiped her eyes. "The longer I waited, the more difficult it seemed." She stopped, straightened her spine, and released a jagged breath. "I was never for one moment ashamed of Johnny. Nicole, human beings are often afraid of what they don't understand, but instead of focusing on their ignorance, they grab onto their fear. Instead of learning about what they fear, they want to destroy what makes them afraid. I wasn't protecting you from Johnny's homosexuality. I was trying to protect you from the people that feared and hated him." Anna held her close. "I know I can't, and I'm glad we talked. Now Johnny is alive in both our hearts."

Nic knew the moon was full. Despite the black silhouette of oak branches that shattered its face into a thousand pieces, she knew it was full. She shut the heavy outer door to the building and headed south, hoping a walk would put the innumerable pieces she'd gathered over the day together to make a whole.

She neared the scoreboard at Wrigley Field and remembered what a great year it had been for the Cubs. They almost made it. They almost won the World Series, losing to Detroit in the final innings of the final game. Chicago sports fans had a saying: 'There's always next year.' There had been no next year for Johnny, nor would there be one for Carolyn.

Solstice, the official beginning of winter, was a month away, and November had been mild, but the Farmer's Almanac predicted heavy snow and cold temperatures at the end of December. Nic hoped they were right. Maybe a thick mantle of snow would hide the ugly things she had learned about people. Maybe enough snow would fall to muffle the awful noises filling her head.

She had never given much thought to why people behaved as they did. Now, life was forcing her to pay attention. To her surprise, instead of being afraid, she felt amused by her waning innocence, ready to open the doors that appeared before her.

A pink neon sign illuminated the wet sidewalk below her shoes. Nic was astonished to see she stood in front of Vera's Diner. She had not noticed how far she'd walked or how cold it was, but a cup of steaming coffee sounded great.

It was at Vera's Diner that Nic, Millie, and others from the area caught buses every morning to ride to the airplane factory west of the city. She shook her head, again amazed at the strange passage of time. That had been less than a year ago, but felt like a lifetime.

"Hey, Honey." Vera shouted from behind the counter as a sudden gust of wind helped Nic push open the metal and glass door. The heavenly aroma of fresh coffee filled her nostrils, and she banished memories of her earlier experience.

"You work at an exciting place. Is that where you got the shiner?" Vera asked. She wore her reputation as a gossip with pride, and Nic fully expected a cross-examination. As long as the coffee was hot and fresh, she would be glad to tell all.

She unbuttoned her coat and looked for a stool, nodding apologetically to patrons near the door who were retrieving napkins and newspapers from her breezy entrance.

Vera had recently installed bright fluorescent lighting, and at the time, Nic wondered if would be bad for business. To her, the harsh light made people look sickly. Judging by the size of the crowd, it had not hurt anyone's appetite.

Vera set a dish in a cart next to where she stood and pointed to a stool usually saved for the help. "Park it here."

The special seat meant she would want an earful. "Let me have a cup of coffee, please. Vera. This," Nic pointed to her eye and explained the circumstances. "But you're right about the station. It's exciting."

Vera kept the cup filled and they talked about the studio, the murder, the spill Nic took on the icy sidewalk, the movie *And then There Were None,* and other events of the last couple of weeks, which, except for the death of Carolyn Park, suddenly seemed unimportant. Nic felt closer to Anna than ever, and knew that recent experiences meant more change, outside and in. Life had stretched her to a new shape, and though it felt strange, she would adapt. At least until the next change came along.

*

Having spent much of the previous day with an overly active brain, Nic intended to keep her mind calm and clear. The trip to work went well, which was why as she opened the door to the lounge with her mind idling, it took a second to understand that Marcy was waving at her from the center of a cluster of women.

"Come here. I don't want to yell." Nic felt drawn like a bee to the hive as she joined the circle and waited with the others for Marcy to speak. "Nora is here."

"Nora is where?" Nic asked.

"In the building. She was on twenty earlier. Amanda," Marcy pointed at a redhead buffing her nails by one of the pedestal sinks, "saw her there this morning."

"Did she have a chance to ask what happened? Why they arrested her?" The question earned a dubious look from Marcy and a few of the worker bees.

"No, of course not."

When the lounge door opened again, Marcy closed her mouth and stared. Nic looked in the mirror and saw what triggered the response. Nora entered, and seemingly oblivious to the crowd, walked to a chair on the other side of the room, parting the women like a biblical body of water. No one spoke as she passed, and the masses filed out until only Nora, Marcy, and Nic remained.

"Are you coming, Nic?" Marcy looked over her shoulder as she pushed open the door.

"I'll be out in a minute." Nic watched Nora pull a cigarette and a gold lighter from her purse. The flame, while igniting the tobacco, shed light on the dark circles under her eyes, illuminating her exhaustion.

When the door closed behind Marcy, Nic watched silently as Nora used a lengthy red finger and thumbnail to dislodge tobacco from her tongue. She continued to stare until Nora looked up and broke the silence. "What are you looking at? Haven't you ever seen a murderer before?" Nic didn't answer. "Look honey, if you have something to say, say it, and leave me the hell alone."

Chapter 8

If Nora had meant to discourage further conversation, she failed. Nic recoiled slightly, but did not retreat. Instead, she sat in the chair next to her. She intended to have a dialogue and since she had not thought through what she wanted to say, she did what came naturally and spoke from her heart. "I don't think you killed Carolyn."

The stream of smoke Nora was exhaling caught in her throat. She stifled a cough, and when her dark eyes settled on Nic, they were less hostile. "You're the only person who doesn't. Why don't you think I killed her?"

Nic responded without hesitation. "When you spoke to me after the first show, I was hurt and angry, but even with that, and even though I didn't know you and Carolyn were companions, I knew you cared for her deeply. I was almost convinced your outrage was at me, but something happened that made me think otherwise. Maybe you dropped your guard, or maybe you ran out of strength, but instead of anger in your eyes, I saw pain, terrible pain. I just didn't know then what it was." Nic controlled her emotions and stayed focused. "You were right. I'll never replace Carolyn as Inez. No one could. I doubt that I could have done the part at all if I hadn't seen her work. I can't fill her shoes, Nora, but having seen her, I have a goal to aim for." She took another quick breath and added a final sentence. "I know you didn't kill her, and I'm truly sorry for your loss."

As the sentence faded, the mask of unfeeling detachment Nora wore developed a crack. Her cigarette fell to the ashtray and pale hands rose to cover the newly exposed pain. Her profile disappeared behind the dark pageboy and she made no sound. Only the movement of her thin shoulders told Nic she was crying. She scanned the lounge for tissue.

"I could never have hurt her. Never." Nora spoke with such force that Nic felt the air around her shudder. "People had no idea what a wonderful person she was. She never discussed the things she did. Not even when they harassed and hurt her." With shaking fingers, Nora took a tissue from the box Nic held and pressed it to her face.

The door behind them opened, but whoever entered, left immediately. Nora struggled to regain control and offered a half-hearted attempt at sarcasm. "Your reputation is at risk being seen with me, you know."

The dark eyes, that only a few weeks earlier had pierced Nic to the core, were sunken and hollow. She seemed drained of tears, anger, and life. Nora had not killed Carolyn, but whoever was responsible destroyed a large part of her with the same bullet. Nic wondered if the pain had been great enough to push her to suicide. "Nora, why did you try to kill yourself?"

Folding the tissues to find a spot not stained with makeup, Nora wiped her face again and looked at Nic. "I didn't. I was hit from behind and pushed into the river. I never saw who did it. I woke up in the emergency room, handcuffed to a bed, with Jones and O'Brian waiting to take me to jail. They said they found a note in my car typed on the machine in my office. I didn't write it. Whoever did, wiped off the typewriter."

"Who called the police?"

"They didn't tell me. Maybe whoever pushed me called them after planting the suicide note. O'Brian said my confession was the icing on the cake. He said that with the rumors of our breaking up, and the jewelry Carolyn had in her pocket, the note proved I'd murdered her."

"Did you tell them you were pushed?"

"O'Brian laughed. When they finally let me make a phone call, my attorney came to the station with the ER report that said the lump on the back of my head was consistent with my story that someone struck me from behind. He also told them that since Carolyn and I've been together for years, it was only natural that she'd have a piece of my jewelry in her pocket."

Nic hadn't thought about the jewelry when she read the article in the paper, but now she realized that conclusion didn't make sense. "If she'd grabbed the jewelry while defending herself, they would have found it in her hand, not her pocket."

"I told O'Brian the same thing, and my attorney told him that the rumors about our breaking up were just that, rumors, but he wasn't listening. He also told him that he couldn't prove I typed the confession. We don't lock our office and anyone could have used the typewriter. They didn't find my fingerprints on the letter, but O'Brian decided that was because I wore gloves to handle it. Why would a person who was about to kill themselves wear gloves to handle the note?"

Nic had more than enough of her own anger at O'Brian. His actions with Nora, though difficult to hear, were not a surprise. "Did he really believe that?"

"No, but he won't let anything like facts interfere with arresting me for Carolyn's murder. My attorney went over O'Brian's head and talked to the district superintendent. He convinced them they didn't have enough to keep me in jail." Unaware of the small pile of tissues on her lap, Nora took another sheet.

"Did you have a chance to read the newspaper article?"

"One of the officers showed me a copy while I sat in that horrid cell." Her voice softened. "The article said Carolyn wanted to end our relationship. That wasn't true. She'd decided to end her convenient marriage, to divorce Cecil."

"Had she told Cecil?"

"I don't know." Nora removed an earring and rolled it in her hand. "I never had a chance to ask. I wasn't in Chicago Thursday or Friday. I was in Michigan talking to my father's attorney about his will and settling his estate. He died the previous week and I'm the only remaining family."

"I'm sorry."

"Don't be. We hated each other and hadn't spoken in years." Her voice at first had sounded almost relaxed. It grew edgier and as she clenched her hands, white ridged knuckles looked ready to burst the nearly translucent skin. "I had to take care of business for a person who despised me while the person I love was murdered. The person who loved me."

"You can prove where you were. Your arrest doesn't make sense."

A look as close to a smile as Nic had seen appeared on Nora's face. "Detective O'Brian suggested that I drove halfway home from Michigan and rented a motel room, then drove to Chicago to kill Carolyn and drove back to the motel. The man may not like me, but he thinks I'm clever." She wiped her red nose and retrieved a compact from her purse. "If I did what he suggests, why would I go to the studio to kill her?" Nora shook her head. "It doesn't make sense. It doesn't make sense that she was at the studio that late. She was supposed to be at the symphony. Nothing about this makes sense. Neither does O'Brian's behavior."

Nodding her head in agreement, Nic had additional disparaging words concerning the policeman's deportment. "To my knowledge, no one has accused Detective O'Brian of making sense."

Nora looked up from the compact. "That's right. You've had the pleasure of spending an evening with the good detective. I heard they took you to the station. Now you know why they say there's no business like show business." She immediately dropped her head. "I'm sorry. I'm sure it was awful for you. I'm afraid I've lost my few remaining social skills."

When Nic stood, it was not because the words offended her. The desolation she saw in Nora left no room for anger. She put the tissue box next to her on the chair and wrote her phone number on a piece of paper. "Call me if you need to talk, or find me, but please, don't try to do this by yourself."

Nora stared at the paper for a second, and thanked her as she clipped on her earring. "Did O'Brian give you the black eye?"

"No, I slipped on the ice, but I'm sure if O'Brian could have, he would."

"You lead an exciting life."

Nic considered the statement as she retrieved her purse and headed to the door. "Only the last month."

When she left the lounge, Nic replayed their exchange and decided it had not gone too badly. She was glad they talked, but had more questions than ever. Who started the rumors about Carolyn and Nora breaking up? Greg had said he first heard it a few weeks before her death, but never mentioned who told him. Had Carolyn informed Cecil of her divorce plans? The person she needed to talk to was Aunt Anna, but that would have to wait until after work.

Nora remained in the chair looking at the phone number she held. The offer of friendship seemed genuine. She was grateful, and sadly, a little skeptical. Why would Nic reach out to her, especially after she made such a horrible first impression? Was it an attempt to mislead her? Had Nic wanted the leading role enough to kill Carolyn? Her head shook at the unlikely scenario. There were a few people at the station that she and Carolyn considered friends, but many had distorted ideas about homosexuality and chose to either hate queers or pretend they didn't exist. Nic spoke without criticism or judgment, and showed only concern.

Sitting in the jail cell the previous evening, Nora had felt more alone than she thought possible. She'd half wished that O'Brian had been right about her trying to kill herself, and that she'd succeeded. She stood looking at the number once more before folding the paper and slipping it into her purse. At least one person seemed to care.

By four o'clock, Frank wished the cast and crew a nice weekend and sent them home. They were on schedule and would not work on Saturday. As Nic walked off the stage, Gerald, who played Inez's assistant, Jeff, tapped her on the shoulder. "Hey, I heard you had a conversation with our local murderess."

Nic's response was fast and fierce enough to surprise even her. "Nora didn't murder anyone, Gerald, and you should be careful about repeating things you hear. That kind of thoughtless remark can be hurtful." She turned to walk away, "even dangerous."

In the time it took her to march off the stage and reach the band area, Nic managed enough deep breaths to settle her nerves and recover from her outburst. Greg and Belia had just returned with the band. "Do you think things will be calming down around here soon?" She asked Greg.

"Entropy, my dear woman. Order leads to disorder. Calm to chaos, not the other way round." Greg put his right hand in his jacket pocket and stroked his barely visible blonde goatee with the left, a pose that left Nic frowning. Undeterred by her response, the philosophical bass player finished packing his instrument and turned to leave. "Good afternoon, ladies. Plant you now, and dig you later."

Nic took a second to interpret Greg's farewell and was grinning as she turned to Belia. The smile faded at the sight of the musician clinging to her violin, a pose that Nic had learned, meant she was frightened. "Nic, I went to the lounge before and see you talking with Nora Hahn. Do the police no longer think she has murdered Mrs. Park?"

"I don't know what the police think, but I don't think she did it. Belia, if you could have seen her. She was devastated, frightened, and lonely."

"I do not think she kill her, but will they look now for someone else?" Belia seemed more anxious than usual.

"What are you worried about?" Nic asked Belia as she sat on the nearby piano bench clutching her violin. Nic thought she understood. She sat next to her. "This isn't Czechoslovakia. The police can't just come into your home and arrest you." For a half a second, she didn't completely believe her own words. "You don't have to worry."

"I did not kill her." Belia replied firmly.

"I know. Don't worry." Nic felt her shoulders relax slightly, as she patted her back.

"Thank you, Nic. Sometimes it is hard to forget what happened to my family."

"I know what you mean, Belia."

When Nic left Studio A, she considered going to the twentieth floor to check on Nora. Instead, she collected her coat and purse and headed for the elevator. If Nora wanted to talk, she'd find her. "Are you going home tonight?" Nic asked Marcy at the reception desk.

She replied without looking up. "I have a few things to finish first. Good night."

"I'll see you Monday." As the elevator doors closed, Nic saw Marcy look over and frown. She'd had no kind words for Carolyn and seemed almost delighted when they arrested Nora. Could it be that because she had stayed in the lounge with Nora, Marcy added her to a perceived list of enemies?

When a seat opened on the train, Nic, who was more exhausted than she realized, gratefully filled it. Outside, the sky had grown dark. Inside the lighted car, faces of other passengers reflected in the windows. She studied the strangers and wondered if she could form an opinion based only on their appearance. Could she judge if the olive-skinned man to her left was good or bad? Could she know by the clothes she wore if the Negro woman in front of her was kind or mean? She had no idea who loved men or who loved women, or why anyone would care.

Chapter 9

"Aunt Anna, are you here?"

"In my office, Nicole."

Three rooms in the large apartment Nic and Anna shared were designed as bedrooms. Two functioned in that capacity, while the third served as an office for Anna. A wooden desk, file cabinet, and two chairs filled the space and matched the varnished baseboard and hardwood floor. As Nic slid into the chair in front of the desk, Anna studied her bruised forehead and black eye. "You're looking better. How do you feel?"

"Good. No students today?"

"It's Friday. You know I try not to schedule students when their attention is challenged."

"That's right, it is Friday. You don't like teaching in the morning, and by Friday afternoon, their focus is on the weekend."

"Right." Nic's summary amused Anna. "Anything exciting happen at work?"

"We're on schedule and I don't have to work tomorrow. That's not exciting, but it's nice. The other news is that I had a long chat with Nora."

"She was at work?" Anna placed her glasses on a pile of papers and leaned back.

"The police released her because they didn't have enough evidence."

"Why did they arrest her before arriving at that conclusion?"

"Her attorney went to the police station and pointed out the inconsistencies of their case. When O'Brian wouldn't release her, the attorney went over his head. If she hadn't had him, she might still be in jail. Aunt Anna, Nora didn't kill Carolyn. She's completely shattered."

"Is that why she tried to kill herself?"

Nic explained how Nora wound up in the river and the fake suicide note.

The story sparked a memory that sent Anna reaching hastily into the canvas shoulder bag that she had used as a Civilian Defense Volunteer during the war. She laid a handful of papers on the desk. "With all the excitement yesterday I forgot to mention the information Darlene found for us."

"What is it?"

"First, let me ask you a question. Did Nora say whether she and Carolyn were breaking up?"

"According to Nora, that wasn't true. The only relationship changes Carolyn had planned was divorcing Cecil."

"Hmm," Anna stared at the papers. "Then Cecil Park had difficult times in his future. I wonder if he knew."

"Knew what?"

Before Anna could answer, the front door opened and Millie marched down the hall wearing a big smile. When she reached the office, she leaned on the doorframe and said, "What number please?"

"What number please?" Nic repeated.

"I have great news. My brother, Anthony, said if I wanted to work for the phone company, they're looking for help and he could hire me as an operator. I'll use my gorgeous voice like my radio star friend." She elbowed Nic.

"Millie, that's wonderful. You'll be glad to be out and involved with people again," Anna told her.

Nic stood to give her a hug. "When do you start?"

"Next Tuesday. I'll work day shift, three days a week. Working part time will be great, because when Joe comes home I'll be a part-time housewife." Millie looked from Anna to Nic expectantly. "Well?"

"Didn't Charlotte Perkins Gilman say a house didn't need a wife any more than it needed a husband?"

Since Anna often said things Millie didn't understand, she offered a nod and a smile before changing the subject. "What are you two doing?"

"Aunt Anna was about to share the research she did yesterday." Nic returned to her chair.

"What did you find out, Anna?" Millie asked.

"I asked Darlene," Anna's tilted head and slightly raised eyebrows directed them to the apartment above, "to see what information she could find on the Parks. Much of it is public record, but Darlene did a great job gathering financial reports along with newspaper and magazine articles about their involvement in the community. She found a good deal of personal information on Cecil Park, whose law firm had a healthy client list until his partner, Jack Sutherland, died two years ago. Many of Jack's clients moved on to other firms. In the meantime, Cecil hasn't added any new ones, and has lost a number of his own, as well as the remaining Sutherland clients. Carolyn's family had been with Jack for years, and his father before him. Even after she married Cecil, Sutherland remained her attorney until his death. It appears that Cecil took over her estate after that."

Nic took a pencil from the desk and twirled it in her fingers. "I wonder why Carolyn didn't let Cecil handle the account after they married. Maybe it was easier to leave things as they were."

"I don't know about that, but I do know that in the last six months or so Cecil's clients have increasingly gone to other attorneys. The war had no effect on the Sutherland firm because it had no effect on most of their clients. If anything, they profited. That means his clients have other reasons for leaving. It might be helpful to discover those reasons."

"Were both Carolyn and Cecil involved with the charities, Aunt Anna?"

"Cecil had little to do with them, and most of the community events he attended were not connected to the foundation. Carolyn was extremely wealthy and had good people helping with her investments."

"That's what Frank told me."

"He was right, Nicole. She supported many of her charities with the interest she made on her investments, but money wasn't the only thing she donated. She gave generously of her time to Hull House, soup kitchens, and other organizations."

"Nora said she was involved." Without thinking, Nic put the pencil in her mouth and clamped down with her teeth. Anna, with characteristic swiftness, removed it. "Sorry. Are you sure this information is public record, Aunt Anna?"

"At least ninety percent is there for the asking."

Nic didn't want to know about her aunt's ten percent illegal activities. She dropped the public record conversation. "Carolyn was the civic-minded Park. Why would she need a husband if she had more money than he did? What did Cecil contribute?"

"To answer your second question, Cecil didn't contribute anything that I could find, certainly nothing financial. As far as why she married him," Anna shrugged. "Perhaps Carolyn believed her charitable work would be compromised because of her relationship with Nora. She might have married Cecil as a cover, as homosexuals have done throughout history. I remember back in the 20s, they called them lavender marriages, but I've also heard them referred to as a marriage of convenience. Nora is the one who can tell us more about that. For all we know, Carolyn may have paid Cecil a salary to act as her husband."

Nic recalled her conversation earlier in the day. "Nora said Carolyn planned to end her convenient marriage to Cecil, so that would make sense."

Anna eyed the gnawed pencil with amusement before dropping it in the drawer. "Cecil isn't a big contributor, but he is a big spender. Before the war, he bought a new Cadillac Limousine every year. That ended when car manufacturers converted their factories to produce weapons and ammunition. Carolyn had her own limo, but even before the war, had it repaired rather than replaced. He wines and dines clients and has a reputation as a ridiculously large tipper, tossing bills at waiters and doormen, but his manners to those who serve him are otherwise rude."

Millie raised a question. "Were Carolyn and Cecil ever seen together?"

"Not often, according to the information from Darlene." Alley interrupted Anna midway through her response by rubbing against her calf. She hoisted the feline to her lap before continuing. "Carolyn attended community events and fundraisers. She was a great supporter of the arts. I remember seeing her at the symphony, and now I realize it was often with Nora at her side."

"What did Cecil do?"

Anna lifted a few papers and summarized what she read. "Cecil appeared at sports events quite frequently. Wrigley Field and the Cubs, Soldier Field and the Bears, hockey, and horse racing." In response to a cry from her lap, Anna returned the papers to her desk and her attention to Alley. "I think Cecil Park gambles. It would explain where the money's going and why he attends those events. A former student of mine who is now with the Chicago Police is checking with area bookies to see if any of them are familiar with Mr. Park. I believe he is also talking to runners in the area."

The words meant nothing to Nic. "What are bookies and runners?"

"Bookies use the odds on sporting events to take bets. They pay out when a bettor wins and collect when he loses. A runner delivers the bettor's money and other information to the bookie. They're illegal, but there are hundreds of them around the city. Do you understand?"

Nic wished she did. "No, but I don't think I'll need them. How do you find a bookie?"

"I don't know. That's why Robert, my former student, is doing it."

"Aunt Anna, what if you're right and Carolyn was giving him money. If she told him she wanted a divorce, he might be afraid of losing everything."

"He certainly might."

Nic guessed by her response that Anna regarded Cecil as a suspect. "Will he inherit her property?"

"Unless there's a will stating otherwise, he'll inherit the entire massive estate." Anna pressed her fingers together in front of her mouth and nodded slowly. "I'm sure she had a will, so the next logical questions are why aren't we hearing about Cecil Park as a suspect and why aren't we hearing about her money?"

*

The following morning, Millie, Nic, and the Green Hornet streetcar arrived at the stop at the same. Millie noted their good fortune as they boarded through the back and paid the conductor. The early hour on a Saturday guaranteed seats, and Nic expected similar sparse crowds at their destination. Thirty-degree temperatures would deter lakefront visitors more than the hour or day, but they did not discourage her. She had been to the lake only once since starting at the radio station and needed to recharge. For Millie, a few hours out of the apartment made the inclement weather tolerable.

Most passengers that unloaded at the end of the line hurried to indoor destinations, away from bitter lake winds. Nic and Millie continued on foot toward the turbulent slate gray waters, bracing against the frigid air with gloved hands buried deep in their coat pockets.

For Nic, the lake offered fond memories and a place to reflect. Her mom had brought her often. She told her that to appreciate the magical powers and beauty of the lake she should see it anew with every visit. To this end, they performed a private ritual. Holding hands, they faced the cluttered city to the west, viewing tightly huddled rows of houses, the massive ever-growing skyline, and streets and sidewalks filled with vehicles and people running in every direction. Slowly, they would spin the half circle to the east and bask in the colors and moods that defined Lake Michigan. As an adult, Nic repeated the ceremony when she visited, but only in her mind.

Millie and Nic arrived to find the beach, like the streetcar, almost deserted. A couple walked arm and arm, indifferent to the frigid air, while a fisherman in a worn yellow slicker, without the warmth of love, yielded to the abusive weather. They watched as he closed his tackle box and broke down his pole, but when Nic turned to Millie, she asked a completely unrelated question. "Did you always know who you were?"

Millie squinted and drew her hands from her pockets to raise the collar on her coat. "I think maybe your brain is freezing. Of course, I've always known who I am. And if I forget, one of my brothers or sisters reminds me."

"No, I mean…oh, I don't know what I mean. Listen, I want to go to the point." Nic indicated the long narrow strip of land protected by massive boulders that extended a few hundred feet into the water. "I know you don't like it out there, especially in this weather. There's a wind block on the other side of the beach. Do you want to wait there? I'll be back in five minutes."

After a quick look at the wind block, Millie agreed, but gave Nic a warning. "I'll wait, but be careful. It looks slick."

"I will, and like I said, five minutes." She waved a gloved right hand with fingers spread to confirm her promise. As she turned onto the path, Nic noticed the yellow slicker of the departing fisherman.

The unstable waters matched a chaotic gray sky and Nic saw fierce storm clouds gathering to the north. As she approached the boulders, waves rose and fell, exploding against the ancient rocks and turning them into an ice fortress. The passing years changed many things, but to Nic, the lake was still mystical.

Anna did not attend a specific church. When Nic moved in, she took her to St. Johns, the church Nic's mom had attended, but when Nic said she no longer wanted to go, Anna agreed. Although she had never organized her thoughts into a belief, Nic sensed that the lake defined her faith. On a calm day, with the surface smooth as glass, every living thing in the water, and the water itself, appeared a part of the whole. Just as when her life ran smoothly, she felt a part of everything. On a stormy day, a ten-foot wave could tear itself from the water and become a separate powerful form, though it remained part of the lake. Life's stormy days gave her the same sense of disconnection, but in those times of separation, it was her undefined faith that kept her connected to the whole.

A sudden blast of wind persuaded Nic to turn up her collar. She pulled her left hand from its pocket, unaware that the zipper on the change purse caught on her glove. As she raised her hand, the wool fiber broke and the wallet flew to the edge of an icy boulder. She inched forward and reached for the purse catching a splash of yellow in her peripheral vision. A sudden blow to her back knocked her off balance and sent her sliding over the boulder toward the frigid lake water below.

Chapter 10

When a being, human or animal, faces danger, response is instinctive, but luck plays a part in survival as well. To her good fortune, Nic found a tree root between the rocks and managed to grab it while placing her feet securely on a boulder below the water line that was clear of ice. She hung there for a minute to regroup and come up with a plan. The top of the boulder was within reach but she saw nothing to grab to pull her body over. Moments later, the lake assisted Nic, providing a large wave that pushed her high enough to scramble to the top.

She crawled from the rocks and stayed on the ground to take deep breaths and figure out what happened. Shock turned to anger when she remembered the blow that sent her sliding across the boulder. She sat up and muttered a promise to pay more attention to her surroundings and spend less time wet and on the ground.

"Nic. Good grief. What happened?" Millie helped her to her feet. "I was worried. You were supposed to be back five minutes ago. You're drenched."

"A guy in a yellow slicker pushed me in. At least he tried to. Did you see where the fisherman went?"

"He ran past me. God, Nic. He tried to push you in the lake?"

As the shock and anger waned, Nic became aware of her wet clothes and the cold seeping into her bones. "Millie, I'm freezing. Vera's is around the corner. I could use a cup of coffee and a warm spot to dry out."

Huddled together for warmth, and hurrying in the direction of the diner, the women found their progress obstructed by a man sitting on the ground holding his head. Scattered around him were a tackle box and fishing pole. "That's the fisherman, but I don't see his coat."

Nic dropped to her knees. "Are you okay?"

"I think so. I was going home and the next thing I knew, I was on the ground." He felt the back of his head and checked his pockets. "Someone hit me, but they didn't steal anything."

Millie came around to ask him a question. "Were you wearing a yellow slicker?"

He appeared puzzled by her question, and that confusion grew when he looked at his chest. "I was. Why would anyone steal that old thing? It ain't worth a plug nickel."

Nic told him only that the person in the slicker bumped her and she slipped on the rocks. As she and Millie helped him stand, they noticed that he wore a number of layers for warmth. He said the slicker was only to keep him dry and when he noticed Nic's wet clothes, suggested that she might consider one. She agreed. After helping gather his tackle and pole, they hurried to the diner where it was quiet, and more importantly, warm.

"Hi, ladies. A little chilly out there, isn't it?" Vera stopped her cheerful greeting and assumed a familiar pose with a hand on her hip and her questioning eyes locked on Nic. "You're soaking wet. What did you do, go for a swim?"

"Not intentionally. I slipped on one of the boulders." She removed her coat and hung it on the silver rack by the door where a puddle immediately formed. "Boy, there's nothing like the smell of wet wool." Nic put her gloves on top of the hat rack and followed Millie and Vera to a booth. "Two coffees, please."

"You're pretty young to be falling as much as you do. Are you sure you don't need glasses?"

"Glasses. No, I.... You know, maybe you're right, Vera. I should have my eyes examined." Vera didn't hear Millie's comment, but Nic did. She chose not to respond.

"I'll bring the coffee in a minute, but you'd better change out of those wet clothes. I keep extras around, and we're close to the same size. Do you want one of the waitress uniforms or a pair of slacks and a shirt?"

Vera was thin, but large-busted. Nic pictured the uniform on her boyish body and knew her shiver was not because of wet clothing. "Slacks would be good."

"While I find the clothes, you can clean that cut and put a bandage on it."

"It was bandaged." Nic felt for the dressing. "It must have fallen off in the water."

"You'll find what you need in the bathroom. Clean it good and put Mercurochrome on it. There are a lot of little creepy things swimming around in that lake."

Nic returned wearing a pair of blue slacks, a powder blue blouse, and a fresh bandage. After she brought their coffee, Vera took the wet coat to the back room and hung it next to the gas furnace to remove some of the water.

Millie had warmed enough to remove her coat, but Nic's narrow escape left her chilled. She leaned across the table and spoke in a whisper. "Nic, this is scary. Someone's trying to hurt you."

During the two years Nic spent waiting for a bus at Vera's she learned that the diner was the heart of the neighborhood grapevine, and she had no desire to be a topic. "You might be right, but let's not talk here. I don't want Vera to know what happened. It'll be all over the city before tomorrow morning."

With their coffee finished and fingers warmed, Nic and Millie decided it was time to make the journey home. The coat wasn't dry, but sitting next to the furnace, it was no longer dripping when Vera brought it to the table. Nic tucked her own wet clothing under her arm and promised to return the borrowed clothing soon.

Except for an occasional reminder to Nic to slow down, Millie and she wove through the neighborhood with little conversation. Nic had her mind on a bigger problem, how and what to tell Aunt Anna. She hoped to avoid the confrontation as long as possible. When they arrived at the apartment, they entered and climbed to 2B quietly enough to avoid disturbing Mrs. Murphy.

After dropping her wet clothes off in the bathroom, Nic joined Millie in the kitchen where she was making a pot of coffee. She sat at the table, barely able to find the top through the collection of photographs scattered about. Millie had been trying, unsuccessfully, to paste them into albums, but every time she came across a picture of Joe, her good intentions gave way to loneliness and a few tears. She gave up and decided to put them in a shoebox and wait until Joe came home to paste them in books. They had not yet made it to the shoebox.

Nic pushed pictures around with an icy finger until she uncovered one of the happy couple right before Joe left for the

Pacific. His navy blue bellbottom uniform fit comfortably over the solid six-foot frame that dwarfed his not-quite-five-foot bride. Before his standard Navy haircut, Joe had the same dark curls as Millie. In the photo, only stubble showed under his white cap. She pushed the photos into a pile and made a space for their coffee cups. "Have you heard from Joe?"

"No, but I'm not worrying. If anything were wrong I'd have heard from the Navy." Millie removed the percolator from the burner, set the grounds in the sink, and carried the pot to the table.

"That makes sense. Millie, speaking of not worrying, don't mention anything to Aunt Anna about what happened at the lake. I don't want her worrying for nothing. Maybe this guy mistook me for someone else. Let's not say anything until we know for sure."

"You don't really believe it was a mistake, do you?"

"I don't know, but if it was, there's no sense worrying Aunt Anna."

Millie hesitantly agreed.

"Hello." Anna yelled from the front door. "When did you two sneak in?"

"How did she know we snuck in?" Millie whispered to Nic and raised her voice as Anna came down the hall. "A few minutes ago. Do you want coffee, Anna?"

"Thanks, Millie." Anna entered the kitchen and looked from Nic to Millie. They avoided looking back. While Millie concentrated on the seemingly difficult job of pouring coffee, Nic watched her intently. "What's wrong?"

"Why do you think anything's wrong, Aunt Anna?"

"Well, for starters, I've never seen two women focus that hard on pouring a cup of coffee. Nicole, you're wearing clothes that don't belong to you. Your hair is wet, and the bandage on your forehead isn't the one you had when you left the house this morning. One of you had better tell me what's going on."

Nic was about to tell Anna that she was simply trying on clothes from her best friend's closet, but as Millie set the cup on the table, her quivering lower lip dropped and her promise to Nic gave way to a frantic account of the morning. "Someone tried to push Nic into the lake. He wore a yellow slicker and we thought he was a fisherman we saw earlier. Whoever it was knocked the fisherman out, stole his coat, and wore it when he pushed Nic off the rocks."

Nic shook her head and stared at Millie, who now sat with her hands over her mouth. "God, haven't you ever heard that loose lips sink ships?" She knew Millie said what she did because she was scared, but recent events were beginning to take their toll. The cold plunge was an awful end to a horrid week and her patience was thin. To add to that, Anna's face was unreadable, and therefore worrisome. "Look, Aunt Anna. I'm all right."

"Nicole, these are dangerous people. Maybe the wisest thing for us to do at this point is to go to the police. We can tell them about the events that have taken place, and let them handle it."

"No." Nic realized how loudly she objected and lowered the volume. "What good would it do? We don't know what he looks like, and he probably threw the slicker away when he ran off. You know how the police are." Nic controlled the volume, but not her frustration. "Really, Aunt Anna. You of all people don't think we should go to the police, do you?"

"I'm not the one in danger."

In the seventeen years that Nic lived with Anna, they had few disagreements. Nic rarely felt enough passion about a subject to fight, and Anna was more persuasive than stubborn. When Nic leaned her crossed arms on the table and rested her chin, her green eyes were resolute. "The police won't do anything, and even if they agreed to investigate, if someone is trying to hurt me, I'd still be in danger. They won't give me a bodyguard. Aunt Anna, I don't want to go to the police. I want to find out who murdered Carolyn."

"I have no great desire to call the police, but I don't want anything to happen to you. Anything worse. To be honest, if this happened to me, I wouldn't call the police, and I'd be just as angry."

The hum of Millie's refrigerator filled the quiet kitchen as the women considered their next move. Anna broke the silence. "Have you had a chance to write down the phone conversation you overheard?"

"No, I haven't, but I have been thinking about it. If the phone call was about Carolyn Park, when he made the comment about pinning it on the girlfriend, he could have been talking about Nora."

"That's a logical assumption. If he is the murderer, I wonder why he's hanging around." Anna considered the thought for a moment, then shook her shoulders and ran her eyes over Nic. "Maybe you should soak in a hot tub and change into your own clothes."

A hot bath with one of the Modern Woman bath oil samples sounded great. "Good idea, Aunt Anna. Millie, I'll talk to you later." Nic jumped from the chair, gathered the pile of wet clothes from the bathroom, and left Millie and Anna to their plotting.

The water streamed into the tub, and after Nic added the recommended amount of bath oil, the room filled with a sweet lavender fragrance. It soothed her considerably. She removed Vera's clothes and grabbed a towel and Dashiell Hammett's latest Sam Spade adventure before sinking into the hot water.

When her bruised knee showed above the water line, she reviewed the car accident and the event at the lake. As nice as the free samples of Modern Woman bath oil were, if the accidents continued, she might have to consider a less violent profession.

Chapter 11

The weekend had not been a total waste, but her unexpected plunge into icy lake waters left Nic chilled. That chill returned when the elevator doors slid open and Marcy looked up and quickly returned to her paper. Nic stood in front of her desk determined to learn the reason for her cool behavior. "Do you want to tell me why you're acting strangely?"

Marcy didn't look up. "I'm not acting strangely. I'm busy. I can't be expected to drop what I'm doing whenever a person steps off the elevator."

Nic examined the newspaper spread across the desk. "I see, and Flash Gordon is a major part of your busy schedule. What is it?"

Marcy fingered the newspaper. "Are you one of them?"

"Am I one of who them?"

"You know, like Carolyn and Nora, queer?"

Nic inhaled a sharp breath and dropped a hand to the desk for balance. The surprising question might have left her speechless, but shock turned to anger and Nic found her voice. "What if I was Marcy? How would that affect you? Are you afraid I'd try to convert you? Do you think I'd turn you into one of us, into a lesbian?" Her volume rose and she came close to shouting, but not close to stopping. "Maybe you're afraid I'd try to seduce you." Nic glared. "Honey, I can absolutely guarantee that will never happen." Her fury persisted, but her words came to an abrupt end. She spun and left Marcy with her paper and her mouth open.

The studio door moved as Nic reached for the handle. George stood in front of her with a spool of wire on his shoulder. "Hello, George." She wondered if she was still yelling, because he gave her a strange look and muttered something indecipherable. Her anger from the exchange with Marcy reignited and Nic directed it at George. She intended to stand her ground until he spoke to her. "Where is Barney, George?"

He stared at the floor and smashed his body and the coiled wire against the wall to move around her. When she didn't let him pass, he spoke. "He had an appointment or something. Look, I gotta take this to the supply room." He hurdled forward, bumping the wire into Nic who had not moved far or fast enough.

"Do I make people nervous?" She saw Jimmy standing by the sound effects box. "I might as well find out." She hurried over and stood in front of Jimmy to block his retreat. "Jimmy, have you heard anything else about Carolyn's murder?" He shook his head.

The little patience Nic had left dissolved. She had no idea what to ask, but her rotten mood required an answer. She improvised. "Did you kill her, Jimmy?"

In a move that surprised Nic, his slouched shoulders straightened, and instead of avoiding her eyes, he glared. "No I didn't, and you'd better back off, lady." He stormed away in an uncharacteristic hurry.

"That didn't accomplish anything." She retreated to the lounge, frustrated and more than a little embarrassed.

"Bravo."

Nic felt her face flush when she recognized that the deep voice belonged to Nora.

"I was dropping copy off in one of the offices and overheard your exchange with Marcy. You're braver than you look."

"Thanks, I think." Nic dropped her purse on a chair and sat beside it. "Nora, why did Marcy dislike Carolyn so intensely? Is it really just because she was a lesbian?"

Nora sat next to her and lit a cigarette. "That's part of it, but another reason involves an incident that happened with Marcy's sister. A year ago, Carolyn was involved in a War Bond drive that took a great deal of her time. She talked the station owners into hiring an assistant to help her for a few weeks, someone to mark the scripts so she could learn her lines, and do little errands. Marcy heard about the job and hovered around trying to convince Carolyn to give it to her sister, Beverly. Marcy begged and although Carolyn was reluctant to hire her, she gave in. Unfortunately, Beverly was awful. If she didn't want to work, she wouldn't show up, and when she did, she spent most of her time in here," Nora indicated the lounge, "or in one of the restaurants downstairs. Carolyn was patient, much more than I would have been, but since she ended up doing the work, she had no choice but to replace Beverly."

"Marcy was angry because her sister lost a job she didn't do?" Nic shook her head. "Maybe it's just me, but that doesn't seem like reason enough to explain her hatred."

"There's more. Instead of admitting that she couldn't, or wouldn't, do the job, Beverly told anyone who'd listen that Carolyn approached her, and when she refused, she had her fired. I don't think Marcy believed it, though she supported the story. Since everyone suspected how Carolyn lived and because she made no effort to defend herself, it became WBAC legend. Plenty of people around here feel like Marcy does about homosexuals and are more than happy to share rumors like that whether it happened or not. It wasn't true, of course. Carolyn is—" Nora stopped and pinched the top of her nose. "I mean Carolyn was a class act, and Beverly…I don't know what Beverly is, but she isn't an assistant."

Nic considered that maybe Marcy did believe the hurtful lies her sister told. Adding that information to her other fears and misconceptions about homosexuals, she had what she probably considered good reason to hate Carolyn. Then again, there were people who simply needed something to hate.

"Listen, Nic. I want to apologize for laying into you after the show." Nora stubbed out her cigarette and removed an earring. "I wanted to check out the new kid. I hadn't planned to say anything, but when I saw you doing her part…. I don't know. I was angry and hurt, and chose the last person in the studio I should have to attack. You didn't deserve that. I thought you might like to know that Carolyn noticed your work. She told me after watching you and Gerald on several commercials that you were a natural, and she was sure you'd do well. After seeing you do Inez, I agree."

That surprised and saddened Nic, because she had rarely spoken with Carolyn. "When I learned about your relationship, I knew it had been difficult for you to watch me do her part so soon after her death. Nora, you don't have to apologize. I'm sorry you've had to deal with so much. Have you heard anything else from the police?"

"No. O'Brian is convinced I killed Carolyn and says he intends to prove it, but my attorney doubts that he can. He's putting information together that should totally disprove

O'Brian's theories. I'll be glad when this is over. Since that push in the river, I'm constantly looking over my shoulder."

"I'm sure you will be glad when it's over. I'm beginning to feel the same way." Nic told her.

"You? Why?"

"I told you that I slipped on the ice last Wednesday." She pointed to her barely visible black eye. "The reason I fell was because I had to dodge a car that had possibly been aiming at me. Then Saturday someone tried to push me in the lake. I believe it's because I've been asking questions about the night Carolyn died."

"Asking questions? Why are you putting yourself at risk, Nic?"

"I'm not trying to be brave, and I wish we could trust the police to take care of it, but I don't think they will. They don't seem to want to look farther than you, and the bottom line for me is, Carolyn's death is the reason I have this job. I can't do much, but I can ask questions and look for the truth. My aunt has a few leads she thinks we should check out."

"Your aunt?"

Nic forgot that not everyone had an Aunt Anna. "She enjoys solving mysteries, and she has resources around the city. Do you think the person who pushed you in the river could be tied in with the stuff that's happening to me?"

"You and I weren't on friendly terms, but I suppose anything is possible."

"The connection would almost have to be Carolyn's death. As I said, I think their interest in me is for asking questions."

"And judging by the event at the river and the note in the car, their interest in me is to make me the killer."

"There's something else." Nic explained the phone call in the lobby. "Of course I don't know if he was talking about Carolyn, or you, but if he was, it would confirm that they are trying to frame you. I thought about telling O'Brian what I heard, but he won't believe me, and if he did, I'm sure he wouldn't think the conversation had anything to do with the case."

Nora re-clipped her earring and took a small card and a pen from her purse. After writing something, she stood and handed the card to Nic. "You're right about O'Brian. He thinks he has his killer and nothing we say will change that. I'd better head upstairs, but here's my phone number. I want to help you and your aunt. I mean it. I have my own reasons for wanting Carolyn's killer caught. I'm glad I had a chance to apologize, Nic, and that I caught your conversation with Marcy."

Nora left wearing an expression Nic had not seen before—a pleased smile. It made her look younger, smoothing deep vertical lines between her eyebrows that Nic had assumed were permanent, and creating new lines from the sides of her eyes and mouth. She wondered if there had been anyone for Nora to talk to when she heard about Carolyn.

Frank seemed in a good mood as he and Alice joined the cast on stage. "Hey, Nic, what are you doing for Thanksgiving? We'll take Thursday off, but have our regular rehearsal on Friday. In fact, I'd better make an announcement before we start."

Nic had completely forgotten about Thanksgiving. It was less than two weeks away and she couldn't remember if Anna and she had discussed it. They usually had dinner together while Millie joined the throngs of brothers, sisters, cousins, aunts, uncles, and anyone else who showed up at her mother and father's house. Nic and Anna had a standing invitation but preferred a quiet meal at home. She saw Nora dropping off papers to one of the actors and ran over. "Nora, what are you doing for Thanksgiving?"

"I hadn't thought about it. I'll probably burn something beyond recognition and call it dinner." She laughed, but not with conviction.

"Do you want to join my aunt and me, and of course Alley, the cat, for dinner?"

Nora had obviously not expected an invitation to dinner. Her brown eyes reflected surprise and caution. "Do you want to check with your aunt first? I mean, she may not want company."

The response was almost a yes, and that pleased Nic. She knew it would please her aunt. "Believe me, she'll love the company. I'll ask Belia, too. She has no family. What do you think? It wouldn't be anything fancy, but my aunt is a good cook."

"If you're sure it isn't too much trouble. I'd like to join you. Tell me what to bring."

"I'll talk to Aunt Anna and let you know. She'll be glad to meet you, and I know you'll find her interesting."

"From what you've told me, I'm sure you're right."

Nic turned to find Belia, but Nora called her before she stepped off the stage. "Nic. Thanks."

"I'll see you tomorrow." Nic saw Belia standing against the back wall in a too familiar pose, clutching her violin as she watched a group gathered in the middle of the room. By the time Nic reached her, Alice, Frank, the engineers, Jimmy, and the sound effects men had finished their meeting and returned to work. Belia relaxed. "Are you all right?"

"Yes. I am fine, Nic. Thank you."

"Did the big guy leave without his instrument?" She pointed to the large case that held Greg's bass.

"He has a job soon where he needs to wear a tuxedo. Mr. Reed will be a little late, so Greg has gone to one of the floors where they rent them."

Nic tried to picture the tall thin blonde in a tuxedo, and decided he might look good. "Belia, do you have plans for Thanksgiving?"

"No."

"Do you want to join my aunt and me for dinner? Nora will be there, too."

For the second time, the response to Nic's dinner invitation was surprise, but Belia's interest was in the guest list. "Nora Hahn who is a friend of Mrs. Park?"

"Yes."

"Marcy said she is not a nice person, and she is a queer."

"She's a homosexual, Belia, not a monster." It angered Nic that Marcy continued spreading hate.

"You said she was mean to you."

"She apologized, and as far as Marcy telling you Nora is not a nice person, it's not true. This is a hard time for her. She's alone, without family or friends."

"Like me." Belia dropped her head. "My family died because we were not people Hitler wanted. My family and Miss Hahn, we are not considered good people." Belia looked at Nic. "If you will forgive my rudeness and would like me, I am happy to come."

Chapter 12

The first of the six brass mailboxes inside the front door belonged to Anna and Nic. Marked simply 'OWEN' it served as a receptacle for their mail and housed the buzzer and intercom for apartment 1A. As she checked the contents, Nic wondered if Millie had heard from Joe. With all the excitement, she had forgotten to ask.

She was glancing at the handful of envelopes as she pushed the apartment door open, but stopped her forward progress at the sight of Anna asleep on the sofa. Papers filled her lap and her glasses rested halfway down her nose. Nic tried to close the door quietly, but a loud meow sounded and Alley poked her head through the papers. Anna opened her eyes.

"That must be interesting reading."

"I was grading a paper until this one decided to park it. What could I do? How was your day, dear?"

Nic settled in the sturdy fabric and wood armchair, the same chair she chose on her first day with Aunt Anna all those years ago. "Did I tell you that Marcy, the receptionist, had been acting strange?"

"Yes, you mentioned that."

"This morning I asked her if there was a problem. She responded by asking me if I was like Carolyn and Nora."

"She meant a lesbian?"

"Yes, and I proceeded to tell her off. I seem to be doing that more and more these days, Aunt Anna. I like it. After years of keeping quiet, I'm speaking my mind."

"Good for you. It isn't good to be a hot head, but you have to stand up for what you believe."

"I went to the lounge later and Nora was there. She said she'd heard our conversation and that I was tougher than I look. I think she meant it as a compliment. She also apologized for the hard time she gave me after the first show. She told me Carolyn thought I was good, and so did she. That was nice to hear, but strange since I'd never said anything but hello and goodbye to Carolyn." Nic looked out the window and remembered another bit of information that she thought might be of interest to her aunt. "I invited Nora and Belia for Thanksgiving dinner. Would you like to join us? I assume you'll be doing the cooking."

"Let me check my schedule." Nic had been right. The news delighted Anna. "It sounds fun. Will Belia bring her violin?"

"We didn't discuss that, but I'm sure she would if I ask. Nora wants to know what she should bring. Aunt Anna, she seemed so pleased that I thought to ask. It was almost sad."

"I'm sure she was pleased, and probably a little surprised." As a reward for rubbing Alley's belly, Anna received a quick swat from a sharp claw. "You little bugger." She moved the offending feline from her lap and stood with two fingers in the air. One had a quickly reddening scratch. "Two questions, Nicole. One, are you being careful, and two, is there any news on the murder investigation?"

Jean Sheldon

"Yes, I'm being careful, and yes, there were a couple of events that we should discuss." As Nic watched Anna head to the back of the apartment, she wondered what, if anything, Detective O'Brian was doing on the case. If he thought Nora killed Carolyn he would not be investigating other leads. Were there other leads? Nora had been attacked, yet O'Brian remained focused on her as the killer, even though the evidence Nora's attorney supplied refuted his arguments. O'Brian's reasons for suspecting Nora, if he had any, came from a source other than known evidence.

The minute Anna returned to the sofa, now sporting a bandage on her finger, Alley tumbled into her lap. "Do you think this cat is spoiled?" She handed a sheet of paper to her smirking niece. "I made a list of the people from the studio that I could remember you mentioning. Do you want to go through it and see if I missed anyone?"

Nic studied the names and commented as she made additions. "George Sokal is Barney's sound effects partner. I've tried to talk to him a couple of times, but he wasn't very receptive. Jimmy Holmes is the copy boy, and I have no idea if he'll talk to me after today."

"What happened today?"

"I asked him if he killed Carolyn."

"You asked him if he killed Carolyn. Why did you do that, Nicole?"

"Right after I talked to Marcy, I ran into George and he practically pushed me out of the way to avoid a conversation. When Jimmy wouldn't talk…" Nic finished the sentence with a shrug. "I was completely out of patience. I'll work on restraining myself from the direct approach. Let's go back to the list."

Anna agreed.

"Daniel Newman, the announcer. I don't remember him saying where he was on Friday. Harold Slashinski and Stanley Janks are the two engineers. I don't know their whereabouts either. Alice Redding is Frank Myers's secretary, and Allen Reed is the band director."

The compact body of Anna Owen may have seen over sixty years of life, but it shot forward with the agility of a teenager. "Allen Reed is your band director?"

"You know him?" After a quick mental slap to her forehead for forgetting that Anna knew half the residents of Chicago, Nic amended her response. "Of course you do."

"I've known Allen for years. When you see him, tell him I said hello, and ask him how his car is running." Anna smiled, and Nic could see it had nothing to do with her.

"Should I know what that means?"

"No."

"Why don't we go on then?" A one-word answer from Anna meant the end of that particular conversation. "The only other person I can think of is Gerald Carpenter. He's Jeff, Inez's assistant on the show. You have the rest of the cast and crew. Why did you put Frank Myers on here?"

"I put all the WBAC employees I could remember you mentioning on the list. I was even going to add you, but thought you were probably innocent."

Nic stared, but her look of disbelief turned quickly to mock irritation. "Probably?"

"I knew you were innocent. Better?" Anna took the list. "I added only people from the studio, but perhaps we should put Cecil Park on here."

"That sounds like a good idea."

"I'll put him on the top until we have more information, but for now, let's discuss the studio suspects. The first step is to eliminate those who couldn't possibly have killed her. Let's start with this fellow, Greg Devens."

"Greg didn't kill her. He's a nice guy."

"Nicole." Anna, on occasion, had a flare for the dramatic. She expressed her impatience by removing her glasses, pinching the bridge of her nose, only to slide them on and look over the lenses to continue. "I'm sure he's a nice person, but right now, we're concerned with facts, not opinions. Did he say where he was when Carolyn was murdered?"

"He said he ate dinner and went to a club on Clark Street where he played with his jazz trio." Nic wiggled out of her shoes and folded her legs to sit on her feet. "According to him, they finished around two a.m."

"We can scratch him off." Anna drew a line through his name. "I doubt if one of the other members could play a solo long enough for him to sneak off to the Mart and commit murder. It would be difficult to disappear for a few hours when you're one third of the band and playing a bass fiddle. The coroner said that Carolyn Park died around ten p.m."

"How do you know that?"

"How do I know what, Nicole? The time of death? A former student of mine is a friend of the coroner. He called him for me. Next we have Marcy Duran."

"Chicago is a big city, Aunt Anna. Are there people you don't know?"

"Some." Anna studied her notes. "But I usually know a friend or relative. Most people don't realize the number of connections they share. Shall we continue?"

Nic laughed. She doubted that most people had as many connections as Anna Owen, and thought moving on was a good idea. "Marcy Duran is the receptionist I told you about. I don't know what her alibi was, but she certainly disliked Carolyn. Hated is more accurate." Nic told Anna what she learned from Nora. "I doubt if Marcy will tell me anything at this point, but maybe I can learn where she was from Frank. I definitely wouldn't take her off the list."

Anna made a notation. "Next is the violinist, Belia Malecek. Did she say where she was at the time of the murder?"

"I hadn't thought about what she said. She was one of the last people to leave and that was around eight o'clock, but she didn't say why she'd been there that late. Belia is afraid of the police. It'll be hard to ask her anything without scaring her. In her eyes, every officer wears an SS uniform."

"If she won't share anything with you before Thanksgiving, maybe after a good meal she'll be comfortable chatting. I'll put a question mark next to her name. Nora Hahn?"

Nic explained Nora's trip to Michigan and her meeting with her father's attorney, and O'Brian's theory about the motel being a phony alibi. "Aunt Anna, I know we are talking facts only right now, but after the conversations I've had with Nora, I simply cannot believe she killed her."

"I'm sure you're right, and unless her lodgings were in the middle of a cornfield with no other guests and the owners went to bed at seven in the evening, it isn't likely that no one would have seen her come or go. Why is O'Brian such an ass?"

Nic gave her an exaggerated look of shock. "Aunt Anna, please, your language will upset Alley."

"I don't know if you've heard such language or not, Nicole." Anna tried to look stern, but it gave way to a playful grin. "But I know Alley has." The unperturbed cat laid a paw over her ear.

*

Any thoughts Nic entertained as she spun through the revolving door, dissolved at the aroma of fresh coffee. She had arrived at work a few minutes early and decided that if the brew tasted as good as it smelled it would be a perfect way to start the day.

The source of the heady scent was a small coffee shop to the right of the elevators. An empty table near the back beckoned. Almost immediately, a steaming cup of coffee sat before her, and the first sip told her it rivaled Vera's special blend. Encouraged and energized, she dug through her purse for the list of people she wanted to approach with questions. Anna and she discussed sharing it with Nora to find out her opinion of the suspects. She decided to make a copy.

After duplicating the names on the bottom of the sheet, Nic ripped it in half and laid them on the table. With the cup resting on her lower lip, she raised her eyes and noticed a vaguely familiar person seated at the counter. She couldn't place him, and assumed he worked in the Mart and that she had seen him in passing. She was returning to her list when he noticed her. To her surprise, he clenched his jaw, threw a quarter on the counter, and almost ran out of the restaurant. The reaction startled her, but she refused to let it ruin a perfectly good cup of coffee. A short time later, she took a final sip, tucked the lists in her purse, and wondered as she rode the elevator to nineteen, whether she should stop in the lounge to see if her appearance was bad enough to frighten people.

The reception desk was empty, and except for George, Barney, and Frank, who were involved in a discussion on the stage, the studio was too. Nic decided not to interrupt and went to the other side of the room to sit in one of the empty band chairs. She filled another with her coat and purse.

"Are you planning to work with the band?" Frank asked.

"Oh. I thought you were busy."

"We were finishing up when you came in. Well, are you?"

"You mean planning to work with the band?" Nic smiled. "If it involves singing, playing a musical instrument, or whistling for that matter, you don't want me for the job."

"You mean to tell me, Miss Owen, there's something you can't do."

"You won't hear many good reports on my cooking either." Nic was sure they had spent enough time talking about her shortcomings. She had a few questions of her own. "Frank, were you here late the night Carolyn was murdered?"

"No, why?"

"O'Brian thinks Nora is guilty and won't pursue anyone else. The killer will go free and an innocent person will go to jail."

"You don't think Nora did it?"

"No, I don't."

"You know I don't either."

"Do you think Cecil Park could have killed her?"

"I have to admit he crossed my mind when I learned about the murder, but that could be because in so many of the mystery and detectives shows it is typically the spouse. Of course, his relationship with Carolyn was hardly typical. Apparently Park was with a client at the Palmer House the entire night, drinking and making a fool of himself."

"Oh?"

"From what I heard, he was at the Empire Room and very drunk—forcing women to dance, knocking into tables, and spilling drinks. The Concierge escorted him out at one a.m. Plenty of people remembered his visit, but my guess is he lost the client."

"With the fortune Carolyn left, he can afford to lose Sutherland's clients and his own and still be set financially for the rest of his life. Does Cecil have connections with the station?"

"He may with some of the owners and sponsors. People with his money have connections everywhere, but he doesn't with me. What's with the interest in Park? You know quite a bit about him."

Nic stood with her coat. "I have an aunt who's a bit of a Miss Marple and we have been discussing people's alibis."

"Miss Marple and Inez Ingles, that's an impressive team." Frank wasn't a bad detective either. He anticipated the conversation's direction. "Before you ask, I left just before seven, drove to the south side, and spent the evening playing bridge with my mom and dad and a beautiful, mysterious woman whose name I choose not to reveal but who looks quite a bit like my wife." He grinned. "I'll see you later, Nic. Good sleuthing."

The arrival of Harold and Stanley provided Nic with her next interview. She headed to the booth as the engineers stepped inside. Both men, like Frank, lived on the south side. Unlike Frank, they made their daily commute on the bus, armed with a lunch pale and a copy of the neighborhood Polish newspaper. She stood in front of the booth and tapped on the large window, hoping they had time to talk. Harold waved as Nic mouthed, "Can I talk to you?" He shook his head and opened the door.

"People do that to us all the time and we have no idea what they're saying." He laughed and invited the blushing actress inside.

"I'm sorry. Now that I've interrupted, do you mind if I ask a few questions?" The men exchanged a shrug. "Were you here late on the night Carolyn was killed?"

Harold answered. "No, we left around six o'clock. Why?"

Nic had no idea how to continue without making them feel like suspects. Stanley came to the rescue. "We leave early on Fridays. We start bowling at eight and the team counts on us, you know."

"That Friday we won the tournament." Harold told her. "I bowled a 288."

Judging by the size of his smile, Nic guessed that 288 was a good bowling score. "Congratulations to you and the rest of your team. How did you do, Stanley?"

It was his turn to beam. "I bowled 275, my all-time high game. It was a great day for us. Not so good for Carolyn, I'm afraid."

"Did you know her, Stanley?"

"Not well. She was what my *beusha*, my grandma, called a private woman. She was kind but never seemed comfortable around people. A nice lady though. I never saw her be mean or rude to anyone, and we see everything from in here."

Nic made a mental note that even if the studio looked empty, she would have to check the booth before adjusting nylons or bra straps. "What about you, Harold? Did you know her?"

"Stosh is right. She kept to herself but was always nice. I hope they catch her killer. I still can't believe they arrested Nora. It wasn't her, that's for sure."

Nic backed toward the door, grateful they were sympathetic to a floundering detective. "Thanks, you two, and again, congratulations."

When she arrived at the lounge, Nic stood in front of the mirror and wondered if an exotic hairstyle would make her feel more like a detective. More importantly, would it make her act more like a detective? She parted her hair in the middle and tucked it behind her ears like Vivien Leigh, but looked more like a teenager than the actress. With the hair combed back and held in a tail, she looked equally youthful, and a tight bun slightly askew on top of her head made her look stern. It didn't look too bad when she held it in curves next to her face copying Nora's pageboy, but when she let go, the chic style returned to her usual shapeless mop. Nic had envied Millie's thick curls since they were kids. All she did was give her hair a quick brushing and a shake. Maybe a permanent was in order.

The door opened and Nic saw Marcy looking at her in the mirror. "Nic." She hesitated. "Look, Nic, can we talk?"

Chapter 13

Nic nodded, put her comb in her purse, and brushed her hair lightly off her shoulder as if she had achieved the desired look. She muffled a groan, knowing that if that were true, it would have been even more depressing. They walked in silence to the chairs Nic occupied with Nora a few days before. "What is it, Marcy?"

"Nic, I like you."

"You mean as long as I'm the kind of person you find acceptable."

Marcy raised her head sharply, but it, and her shoulders, fell as the response she meant to deliver dissolved. "I suppose it might seem that way. It is true that I don't understand relationships like Carolyn and Nora had. You heard about my sister?"

"You mean Beverly?"

Marcy raised her chin to confirm. "I didn't completely believe that Carolyn approached her. Beverly never could keep a job. About six months ago, she married a guy who lets her sit around all day and do nothing. She's perfectly content."

"Then why, Marcy, did you support the lies she told around the studio?"

"She's my sister, no matter what."

Nic responded irritably. "I don't have sisters or brothers, and don't understand a relationship where no matter what a person does, even if it hurts another person, you support them. Should I hate you because you have a relationship I don't understand?"

"I don't know if that's the same thing, but I wasn't doing it just for my sister. I didn't like Carolyn. All that money made her think she was better than the rest of us."

"Maybe she didn't think she was better. Maybe she had to protect herself from cruel things people said to and about her. Imagine how it would feel to come to work knowing people hated you or made fun of you because you were you. How would you behave? Who would you talk to?" Nic kept her voice low. It made no sense to shout. No matter what the volume, Marcy would never understand. "As much as you don't understand their relationship, I don't understand senseless hate. Anyway," she nearly put a hand on Marcy's knee, but thought better of it. "I'm glad you wanted to talk. I don't think I'd do as well as Carolyn did if no one talked to me."

"I'm glad we talked too. I do like you, and hope we can be friends."

The conversation had been agreeable enough and a relief in a way, but Nic saw little chance of a blossoming friendship. Nora popped into her mind and reminded Nic that hers was a friendship she would like to develop. That thought naturally led to Carolyn Park and reminded the detective that she wanted to ask Marcy about her alibi for the night of the murder. Not sure how to bring up the subject, Nic was delighted when Marcy stood at the mirror to check her makeup and supplied the perfect opening.

"I've heard you've been asking questions about Carolyn's murder. I know you don't think Nora killed her, but who do you think did it?"

Nic had a list of those she thought were innocent, but never decided which of the suspects she believed actually killed Carolyn. A name popped into her head. "Cecil Park."

"Really?"

Cecil had an alibi, but Nic wanted to keep her talking. She took a chance that although Marcy knew about everything that happened at the station, she had not heard about his adventure at the Palmer House. "They say it is often the spouse, and he doesn't have an alibi."

"Cecil doesn't have an alibi?" Marcy sounded surprised but continued penciling a raised reddish eyebrow. "I'm certainly glad I have one. My sister, Beverly, was having another crisis. She called when I was leaving the studio, around five thirty, and asked me to come by. I stayed with her until shortly after midnight." Marcy turned from the mirror to Nic. "The crisis was that her husband had to work overtime. I told you she was something." She returned her makeup bag to her purse and snapped it closed. "I'm supposed to be at the reception desk. Thanks for talking to me, Nic."

Beverly could confirm Marcy's alibi. Of course, if she thought the way Marcy did, she would cover for her. Perhaps the sisters plotted to do Carolyn in together. Nic found it a little difficult to picture that. Marcy may have been a narrow-minded hypocrite, but she didn't strike her as a murderer.

By four thirty, the cast had finished for the day and most left in a hurry. Nic saw Gerald on stage. "Do you have a minute?"

"Sure, Nic. Listen, I apologize for the remark I made about Nora. I was trying to be funny. I met Carolyn and Nora when I started, and they both treated me great. I may have a strange way of showing it, but I know that Nora didn't kill her. What can I do for you?"

Gerald's charm had surely broken a few hearts, but Nic sensed his sincerity, and his apology made her feel better. "Did you notice anyone in the studio the Friday Carolyn died? A person who didn't belong, or maybe someone who did belong but behaved strangely."

"I'm afraid not. I shot out of here as soon as we finished. I had a hot date and headed home to change. In fact, I rode the elevator with Carolyn. I asked where Nora was and she told me she was out of town for a few days."

That was new. "Did you talk to her about anything else?"

"No, that was pretty much it. She seemed preoccupied. I stopped to buy a paper and when I went outside, she was getting in her limo."

Carolyn left the building. "Thanks, Gerald. I hope your hot date went well."

"It did." He winked and hurried out. Before the door swung closed, Frank came in, followed by the ever-faithful Alice Redding. Nic hoped Frank knew Alice's whereabouts on the night of the murder. She would prefer not to make enemies of the entire studio.

As they approached, Alice took several sheets of paper from a clipboard in Frank's hand and left for the engineer's booth. Frank joined Nic on stage. "Rehearsal went well."

"I thought so." Nic was more focused on Alice's departure than Frank's arrival and sounded distracted enough to prompt a question from her boss. "Is there something on your mind, Nic?"

"Well, I was, I mean I wondered if Alice. See I'm trying to find out if…"

Frank managed to translate Nic's incoherent request. "Alice went home early on Friday. One of her kids was sick and she took a cab to pick him up at school."

Nic knew her face was red and avoided looking directly at Frank. "Sorry. I guess if I expect to be a detective, I'd better learn how to ask a question."

"I'm sure you'll figure things out. You seem to be a pretty quick study."

Nic turned and saw his smile, but detected an unease, which he confirmed. "Nic, I won't ask you about your investigation, but I will ask you to be careful. Your understudy isn't ready to play Inez just yet." He squeezed her shoulder and left to join Alice.

While she appreciated Frank's concern, Nic thought it was unwarranted. Still, she might have given it more consideration had she not seen Allen Reed putting on his coat to leave. She barely knew the music director. Asking him where he was on the night of the murder might not make her a new friend, but at least she wouldn't lose one. "Hi, Allen."

Allen pressed a burgundy silk scarf inside the lapels of a knee length black wool coat. Both the scarf and coat looked stunning in contrast to his white hair, but Nic suspected he would look distinguished in a pair of overalls. He was one of the tallest men at the station at six foot four, and though he exhibited youthful energy, Nic thought he might be in his mid sixties. He was slender, and wore tailored double-breasted suits and highly buffed black leather shoes. The Italian style meant they were several years old, because leather shoes were not available from Europe since before the war.

"Miss Owen, what brings you to this corner of the world? How is that cut healing?"

"It's fine. Thanks, Allen." Nic remembered the question from Anna. "I have a message for you from my Aunt Anna. She said to say hello and to ask how your car is running."

From his lengthy bemused stare, Nic wondered if he was not the Allen Reed Anna had known. She was about to apologize when his eyes doubled in size and a smile exposing a mouthful of radiant white teeth showed recognition and delight. "Nic, you're Anna Owen's niece Nicole. Oh, my stars, I never put it together."

Nic smoothed her clothes, and tried to look unruffled when he released her from a lengthy and enthusiastic bear hug. His fervent response continued. "Your aunt is one of my favorite people on the planet, maybe in the solar system, quite possibly the universe. How is the wonderful woman?"

"Aunt Anna is well, but I'll never adjust to the fact she knows most residents in the city of Chicago."

"She does have a way with people. Please give her my regards and tell her we must reconnect soon. Oh, never mind that. I'll call her." The last three words, spoken almost in a whisper, gave him another idea. "Would it be terribly rude of me to ask for you for a phone number to reach Anna?" Allen flushed a few shades closer to the color of his scarf.

His red face reminded of Nic her own recent uncomfortable moment. She hurried to his rescue. "Not rude at all. I live with her. Let me write it down." She found her script on stage and wrote the number, tearing off the section for Allen. "I'm curious, Allen. Why does my aunt want to know about your car?"

The color returned, along with the smile. "Years ago I owned a Stutz Bearcat which I bragged about quite often to Anna. After months of trying, I talked her into taking a ride. I let her believe that I knew everything there was to know when it came to engines and automobiles."

"You didn't?"

Allen was lost in a memory. When he returned to the present and rolled his eyes, they held a mix of mischief and laughter. "No. I knew almost nothing, but I was determined. We headed to the Indiana Sand Dunes and three quarters of the way there, the car stopped. I had plenty of gas and knew it wasn't that, but truth be told, I didn't even know how to open the hood."

Nic pictured Allen and Anna driving in a shiny Bearcat. An image that, had she not remembered her manners, would have made her giggle. "What did you do?"

"After admitting I knew nothing about cars, I told Anna I'd go for help. She had become rather cross and chose to stay with the car while I walked to where we'd seen a service station. I'd gone maybe a mile when I heard a car behind me. The driver honked with great enthusiasm." Allen shook his head. "It was Anna Owen. She'd fixed the car and come for me. She was delighted with herself and assured me that I'd never live it down. Anna being Anna, I knew I could count on that."

"She fixed the car? I can't wait to hear her story. Did she say how she fixed it?"

"She wouldn't tell me, and I never asked again. But she was kind enough to show me how to open the hood."

When Allen disappeared once again into pleasant memories, Nic interrupted. "Do you mind if I ask you a question, Allen? Did you know Carolyn well?"

The laughter in his eyes faded. "Yes, I did. She came to performances I conducted and was a great supporter of music and the arts. Why do you ask, my dear?"

"I don't think Nora killed her, but the police aren't looking for whoever did. I'm trying to see what I can discover."

Allen looked at the stage. "Nora didn't kill Carolyn. O'Brian is a fool. He wasn't convinced my alibi was legitimate. I conducted the City Theater Orchestra that night in front of six hundred people. He suggested that I hired a double to conduct since anyone can twirl a stick." After a brief silence, Allen's gaze returned to Nic. "Carolyn had planned to be at the concert. She usually came with Nora but told me she had business out of town and that she was coming alone. I left here around six thirty and there wasn't time to look for her before the show. I didn't think about not seeing her until Frank called the next day. We have lost a fine human being."

"Thank you, Allen." Nic touched his arm. "I'll give Aunt Anna your regards."

Allen donned his fedora and tipped the wide brim at Nic. As he made his way to the exit, his eyes drifted to the empty stage where, to the memory of his friend, he tipped it once more.

Chapter 14

The following morning, to Frank's delight, the cast walked through two scenes with sound effects and few problems. Frank rewarded the group with an unplanned break. He and Nic were leaving the stage when the back door crashed open.

"Myers. What the hell is going on around here?" The words, delivered at a volume that nearly matched that of Detective O'Brian, echoed off the towering walls.

"Oh no." Any additional comments Frank made were unintelligible as he ran to intercept a short round man that he was not overjoyed to see.

His red cheeks and labored breathing suggested the visitor was either out of shape, angry, or both. Frank and he met in the center of the studio, where he took a long fat cigar from his teeth and used it to stress each word as he repeated the question. Frank grabbed his elbow and led him with a firm hand, into the engineer's booth.

Nic had watched the entrance and brief conversation with interest until they went into the booth. When she saw Greg returning to the band area, she hurried over with a question. "Who is that?"

After a long look at the engineer's booth, Greg gave a short answer. "Cecil Park."

Muffled shouts escaped from the booth through its slightly open door.

"Why would he be yelling at Frank?"

"Maybe he's angry because the murder investigation isn't over. Or, maybe he just needed to flex his muscles. I've heard he has a bad temper. Look how red his face is. If he keeps it up much longer, he might explode." Greg left the bass in its stand and plucked softly while he and Nic watched the exchange.

Inside the booth, Park stood with his overcoat draped on his left arm and held his hat and a glove in a gloved left hand. His right hand gripped the cigar he continued to brandish at Frank.

"Look, Mr. Park, I'm sorry about Carolyn. We all are, but the police are in charge of the investigation, not us. Now, if you will excuse me. We have a show to do." Frank placed a hand under Cecil's elbow to encourage his departure but he swept it away.

"We'll see how long you have a show, Myers."

Cecil Park had not, in all probability, meant to reshape his hat when he smashed it on his head. If he had, he might have realized how comical he looked when he slammed open the door to storm from the booth. Had he been calmer, he might have noticed the two-foot high wooden box of sound effects that sat in his path. He did not, and with nothing to grab for balance he tumbled over the side.

When Park regained his footing and climbed from the box, he snorted and grabbed a fistful of objects, hurling them across the room. He stomped to the door and threw it open, slamming it against the wall with enough force to rattle its hinges, but his forward motion stopped suddenly and he returned to the box to recover his hat. In what might have been a final attempt to preserve his dignity, Park stormed into the hallway taking half the air from the studio with him.

Barney, like most who had returned during the exchange, watched from across the room. After Park's exit, he gathered the scattered sound effects and checked them for damage before tossing them in the box.

Nic and Greg had managed to control their reactions when Park fell into the box. They stayed in control during his extended exit, but when the back door closed, they burst into laughter. Frank sat in the engineer's booth wearily shaking his head until rehearsal resumed.

On the train ride home, Nic could not help but chuckle at the image of Park floundering in the box. Nor could she resist sharing the story with Anna as soon as she arrived home. Unfortunately, Anna did not react as Nic expected. After a detailed and amusing description of the event, her distracted aunt only smiled and said she needed to change her clothes.

"Are you going out?"

"No." Anna left and Nic decided it might be a good idea to put the day, and Anna's strange behavior, out of her mind by reading the paper. The empty sofa offered her a place to stretch out and scan for stories about places other than WBAC. Five minutes into her search, the front buzzer interrupted.

When Nic saw the person responsible on the porch, she buzzed him into the building and stared through the open apartment door until Anna returned. "Who's there, Nicole?"

Nic stayed quiet but the visitor's excited voice came through the door. "I hear the voice of an angel."

"Allen!" Anna screamed and pushed her niece aside. "Why didn't you invite the man in?"

Nic remained in the doorway and watched Allen Reed rush in and grab Anna around the waist, swinging her in the air. No one noticed Millie in the front hall until she tapped Nic's shoulder. "Who's the tall guy?" She edged into the doorway next to Nic.

"That's Allen Reed. He's the musical director at the radio station." Nic kept her eyes on the elderly pair. "Aunt Anna fixed his car."

"He seems pleased with her work." Millie folded her arms in front of her chest and leaned on the doorframe, where she and Nic remained for the several minutes it took the couple to stop spinning.

"Aunt Anna, would you like Millie and I to make coffee?"

"That would be wonderful, Nicole." When Nic and Millie left for the kitchen, Anna hooked Allen's arm and led him to the sofa. "Nicole sees you every day. It's my turn." She patted his jacket sleeve. "You look wonderful, and if it's possible, more handsome than the last time I saw you."

"Stop, Anna. You'll make an old fool blush. You, however, are more radiant than ever, which comes as no surprise."

Friends lose touch for a variety of reasons. For Anna and Allen, volunteering with numerous groups and organizations while maintaining their full time jobs left too few hours in the day. Adding to that, the complications of a depression, a world war, and the unexpected changes that were a natural part of life, the gap became insurmountable. The friendship slipped from daily thought, but waited in their hearts for rediscovery, and after a separation that felt like days, not decades, their memories of each other matched the faces before them, unchanged by time or adversity.

"Do you still enjoy teaching?"

"I'm not teaching at the university anymore. I realized I would never make full professor and took an early retirement to teach at home. The simple answer is yes. I enjoy teaching. It isn't a choice it's a passion. And speaking of passion, Allen, when Nicole told me you were the musical director at WBAC, I was thrilled, not only to see you again, but because she had the opportunity to meet you and share in your passion for music."

Millie and Nic arrived with the coffee and Nic overheard Anna's comment. She knew Anna well enough to suspect she had other plans for Allen. "Don't let her fool you, Allen. Ask Aunt Anna if there's another reason she's glad to see you."

He turned from Nic to Anna. "You have a reason beyond my good looks and charm? My dear, Anna, don't keep me in suspense."

She leaned closer with a conspiratorial look and a twinkle in her eye. "You were friends with Carolyn Park, weren't you?"

"Yes, I was. You knew she was a big contributor to the arts." Allen stopped to study Anna. "Wait. Don't tell me. You're still an amateur detective and you've added Nic to your team." He turned to Nic. "That's why you've been asking questions around the station." When Nic didn't reply, he turned back to Anna. "Yes, it is, and you two want me to assist, don't you?" Her soft nod and Nic's smile were all Allen needed to see. "Is it any wonder that I've missed having Anna Owen in my life? There's never a dull moment." The music director rubbed his hands and gave the women a complicit grin. "What's my assignment?"

*

The following morning, when Nic entered the studio she spotted Allen examining a stack of musical scores. "Did you and Aunt Anna get caught up after Millie and I went upstairs."

"Hello, Nic. Yes, we did, but I didn't mean to drive you from your own home."

"You didn't. I'm glad you two had a chance to visit."

"You have no idea how extraordinary it was for me to see Anna again." Had Allen felt the need to hide his true feelings, his eyes would have given him away. They sparkled. "Such a treasure, and she's still dabbling in detecting."

"Nothing makes Aunt Anna happier than a new puzzle to solve. Were you really okay with being drafted?"

"I was, and that glorious twist of fate means I'll be spending time with the dear woman. She does love a mystery."

"Yes, she does." Nic wondered if anyone who could resist her aunt's charms. "I'll see you later, Allen."

It was nearly six before rehearsal wrapped up, and it was only then that Nic realized she hadn't seen Barney all day. She returned to the stage. "Frank, where's Barney?"

"He'll be off for a couple weeks, Nic. I'm trying to find help for George."

"Is he all right?"

"They're checking him at the Veteran's Hospital. That's all I know. I called, but they won't tell you anything unless you're a family member."

Nic found her coat and headed for the elevator. The reception desk was empty and the offices dark, making the ding of the arriving elevator louder than usual in the quiet space. Sam was gone and Nic didn't know the present operator, which was fine. She had no desire to chat. She leaned on the wall and thought about Frank's news. What could be wrong with Barney? He'd seemed fine all week. Why had he suddenly gone into the hospital? It would have to be something serious if he was going to be off from work for a couple of weeks.

The elevator stopped at nearly every floor and as the car filled, Nic's thoughts turned from Barney to her present environment. She recalled the first time she stepped inside one of the buildings lifts. Before that, elevators were no more than a form of transportation—a way to travel from one place to another—not an elegantly designed room.

The top half of the car had strips of rosewood and mahogany inlaid in a herringbone pattern and polished to a lustrous shine. On the back wall, a white glass sconce cut in layers and stretched like plumage, bathed the passengers in diffused light and shimmered on the soft fabric that began where the wood inlay left off. A brass panel above the doors matched one on the outside, with etched numbers and a buffed brass arrow. When the car stopped and the arrows inside and outside the door came to a rest on the number one, both Nic and the elevator released a sigh.

*

The view of Lake Michigan from the chaise lounge made it Nora's favorite seat in the apartment. At least it was when Carolyn shared it. Then, the quiet isolation of living in a high rise was a comfort. Their safe space above the cruel and hateful people that sometimes crossed their path brought peace and contentment. Without Carolyn, room after room of empty silence made Nora want to scream. To fill the hole left inside with her rage, her pain. She did not scream. A scream required energy and she had none.

She pulled the cigarette case from her purse and watched a piece of paper float to the floor. Her focus and concentration had suffered much in recent weeks. She had no clue what the note contained and even after unfolding it, needed a second to recognize it as the list of suspects Nic had asked her to look over.

Nic and her aunt's interest in finding the murderer surprised Nora. Most people felt nothing, or like Marcy, believed the murder of a queer was acceptable, maybe warranted. The Owen women were cut from a different cloth. She stared at the list, cringing at the first entry, Cecil Park. Nora knew all she needed to know about him—he was a pig.

Carolyn met Cecil when he joined the Sutherland Law firm. Sutherland's had served her family for generations. Jack Sutherland helped her start the foundation and personally selected a financial firm to invest her money, a firm that lived up to his expectations. Once Carolyn felt comfortable that support for her charities was in place, she took a break from all things connected to her family and enrolled at the University of Chicago. At the beginning of their senior year, she and Nora began a relationship that would last fourteen years.

Four years earlier, Carolyn had gone to the law firm for a meeting with Jack. As she was leaving, Cecil called her into his office. He had become a partner the previous year, and although Jack had introduced them, Carolyn knew nothing about Cecil Park. He knew a great deal about her.

He claimed that he wanted to help her. He knew how much Jack cared for her and he wanted to make sure that neither of them was hurt. When she inquired how that might happen, he explained that he had overheard conversations at his club concerning her relationship with Nora. Some members who donated to her charities had moral and religious beliefs that could not support her lifestyle. He suggested she marry him to convince those who were suspicious they were mistaken. All Carolyn had to do was pay him a regular salary. She could live her life as she wanted, and support her causes without fear of exposure.

Carolyn thought it was a good idea. She did not particularly like the man but wanted to protect her foundation and felt the arrangement could provide that security. Nora never believed a word of it. She thought Cecil had created the story to blackmail Carolyn, but she also realized that it would ease her mind. Carolyn agreed to Cecil's 'proposal.' She and Nora continued to live at their apartment, but she bought a home in Evanston for Cecil to occupy, and, on occasion, to entertain donors.

Recently, Carolyn had uncovered information about his gambling activities that troubled her. When Nora shared that information with O'Brian, he accused her of lying.

She was frustrated with the police for not finding Carolyn's killer and with herself for feeling utterly helpless. She looked again at the list of names. Helping Nic and her aunt would not end the pain, but perhaps it could help end that frustration.

Chapter 15

The outer door of the apartment building groaned as Nic entered and pushed it shut. She stopped to take a handful of mail from their box and heard Millie padding down the stairs. "How was your day, Inez?"

It wasn't until they went inside that Nic answered and had a question of her own. "Things are good at the station, but aren't you behind on the news?" She threw the mail on the coffee table and turned to the mass of dark curls that followed her in.

"Nope. I'm caught up, thanks to Miss Marple."

Nic considered the statement for a moment and smiled. "You mean Aunt Anna? That's funny, that's what I called her to Frank."

"I don't suppose you two could come up with a younger detective to play my part." Anna heard the conversation as she approached. "Marple is in her eighties."

"Hi, Aunt Anna. We were just talking about you."

"I know." Her playful frown disappeared as she added a handful of papers to the cluttered coffee table.

"Allen said you've hired him on. He seemed delighted." Anna's expression and lack of a quick response spoke volumes. "I'm guessing he's not the only one."

"No, you're right. I couldn't be happier about joining forces with Allen, but since I spent last evening breaking in a new cadet, you need to bring me up to date on the case. What did you find out yesterday, Nicole? You mentioned that Cecil Park showed up at the studio, but I'm afraid I was a bit preoccupied with Allen's arrival." She took Nic by the hand and escorted her to the sofa. Millie settled in a chair.

"First, let me tell you what Frank told me today. Barney is in the VA Hospital. Frank called to find out how he was, but they won't tell him because he isn't a member of Barney's immediate family."

"Has he been sick?"

"I don't think so. At least he seemed fine the last time I saw him. I'd like to find out what's going on. He's been great to me and I want to see if there's anything I can do."

"I have friends at the VA Hospital from when I volunteered, and Mary Rose is still head nurse at the psychiatric unit. I'll see what I can learn. If it is an emotional problem, he might be there."

"I'm sure your friends will be glad to share whatever they can. You have a history of being nosey. Even Allen remembered that."

"Nosey is such a harsh word, Nicole. I like to think of myself as having an active interest in the welfare of my fellow human beings."

Nic smiled. "You're actively interested in the welfare of your fellow human beings. Aunt Anna, you just redefined the word snoop."

"I guess I did. Okay, let's do what snoops do best and figure out what's going on. Why don't we go over the conversations you had with people on Tuesday?"

Nic repeated her discussion with Marcy. "The thing is, the sister who can provide her alibi started the rumor that Carolyn fired her because she rejected a pass. The police might not know about that."

Millie's short legs disappeared beneath her as she snuggled into the armchair. "Someone might have passed along the office gossip to the police."

Anna nodded without looking up. She either agreed with Millie, or was confirming the comment she wrote on her list before reading the next names. "What about the engineers, Harold and Stanley?"

"I'm sure Harold and Stanley told the truth about where they were." Nic shared the bowling tournament story. "I mean, why would anyone lie about being at a bowling alley if they weren't there?"

Although not in complete agreement with Nicole's conclusion, Anna nodded and read the next name. "Frank Myers."

"Frank played bridge with his wife and parents on the south side. That would be easy to confirm. Frank did tell me that Cecil Park has an iron-clad alibi." Nic explained Cecil's exploits with his client, and filled Anna and Millie in on his volatile visit to the station. "I told Marcy I thought Cecil did it, but that doesn't seem likely, even though he does have a temper, and possibly a great deal to gain."

Anna sighed and slipped on her glasses. "Did you have a chance to talk to George Sokal?"

"Not since he brushed me off the other day. I'll try again."

"What about Jimmy Holmes?"

"No." Nic groaned. "He won't talk to me. Maybe Nora can have a discussion with Jimmy."

"That's a good idea. Do you know if she had a chance to go over the list of names?"

"No. We haven't talked since I gave her the list. What do you think is going on with Barney, Aunt Anna?"

"You said he seemed healthy, right?" Nic nodded. "I'm only guessing, but since there's been no report of an accident or illness, it might be an emotional problem. Physical or emotional, he's at the hospital where he can get the help he needs. Anna leaned back to read a flyer that topped the stack of mail. "They're having a sale at Field's tomorrow. Maybe we should take a break from detecting to investigate that."

*

During the week, people and vehicles swarmed downtown Chicago, an unending stream of rubber and metal, and flesh and bone. Cars and buses vied for position on busy streets, and for passengers crammed into public transportation, each stop presented a challenging game of musical chairs, without the music. On Saturday morning, despite brisk and windy weather, Nic, Millie, and Anna had a pleasant ride to the Loop in a train car that offered both seats and a working heater. For Nic, the shopping excursion was a way to celebrate one of the more lucrative benefits of her job, her sizable paycheck. Seventy-two dollars for a week's work was more than twice what she had made as a riveter at Douglas Aircraft, and that had exceeded her pay as a counter girl at Marshall Field's considerably.

Climbing from the subway at State and Lake, Millie, Nic, and Anna, braced for the wind. It was common in the concrete and steel heart of the city for lake winds, forced between massive immovable structures, to increase in velocity if for no other reason than escape.

The last few weeks of pleasant fall weather were the stuff of memories, replaced by plummeting temperatures and arctic breezes. As Nic took Anna by the arm to keep her from blowing away, she nearly collided with a paperboy. What froze her in place was not the appearance of the young man or the frigid air, but rather the two-inch headline on the newspaper he waved. "MURDER GUN BELONGED TO MRS. PARK." She paid for her copy, but quickly realized the high winds made it impossible to read.

"Nicole," Anna yelled over the roar. "Let's go inside for a cup of coffee." She took an arm of each of her cohorts and hurried them into a deli where the warmth and wonderful smells of baking bread, pastrami, and most importantly, fresh coffee, made the hostile weather a quickly forgotten memory. Millie and Anna went to the counter while Nic found an empty table. Her head remained bent over the article when the women arrived with their beverages.

"What does it say?" Millie passed Nic a mug, but she didn't respond. "Hello, Nic. What does it say?"

"Sorry." Nic read from the paper. "Police discovered the gun that killed actress and community leader Carolyn Park in a box of sound effects in the studio where her body was found. Cecil Park identified the weapon as belonging to his wife. He said she bought it a few years earlier to carry for protection. Police went on to say they found partial prints on the weapon that they hope to identify." Nic took a sip of coffee. "Why didn't they find it when they searched the studio the first time? They were there long enough."

The small table, cluttered with three coffees and a newspaper, left little room for Anna to prop an elbow, but she found a spot and leaned over the paper. "That's a good question, Nicole. I suppose they could have missed it, or they could have done a lousy job searching. Did you see anything that explains why they decided to search again or if O'Brian is in charge of the second investigation?"

"No, I didn't. I hadn't thought about that, Aunt Anna, but that is odd, isn't it? Why, after all this time, would they think to look in the sound effects box?"

"Everything about this case is odd, Nicole."

Gun or no gun, Millie had been patient, but was ready to experience the point of their outing. She put on her gloves and rubbed her hands together. "Well girls, there's no reason we can't discuss this information while we shop. Next stop, Marshall Field's."

Earlier in the week, Nic had passed a newsstand in the Mart and seen a Norman Rockwell drawing on the cover of the *Saturday Evening Post*. It showed a man setting the time on one of the giant clocks in front of the store. She couldn't help but smile as they approached the timepiece.

Nic had been back to Field's a time or two since she left to work at the factory, but this was her first visit since starting at the radio station. She felt different somehow, a little more confident. "Aunt Anna, I want to look for trousers. I don't have a pair nice enough to wear to the station. They're more comfortable than dresses and stockings, and it must be okay, because I saw Nora and a few other women around the studio wearing them."

"Things have changed since the war. Do you remember a few years ago when a woman was arrested on her way to work at one of the plants for wearing pants? I think there was a law about women 'dressing mannishly.' With the number of women working in boots and coveralls, they had to pass a new law allowing women to wear pants in public." Anna examined a full-length wool coat as she continued. "Today, the only time you need a dress is for a wedding or a funeral, and maybe not then."

Nic had not moved passed Anna's previous statement. "Men passed a law saying they would *allow* women to wear pants? No one ever stopped me for wearing pants when I worked at Douglas."

"I think most people, including the police, tended to ignore it, but yes, it seems rather silly, doesn't it?"

Two hours later, they settled into their seats, glad to be out of the icy weather and on the train heading home. Millie's hair was huge, her curls inflated by the winds. Nic's brown locks were scraggly and knotted, while the tight braid Anna wore had hardly a strand out of place.

The women huddled together to compare their purchases and Nic removed a pair of pants from the brightly colored Field's shopping bag. "I really like these, two dollars and fifty cents a pair, but the clerk told me they're well made. Did you notice the pair she wore? They're the same pants."

"I did. They looked good on her and you." Nic had tried them on at the store and would have made the purchase even without Millie and Anna's unanimous approval, but she was glad they agreed.

When each of their purchases had received sufficient praise, the women returned them to their bags and settled in to enjoy the ride. Nic retrieved the folded newspaper and as she reread the story, decided to ask Nora what she thought about the gun. She would have known if Carolyn owned it. She wondered again if there had been anyone for Nora to talk to after Carolyn died and felt an overwhelming sense of sadness for her new friend. At least she hoped Nora considered her a friend.

Chapter 16

Nic stumbled, just managing to avoid a book lying open at her feet as she hurried to answer the phone. The book's presence on the floor next to the sofa and the momentary confusion as she lurched for the receiver suggested she had been sleeping, not reading, as was her usual Sunday morning ritual.

"Hello."

"Hi, Nic. It's Greg. Am I disturbing you?"

"No. I was reading. Sort of. What's going on?"

"Great news. The band they hired to open at the Empire Room tonight can't make the gig. Their bus broke down in St. Louis."

Although groggy, Nic was awake enough to cast a doubtful look at the receiver and ask what she considered a reasonable question. "Greg, how could that possibly be good news?"

"Oh. Well it's not for them, but my band is subbing. We're playing the opening show. Isn't that great? It's only an hour, and only one night, but it's the Empire Room!"

"That is terrific. You'll have to fill me in on how it went at work tomorrow."

"No, Nic. That's why I called. A friend of mine booked four tables and there are plenty of seats left. You could bring a few guests. What do you say? Please come. I need as many friendly faces as possible."

Nic leaned on the earpiece, remembering Cecil Park's bad behavior at the Palmer House the night Carolyn died. "Actually, this could be perfect. What time do you start?"

"You're the best. We start at eight, and the only requirement is that you clap whether you dig the music or not. Can you whistle?"

"Not well, but I think my aunt can." Nic made a quick mental list of people who might be interested in joining her. "I'll see you tonight."

She found Anna in her office eyeing Alley, sprawled comfortably on top of her desk. "Do you believe this animal? As soon as I put the papers down, she plopped on top and went to sleep."

"Have you considered moving her?"

Without twitching a whisker, Alley gave Nic a look and Anna leaned back in defeat. "I heard the phone, Nicole. Who was it?"

"Greg. He invited us to listen to his jazz band tonight at the Empire Room. They start at eight."

"Are we going?" Anna's eager response came as no surprise. She celebrated life at every opportunity.

"Yes we are." Nic described Greg's good fortune and explained her other reason for attending. "It might give us an opportunity to talk to the waiters and doormen. Maybe one of them will remember something unusual about Cecil Park's visit. We'll have fun while we investigate. What do you think?"

"An excellent idea."

"Aunt Anna, I thought I'd give Nora a call to see if she'd like to join us. She wants to be involved in the investigation, and my guess is she could use the company."

"Another good idea, Nicole. You have a kind heart." Anna stroked Alley as she stood and rounded the desk.

"Where are you going?"

"To find my dancing shoes."

As Nic watched her slip spryly out the door, she addressed the now awakened feline. "Alley, I don't know who is more peculiar, you or your mother." Alley leapt from the desk, followed Anna out, and left Nic muttering. "Fine. Abandon me. See if I care."

Nic phoned Nora and was pleased when she agreed not only to join them, but also to drive. That left only Millie to invite to the growing party. She headed upstairs. "Morning, Sleeping Beauty. Are you up?" Nic yelled as she walked to the kitchen where Millie sat at the table behind a book. "What're you doing?"

"I borrowed this from Anna. After seeing *And Then There Were None*, I decided I wanted to read more Agatha Christie. This one is *Murder on the Calais Coach*. I'm on the second to last chapter, but I can't guess who killed this Ratchett guy. What's up? Been detecting this morning?"

"No, but you, Aunt Anna, Nora, and I will be tonight if you want to join us. Greg, the bass player at the radio station, invited us to hear his band at the Empire Room. It'll be fun. Aunt Anna is so excited she's looking for her dancing shoes."

"Why do you think it will be fun? Have you heard Greg's band?"

"I just assumed they'd be good if they're playing at the Empire Room. He's good with the studio orchestra. By the way, the one stipulation is that we applaud madly. Nora volunteered to drive. She'll pick us up at seven."

"I'll be ready." In what was becoming a too common sight, Millie rose and walked to the front door.

"That's it. I've had enough of people leaving. Where are you going?"

"To see if Anna found her dancing shoes."

A parking attendant appeared before Nora brought the Chevy to a complete stop. "Good evening, Miss Hahn." She and Carolyn were frequent guests at the various Palmer House restaurants and clubs. She climbed out and handed him the keys, but cut her conversation short when she saw the other three women at the hotel entrance.

Nic wanted to find a doorman who worked the Friday night Carolyn died, and was about to ask the uniformed young man holding the door. Before she could, he spotted Anna. "Miss Owen. Are you here to cut a rug?"

"Thomas. I didn't know you worked here."

"I've been here a month and only work on the weekends. Do you come here often?"

The smile and wink on his young face amused Anna, who responded with a grin and a wink of her own. "Not often enough, I'm afraid. Thomas, do you think when you have a break we can talk?" She waved her finger at the group of females.

"Sure. I take a break at nine. Do you want to meet me in the front lobby?"

"That would be perfect. Thank you."

Potter Palmer presented the Palmer House to his new wife, Bertha Honoré, in 1871, as a wedding gift. Two weeks later, flames from the Great Chicago Fire reached its doors and devoured the entire structure. Waiting only for the smoke to clear, Palmer rebuilt, and in less than a year, guests entering the new Palmer House marveled at its opulence. Seventy-three years later, Millie made her first visit to the marble-walled lobby and viewed its neoclassical style art and architecture with the same awe.

Lined with pillars lit by intricately sculpted bronze wall sconces, the lobby that welcomed guests conveyed the feel of a lavish but cozy drawing room. Each of the columns stood two stories and joined a fifty-foot mural of mythological Greek figures and designs at the top. Artist Louis Pierre Rigal created the painting in sections at his studio in France and Palmer installed the twenty-one canvases in 1926.

"Who is Thomas, Aunt Anna?" Nic asked.

"He's one of my students. We'd better see where we're going before the band starts." Nora, with firsthand knowledge, took charge and led the way.

The Empire Room opened in the Palmer House in 1925. When the World Expo came to Chicago in 1933, the room re-emerged as a dinner club and quickly became the place to "see and be seen" for dining, dancing, and enjoying top entertainers from around the world. For Nora and Carolyn, and their community, the Empire Room and the Palmer house, like the Tip-Top-Tap and the Allerton Hotel, were popular spaces that welcomed a diverse clientele.

Nic followed Nora to the top marble step and looked in the black door to the Empire Room. One look told her why Greg wanted a few friendly faces. The room was daunting. Six massive crystal chandeliers trimmed with gold leaf bathed the room in dazzling light. Under them, surrounding a dance floor and stage, were dozens of tables filled with revelers. At one, to the right of plush green velvet stage curtains, Nic spotted the bass player. "He's over there. Are you ready?"

Her three companions nodded and Nic prepared to navigate the sea of white cloth-covered tables. The narrow space available for foot traffic offered a few minor roadblocks—a misplaced chair, a too exuberant guest—but the determined radio star pushed through and arrived at Greg's table just as he slid back his chair.

"I'm sorry." He turned to see who he'd hit and jumped to his feet. "Nic, you made it. Nora, you too. I can't believe you came. Thank you."

"Greg, this is my Aunt Anna, and my friend Millie."

"Definitely cool to meet you." A resonant chord from the piano on stage interrupted his handshakes. "Oh, oh. Gotta go." As Greg departed, he reminded them why they were there. "Don't forget, clap loud, and enjoy the clambake."

"What did he say?" Millie asked. "Are they having a clambake?"

Nic assured her that Greg would translate later, but thought he meant they should enjoy the show. As the band set up, the rest of the party introduced themselves and the waiter took orders and brought drinks.

The Torrance Trio consisted of a piano, bass, and drums. 'Rapid Jack' Torrance, aptly nicknamed for the lightning speed at which his fingers navigated the keys, led the group. The band's drummer, Derek, pounded out rhythms literally without missing a beat, and Greg, who both bowed and plucked his bass, gave the band a unique sound. He was the tallest member of the group and the only Caucasian.

Nic felt pleased and relieved at how good they were, and had no trouble delivering her promised applause. As they played their last song, a Duke Ellington classic, 'It Don't Mean a Thing if it Ain't Got that Swing', the audience, particularly those who came to see the trio, showed their appreciation.

Near the finale, Anna tapped Nic and pointed to her watch. "Thomas has his break at nine and I don't want him in trouble. Do you want me to go alone?"

Millie volunteered to go along and after agreeing to meet in the lobby, Nic and Nora waited to congratulate Greg. He came from the stage glowing. "Man that was hot."

"Greg, you were great. I'm glad you asked us to come."

"Thanks, Nic."

"She's right, Greg. You guys are better than the last time I saw you." Nora added.

Nic noticed another band setting up. "We should probably leave. We're not staying for the next band, and I hate to leave while they're playing." Nora agreed and followed Nic to the lobby where they spotted Millie and Anna talking to Thomas. Comfortable that the investigation was in good hands, they retired to nearby seats. Five minutes later, Greg joined them.

"Guess what? The person who booked the job wants to talk to our manager." His words indicated that was good news, but his face didn't express overwhelming joy. "That would be great if we had a manager."

"How do you go about finding one?" Nic asked.

"I don't know. Neither do the other guys, which might explain why we don't have much work."

"Would Allen Reed know?"

"Good idea, Nora. I bet he would. I'll talk to him Monday. Oh, man, that's tomorrow isn't it? I doubt I'll sleep tonight."

The glance Nic and Nora exchanged said they agreed, but as Nic was about to comment, Anna and Millie appeared. "You cats were aces." Anna told Greg with a grin.

He bowed to the elder fan. "Thanks, Miss Owen. Nice to find another jazz aficionado."

The exchange between her aunt and the musician amused Nic. She was pleased at their mutual admiration, but it occurred to her that Greg was not the only one who had to work in the morning. She suggested they call it a night and the rest of the group reluctantly agreed. "I'm glad you came, Nora," she told her as they watched the Chevy arrive at the curb. "If you're too tired to drive us to the apartment, we can take a cab."

"Don't be silly. In fact, if you don't mind my stopping in for a few minutes, I can tell you what I learned."

Anna approved as she crawled into the back next to Millie. "Good. Then we'll fill you two in on our conversation with Thomas."

They settled in the living room where Nic, Nora, and Millie filled the sofa, while Anna occupied the chair with Alley. "Greg's a nice young man, and an extremely good bass player. Allen still knows how to pick them."

"He is good, Aunt Anna. I mean, I knew he played well with the studio band, but his jazz is different. He seems completely absorbed when he plays." Nic turned to Nora. "Where did you go during the performance?"

"I know a few people at the hotel. I thought I'd see if anyone noticed anything that night. I mean if they noticed anything unusual about Cecil and his client. I should have thought to do it sooner."

Nora's last comment sounded self-critical. Nic realized that although Nora seemed in control, she was in a great deal of pain. That could have been her first trip to the Palmer House without Carolyn. She squeezed her hand and spoke to the first remark. "Could anyone help?"

"Jack Larson is an old friend. He manages most of the night crew—the doormen, parking attendants, cigarette girls." At the mention of the cigarette girls, Nora lit one of her own, exhaling and clicking the lid of her gold lighter before she continued. "He was there when Cecil came in and noticed what he considered strange behavior."

"What did he do?" Anna asked.

"He wandered around the hotel talking to patrons and staff. That was out of character for Cecil Park, who has a reputation for ignoring staff or treating them badly. Jack watched him do that for a good fifteen minutes before his client arrived." Nora shrugged. "I don't know what it means, but it ranks as unusual."

"I agree." Anna adjusted in the chair, unleashing a cry from her furry lap warmer. "Oh hush, I'll put you on the floor. Let me tell you what Thomas told us. He didn't start until ten that night, and didn't see Cecil's entrance. He said he didn't notice anything other than Park's belligerent drunken behavior. Since that was the first time he'd seen him, he didn't know if that was out of character or not. The other boys we saw this evening didn't work that night."

Millie had slumped into a relaxed position on the sofa, and rather than sit up, rolled her head to share her information. "Thomas did mention another strange incident. The limo and driver that dropped Park off wasn't the same one that picked him up. Thomas wanted to see his limo because one of the guys told him it was cool. When the driver showed up, Thomas asked the kid why he thought the car was cool because he didn't think it was anything special. His friend said it wasn't the same car or driver. When they escorted Cecil out at the end of the night, Thomas held the door while the concierge poured him in the back seat. He couldn't see the driver's face, but thought it was strange that he didn't help with Mr. Park." Millie added a final observation. "Thomas was excited to be involved in a mystery with Anna."

"I should say so. He's eighteen." Anna laughed. "He's excited about everything but studying. Thomas promised he would talk to the other boys who worked that Friday to see if they could describe the driver. I also asked him to find out the name of the client who met with Mr. Park."

As the hour grew late, Nic found it difficult to hold a comfortable position. She pulled her knees to her chest and wrapped them in her arms before speaking. "That was a good idea, Aunt Anna. Do you think there's any significance to the different limousine?"

"It does sound rather strange, especially the part about him not helping. A competent driver would have helped the concierge. I'm interested to hear what the other boys say." Anna turned to Nora. "Thank you for driving, Nora, and I'm very glad you were able to join us."

"I'm glad to be involved, Anna. I'll do anything I can to help."

"Good. You're sure to have information that isn't available to us. Which reminds me, did you have a chance to read the article about the gun the police found?"

"I did. I knew Carolyn owned a gun, but she didn't carry it around. I thought maybe the newspaper, or the police," she added with a note of disgust, "were wrong about it belonging to her." She rose. "I wish I could tell you more, but I'm as puzzled as you that her gun was there. I'm also worn out. I'd better go or I'll be sleeping on your sofa." She turned to Nic. "Thanks for asking me along. It was good to be out of the apartment for a while and not at work or in jail."

Millie stood and followed Nora to the door. "We didn't do too badly, but maybe we should put in another hard night of detecting at the Empire Room." She pulled it closed. "Goodnight, Mrs. Murphy."

Chapter 17

"Morning, Sam."

"Good morning, Nic. You're looking pleased this morning. I take it you had a nice weekend."

"I did, thank you." The unsettling events of recent weeks had not dampened her spirits. Nic was pleased. She had never been social and the previous forty-eight hours came dangerously close to her saturation point for human contact, but she could not remember having more fun in one weekend. The trip to Marshall Field's with Millie and Aunt Anna, hearing Greg's band at the Palmer House, and even her new trousers made her smile.

Nic was early and not surprised when the elevator opened to a dark reception area. Voices came from Frank's office and she saw that he had a visitor. When he heard the elevator and looked out, he waved for her to join them. The other person was Nora, who looked as though she had not slept.

"Hi." Nora greeted Nic and slid to the adjacent chair to let her sit. "You're here early."

"Good morning. What's going on? You two look serious."

"The police arrested Barney." Nora told her.

Frank nodded and leaned back, allowing Nic to see that he was not in much better shape. "Last night one of the station's reporters called to let me know. I called Nora and we went to the police station to find out what happened."

"But isn't Barney in the Veteran's Hospital?"

"He is. Now he's there under arrest. We spent half the night waiting at the station until an officer told us he wasn't there and we couldn't see him at the hospital." Frank made an annoyed gesture with his hands before folding them on the desk.

"Why was he arrested?"

"They're charging him with murder. They believe he killed Carolyn."

Nic needed a second to absorb the news. "Why would they think Barney killed Carolyn? He liked her." She added to Nora, "and you. He told me how fond he was of you both."

"Did you read the article in Saturday's paper about the gun?" Frank asked.

"Yes, but it didn't mention Barney."

"The smudged prints they found on the handle are his." Nora told her.

When the smoke from her cigarette made its way to Nic, a strange request followed. "Could I have one of those?"

"Could you have one of what?"

"A cigarette." She pointed to the one Nora held and studied her puzzled expression. She either had not heard correctly, or did not want to share. Her hesitation gave Nic a second to reconsider. Not only was she unsure why she had asked, she wouldn't know what to do with a cigarette if she had one. "Never mind." She couldn't explain, so it seemed like a good time to bring up what Anna and she had discussed about the newspaper article. "Why did the police decide to search the studio again?"

"An employee from the station called in an anonymous tip. Whoever it was said that they knew the gun was in the box."

"That doesn't make sense." Nora had extinguished her cigarette after Nic's request. She glanced at the ashtray before continuing. "Isn't it more likely that the killer called in the tip? How else did he know the gun was there?"

"According to Detective O'Brian," Frank ignored the groans and rolled eyes. "A concerned person from the station discovered the gun accidentally and wanted to see the killer brought to justice, but didn't want to be personally involved."

Nic was about to express her opinion of O'Brian's theory, but Nora beat her to it. "That man is such an ass. Who would be digging around in the sound effects box and find a gun? And why were only Barney's fingerprints on it?" After a few seconds of silence, she raised a dark eyebrow. "The timing of this is interesting. When I arrived home from your place last night, Nic, my doorman had a telegram from my attorney. The owners of the hotel signed sworn statements yesterday that I was there all night. They're willing to testify in court if that becomes necessary, as are the two guests who said my car never moved after seven."

"That explains why they've decided to harass Barney." Nic couldn't believe O'Brian would go after him while he was in the hospital. "Frank, do we even know what's wrong with Barney? Is he well enough for them to take him to jail?"

"I still have no idea why he's there, but I do know that until his doctors release him, he'll stay put. He's in a private room with a policeman at the door."

Nic understood the futility of anger, but felt her control wavering. She took a breath and remembered what Anna told her about her struggle to forgive the people who killed Johnny. At times, she felt close, but whether forgiveness would ever be complete, she didn't know. What she did know was that anger separated her from humanity. She cared about people far too much to allow that. So did Nic. "Has Barney talked to anyone about the gun?"

"If he has, the police didn't tell me." Frank told her.

Nic was sure that Barney didn't kill Carolyn. She suspected Frank felt the same way. "Do you think he did it?"

"Absolutely not."

He posed the question to Nora who snapped on her earring with as much assurance as her reply. "I'd believe it was me before I'd believe it was Barney."

"Me too." Nic agreed with a bit too much conviction. Her response brought stares from Frank and Nora. "No, that wasn't what I meant. I mean that wasn't how I meant it. Forget it." For Nic, the morning had taken a definite and extreme turn for the worse, but her remark had given Nora and Frank their first reason to smile in a number of hours.

Nic left the office and saw Greg headed for the studio. Remembering his excitement the previous evening, she cheered considerably and joined him. "I had a good time last night, and Aunt Anna was right. Your band is aces."

"I'm glad you came. Your aunt is eighteen karat."

They entered the studio and Nic noticed the empty spot next to the engineer's booth where the sound effects box usually sat. "Greg, did you know they arrested Barney for killing Carolyn?"

He stopped short. "Barney? Why would they think he killed Carolyn?"

"Frank said they found partial fingerprints on the gun that killed her, and they're his."

"I thought Barney was in the hospital."

"He's in a room with a guard." Nic saw George standing against the wall and left Greg to ask him the same question. "George, did you hear they arrested Barney? I can't believe they think he killed Carolyn. Do you think he did?"

George straightened and ran a hand through his red curls. He shifted from his left foot to his right and back again before crossing his arms and taking a long look around the room. When the performance ended, he responded. "You wouldn't think he could, but if he's nuts...." He shrugged.

"What do you mean, if he's nuts?" Nic glared, and George looked everywhere but at her, even though she now stood only inches from his face. "Why did you say he's nuts?"

Her close proximity and increased volume made him more uncomfortable. "I don't know if he is or he ain't, but that's what the cops are saying."

Nic realized she had drawn unwanted attention to their conversation. She backed away slightly and kept her voice down. "Were you here late with Barney on the Friday Carolyn died?"

"Not late. I mean I wasn't here late. Barney left early to take care of something, and I didn't see him or Mrs. Park when I left."

"What time was that, George?"

"Around seven I think."

"Where did you go when you left?" Nic pressed, but George appeared to have had enough.

"Hey, I told the cops where I was and what I done. I don't gotta tell you nothin'." He left the studio without looking back.

"Nic." Frank stood behind her. "Are you ready to do the run through?"

Frank's question registered as she watched George depart. "Sure. Whenever you're ready. What will George use for sound effects if the police still have the box?"

"We've borrowed a few things from the *Mystery* show. They won't need them until tomorrow. They're also loaning us one of their sound people."

"Frank, why did George say Barney was nuts?"

Frank had been on his way to the stage when he heard the question. He turned back, his jaw tight. "He said that?" Nic nodded. "Barney was discharged from the military because he had a nervous breakdown. A breakdown caused by the war. Barney is not nuts, and I have no idea how George found out about his service record. I'll have a talk with him."

Before Nic had a chance to process the information Frank shared, she saw the rest of the cast on stage and joined them. They had a solid rehearsal and after a twenty-minute break, Frank called them for the live performance. The 'On the Air' sign lit, the theme song faded to a ringing telephone, and Nic cupped her hand over her ear as she leaned into the microphone. "Hello, Inez Ingalls, Private Eye."

Nic stepped from the Mart into the cold November evening and saw an inch of snow on the sidewalk. She loved the natural blanket. It softened sharp edges and muffled the continual urban symphony of voices and traffic. If only briefly, it transformed black streets and alleys into a sparkling wonderland.

The most vivid snowfall in her memory was one of her earliest. Outside the kitchen window of their home, the iridescent world excited and frightened her. Her mom shared her excitement, but giggled as she dressed her little girl in boots and clothes that hardly allowed her to bend. To Nic, the postage stamp lot that was their backyard looked huge when filled with pristine, untouched snow. The moment they stepped off the back porch, her mom dashed to the middle of the yard and lay face-up, moving her arms and legs to make a snow angel. Nic hurried to her side to make one of her own and burst with pride because although considerably smaller, it looked the same.

Screeching steel wheels announced an approaching train and ended Nic's reverie. She slipped the attendant a dime and ran up the stairs, arriving with a few other stragglers before the train reached the platform. Once on board, she saw there were no empty seats and clung to a pole to catch her breath.

When they reached Belmont, Nic saw her connecting train had not yet arrived and joined dozens of bundled passengers on the shadowy platform. Almost immediately, the whistle of an approaching engine drew her to the edge of the tracks. Over the howling wind and the arriving train, Nic thought she heard her name. She turned and saw a dark figure running straight at her.

Chapter 18

Nic had managed to take a step back, and as the figure made contact, it was with her shoulder. The minimal impact spun her away from the track instead of in front of the approaching train. She stumbled and might have fallen but for a nearby Good Samaritan who grabbed her coat sleeve and helped her stay on her feet. The dark figure descended the stairs two at a time without looking back.

The man that intervened helped Nic to a seat, departing only after she assured him she was fine. Except for legs that trembled more than the rattling car warranted, she thought she was. She focused on convincing her mind and body that when she arrived at her stop only minutes away, she would be able to walk.

When the crackling voice of the conductor announced Irving Park, Nic rallied. She grabbed the seat in front of her, rose with purpose, and made her way out, surveying the platform for dark figures before she hurried down the stairs and ran the two blocks home. In the safety of her apartment, she collapsed in the stuffed chair, still wearing her coat and gloves. Seconds later, Anna came from the kitchen.

"Nicole, what happened? You're white as a sheet."

Nic had hoped for a minute to compose her thoughts. Instead, as often happened when confronted by Anna's questioning blue eyes, the levee gave way. "A man came out of nowhere and almost knocked me in front of the train."

As she described the event to Anna, including the kind stranger who kept her standing, Nic felt calmer. She even warmed enough to remove her gloves and wiggle out of her coat, but the shiver continued. "It was frightening."

"I'm sure it was." Anna touched her knee. "You're shaking. Would you like a cup of tea?"

"No, I'm okay. I'm better just sitting here."

"You couldn't see him at all?"

"No. He was bundled in a coat and hat. I saw nothing but a dark moving shape, but I know he wasn't running for the train. After he bumped me, he ran from the platform."

"Nicole, I know I don't need to say this, but I will anyway. Keep your eyes open at all times. I couldn't bear it if anything happened to you." Anna hugged her. "Do you want to lie down before dinner? There's time. I made tuna casserole but haven't put it in the oven yet."

A loud crash from the back of the apartment sent Anna running to the kitchen. She found her casserole on the floor and Alley in the middle of the mess nibbling on the splattered tuna without any noticeable repentance.

Nic hurried in behind Anna. "What is it?" Her previous ill humor disappeared at the sight of Alley dining on the spilled casserole. She laughed and shook her head before pulling rags from the pantry and handing one to Anna.

"I left it sitting on a towel. It must have been hanging over the table enough for her to drag it down. Why do I keep thinking I'm smarter than that cat?"

Except for the portion eaten by Alley, the casserole went in the trash and the Owen women ate cold-cut sandwiches for dinner. Afterward, Anna and Nic gathered their notes and spread everything on the coffee table in the living room. Anna sat on the sofa next to Alley who was involved in an after-dinner grooming session, while Nic sat opposite them on the floor.

"Are you feeling better, Nicole?"

"I am. All I have to do is picture Alley with the casserole and I can't help but laugh. I should buy one of those Kodak Brownie cameras and take pictures of her antics." Alley stretched in another great pose. "Aunt Anna, what do you say I give Nora a call and see if she'd like to join us? She wants to help with the sleuthing."

"I'd say that sounds like a good idea."

Nic found the card with Nora's number by the phone and dialed. "Hi. We were about to work on the case. Do you want to join us? Great. We'll see you in a bit." She gave Anna the news. "Nora will be here shortly and that makes me happy. I want all the deputies we have available to solve this. Inez Ingalls may be brave enough to live this way, but Nic Owen is not there yet."

"Don't forget, Inez's life is scripted. There are no surprises. Mere mortals aren't that lucky. Nicole, would you go to my office and grab a handful of index cards from the drawer on the right side of my desk?" Nic returned with the blank cards, which Anna split into two stacks. "We'll put each potential suspect's name on one of the cards. Make it small. Some will have quite a bit of information."

As they finished the names, a brief, but brisk, knock sounded on the front door and Millie came through with Nora right behind her. Nora smiled, but the extended lower lip and sharp set of her brow indicated that Millie was less than happy. "You could have told me they all killed him."

"What?" Nic faced the two new arrivals and saw Nora wearing a look of confusion that she suspected matched her own.

"You could have told me they all stabbed the old man." Anna chuckled and Nic realized the cause of her displeasure, but Nora appeared not to have a clue.

Millie had come down the stairs as Nora arrived at the outer door. She let her inside, but did not explain that the reason for her foul mood was the unsatisfying ending of a book. Nic explained to Nora as she helped her with her coat.

"Thanks Anna. Do you want me to put it in your office?" Millie held *Murder on the Calais Coach* in the air.

"Just leave it on the windowsill, Millie. I'll take it back later. Hi, Nora. I'm glad you could come."

"I am too. So the killers she's talking about are in the book." Nora pointed at the tome on the windowsill and watched three heads nod. "I've never read mysteries, but I'm thinking maybe I should start."

"Don't read that one." Millie suggested as she sat on the arm of the chair. "I ruined the ending. What's going on with the case?"

Nic explained her experience on the train platform to Nora and Millie, and filled Anna and Millie in about Barney. Throughout her recitation, Millie grew more serious. When Nic finished, her best friend had a few words of her own. "You two need to be careful. Nic, you shouldn't take the train alone anymore, and both of you should leave the Mart before dark, and maybe you should…."

Nic interrupted. "Millie, I appreciate your concern, and I promise we'll keep our eyes open."

Although Millie didn't look convinced, she moved on. "Could Barney have killed Carolyn?"

"Nora and I don't think so. What about you Aunt Anna?"

"I called the hospital earlier in the day. Mary Rose told me that Barney is on her unit. She has some information, but with the police around, she preferred coming by after work to tell us in person. Why don't we see what she has to say before we discuss Barney? Let's keep working on the other suspects."

Anna divided the index cards with the suspects' names into four stacks and passed them out. The women wrote alibis on the cards of those who had them. When those were complete, Anna described the next task. "Write the time each person said they left, whether they had an alibi or not." As they completed each suspect, Anna retrieved the cards and lined them up on the table. "So, we have Marcy leaving for her sister's at five thirty. Frank left around seven to play bridge with his parents. Greg left shortly after six, and Nora you were in Michigan. Alice left in the afternoon to pick up one of her children, and Harold and Stanley left around six to go to a bowling tournament. Allen Reed left around six thirty to conduct the City Theater Orchestra."

"Aunt Anna, did Allen tell you what O'Brian said about his alibi?"

"You mean that a person who looked like him could have been conducting? Yes, he did." Anna shook her head, but made no further comment and went back to work. "Who do we have left?"

Millie read the remaining cards. "George Sokal, Barney Mills, Jimmy Holmes, and Belia Malecek are the only ones left without alibis."

Nic remembered her conversation with George. "I don't know about his alibi, but George said he left around seven."

While Millie added the information, Nora mentioned another suspect. Her voice was soft but firm. "We don't have a card for Cecil Park."

"Right." Anna handed her a blank. "Put him down and we'll add more to his card later. Nicole, do you remember Robert, the policeman I told you about who is checking on bookies?"

"Yes. Did he find someone involved with Cecil?"

"Not yet. He's still working on it, but he promised to get back to me in the next couple of days with what he finds. Maybe we'll have more to add to Cecil Park's card when he does."

After Nora wrote Cecil Park and the Palmer House on the card and handed it back, Anna noticed the time. "Nicole, Mary Rose should be here soon. Would you mind putting on a pot of coffee?"

Nora and Millie volunteered to help, and in a short time, Nora returned carrying cups, followed by Millie with cream and sugar. Nic arrived with the coffee as the buzzer sounded.

Millie was closest to the door and opened it for a grey-haired woman no taller than she and twenty pounds heavier. "Hello, Millie. It's good to see you. How is Joe?"

"He's good, Mrs. Brenner. Thank you."

Anna joined them at the door and she and Mary Rose exchanged a hug before Nicole helped remove her coat. "Nic, you're a big celebrity I hear, and working at quite an interesting place, at least according to the newspapers."

They exchanged hugs and Nic showed her to the chair. "It has definitely been an experience, Mrs. Brenner."

Before Mary Rose sat, she acknowledged the one person she did not know personally. "You are Nora Hahn. I was sorry to hear about Carolyn. She's done a great deal for our city." Nora extended a hand, which Mary Rose shook before waving around the room. "You have found good friends here."

When Mary Rose sat on the straight back chair that Millie brought from the dining room, her nurse's uniform rose above the rolled stockings that stopped short of her knees. Her white nursing shoes, designed for comfort and endurance, were scuffed from a day's wear, and her grey hair bore an indentation where a hat rested before she'd donned her scarf for the cold trip home.

Mary Rose and Anna had known each other since childhood and Mary Rose adored Anna. Serving as a Red Cross nurse on the frontlines in World War I, she saw firsthand the reality of war. Those images stayed with her, as they did all who experienced it. Anna helped her remember the good things in life. The things she did not often see in the war, or on the psychiatric ward of the Veteran's Hospital.

Alley waited until Mary Rose settled in, and jumped in her lap. "You haven't forgotten your old friend. How are you, Alley? Still spoiled I'll bet." The cat didn't seem to mind the comment from Mary Rose and curled up contentedly. "So, Anna, we're detecting again, are we?"

Anna chuckled. "Nic considers Barney a friend, and we don't think the police are working to solve Carolyn Park's murder. At least they're not working in the direction we think they should."

"I've been following the story. It may be that Mr. Park has been applying pressure for a solution and the police are anxious to relieve that pressure." Mary Rose offered.

"That would explain why they're grasping at straws." Anna had voiced her dislike for O'Brian when she met him. That dislike intensified when Nic shared her experience at the police station. "I met two of the detectives involved in this case when they interviewed Nicole. They didn't inspire a great deal of confidence. Nic and Nora have had enough frustrating encounters with O'Brian and Jones to last a lifetime."

Mary Rose shook her head. "Their behavior at the hospital was cruel and unprofessional. Barney is my patient, not a suspect, and I will do what I can to see that he gets the help he needs."

"Can you tell us what happened to him, Mary Rose?" Nic asked.

"I'm comfortable sharing his story because he is quite open about what happened to him in France. He knows that talking about the experience has helped him heal, and when he shares it with others, it helps them. Barney had an emotional breakdown. He saw terrible battles, bombs exploding, people dying all around. It ended for him when an attack on his squad left many dead and the rest scattered around the countryside. Separated from the rest of his group, Barney entered a village and found the entire community in an open grave."

Mary Rose scratched the snuggled kitty while she spoke. "Another platoon arrived three days later and found him in a corner of the church, rolled in a ball and unable to speak. He stayed with us for three months and although doctors didn't think he'd recover, Barney proved them wrong."

Nic had tears in her eyes. "What happened? Why is he back in the hospital?"

"We don't know for sure. After Barney left us and returned to work, he came twice a week to see his doctor and talk with other soldiers. That's where he was supposed to be the Friday Carolyn Park was killed. He attended every session without fail, so I was surprised to learn that he hadn't shown up. I was more surprised when I heard that his fingerprints were on the gun. Barney's doctors are convinced that he would have a difficult time even holding a gun. He showed up at the hospital a few days ago, in a confused state."

"You said the doctors didn't think Barney could use a gun. Surely they told O'Brian."

"Anna, they spent an hour trying to convince O'Brian to listen, but he wasn't having any of it. He thinks Barney faked the breakdown to get out of the army. Mr. O'Brian has some nerve since he was never in the service."

"How is Barney, Mary Rose? Can we visit him?" Nora asked.

"No, the police won't let anyone see him, not even his wife or family."

"How can he heal if he can't see his family?" Nic asked as she sat next to Anna.

"We need to find the killer." Anna put an arm around Nic. "That's the best way we can help Barney."

"Do you suppose he'll ever forget what he saw, Mary Rose?"

"I doubt he will ever forget, Nic, but he will find a way to deal with it, as he did before. He doesn't have a choice."

When Mary Rose finished, the others, encouraged by her certainty, wanted to work on the case. They decided which of the suspects needed further scrutiny and who would do the scrutinizing. Nic and Nora received multiple warnings that they exercise caution, and after both agreed to a final warning from Millie, Nora stood. "I'd better go. It was nice meeting you, Mary Rose. Please tell Nic or Anna when we can see Barney."

"I will, dear. Do take care of yourself."

Nic walked Nora to her car and returned to find that Anna, too, was finished investigating for the day. "Why don't you and Millie take these dishes into the kitchen? Mary Rose and I would like to visit for a bit before she goes."

Nic and Millie recognized their dismissal.

Chapter 19

The following morning just after 8 o'clock, Millie entered the Owen apartment holding the hem of a red pleated skirt and spinning on a pair of matching pair of one-inch heels. "How do I look?" The other half of the ensemble was a navy blue blouse with three-quarter length sleeves sporting a white sailor tie, which she waved at Nic. "This is for Joe." She had tamed her curls, and her hair fell to her shoulders in waves, adorned above her right ear with a bow that matched the skirt.

Few people noticed Millie's good figure because of her limited stature and round face. It was even less apparent in her usual attire of baggy pants and one of Joe's shirts. A wide belt accentuated her soft curves, and the light olive tone of her face glowed against the navy blouse.

"Millie, you look wonderful." Nic told her as Anna joined with similar praise.

"You look fantastic. Too bad your customers won't see you. I don't remember you wearing that outfit before."

"My sister, Nona, loaned me a few things until I can buy my own. I don't think Anthony would approve of my wardrobe from the factory."

"You're probably right about that. What time do you start?" Nic asked.

"Not until nine, but I'm so excited I couldn't sleep. I've been up since six and dressed for an hour."

"I made coffee. Let's have a cup. You too, Nicole. You have time, don't you?"

"I do."

"Come on, I'll pour." Anna led the way to the kitchen. "Thank you for walking Mary Rose home last night, Millie. She would never have asked, but I'm sure she appreciated the company."

Millie fingered the tie. "It was nice talking with her. She told me about what makes some soldiers break down and what they do to make them better. One of them I'd never heard of before, shock treatments."

"What are shock treatments?" Nic asked as she sat.

"They take a belt with couple of metal buttons and wrap it around your head with the buttons on your temples." Millie held a finger to each of her temples. "Then they plug electrical doohickeys on the buttons and hit a switch to give your brain a shock."

"What?" Nic looked at Anna who was nodding in agreement. "They electrocute you?"

"No. It's not a big shock, just enough to move things in your brain." Millie explained.

"Aunt Anna, is that true?"

"Yes, it is. Although I'm not sure I agree with the treatment or Millie's colorful description." Millie shrugged and Anna went on. "There are scientists who think because our brains are filled with electrical currents and impulses the shock can start things flowing and fix certain problems. Of course, there are other scientists who don't agree."

"What do you think, Aunt Anna?"

"Whether or not the treatment is effective is only one of my concerns. Another is how it's used. Mary Rose told me that some state hospitals use it to keep patients sedate and easier to handle. It is also used to cure homosexuals." Anna filled her cup. "As far as I can tell, they've never proven that electric shock cures homosexuality, and to my knowledge, they've never shown that homosexuality needs curing."

Nic stood. "I'd better go or I'll be late. Aunt Anna, it never ceases to amaze me the things you know."

"Keep your eyes open on the train platforms, Nicole, and everywhere else."

"I will. Thanks for giving me something to think about on the way to work." She hugged Millie and wished her luck as she ran out.

"Millie, when do you have to leave?"

"A few minutes before nine, Anna. I'm working in the office around the corner. Can I have another cup of coffee?"

When Millie left for her new job, Anna dressed and caught a streetcar to the Veteran's Hospital. After having volunteered in every part of the hospital at one time or another, Anna knew where to find the entrance to the psychiatric wing. Mary Rose came from her desk and let her in.

"Mary Rose, I don't want you in trouble for this. If you have any doubts, say the word."

"Anna, I'm far too old to worry about being in trouble. I like Barney and want to help. Let me tell you what I have in mind. The officers guarding him change at noon and they're punctual. I'll take you the back way to wait in a supply closet around the corner. At ten minutes to twelve I'll call the officer to help me fix something while you sneak into Barney's room."

"Fix what?" Anna asked.

Mary Rose removed a wheel from the base of her heavy wooden chair and dropped it to the floor. "Here's the key. As

She Overheard Murder

soon as he comes to help me, you go into the room. Barney's lunch will come at 12:15, so you can't stay any longer than twenty minutes. At ten minutes after twelve, when the new officer is at the door, the wheel will fall off again. I'll call him to come and assist this helpless old lady."

Anna smiled. Both of them knew that people saw older women as weak and helpless, if they saw them at all. As far as Anna was concerned, there were times when being invisible was fine. This was one of those times. She peeked around the corner and saw the officer stationed by Barney's door. He wouldn't be able to see the area when he came to help Mary Rose. "I hope Barney will talk to me."

"If anyone can get him to talk, it's you, Anna. Did you tell Nicole your plan?"

"I thought it best to wait. She'd be a nervous wreck. I have one more question, Mary Rose. I know that after I talk to Barney, I'm to leave out the back door, but what should I do with the key?"

"Put it under the Bible on the desk. I have another, and I'll pick that one up later. The door will lock behind you when you leave." Mary Rose and Anna took a back route to the supply closet around the corner from Barney's room. "Good luck, Anna," she whispered as they hugged.

At ten minutes to twelve, Anna heard Mary Rose call the officer and slipped out of the closet. She entered the room and found Barney sitting on the bed with his feet on the floor. He glanced up as the door closed. Whether because of the finger she held to her lips, or because he was surprised, Barney watched her arrival in silence.

Anna had never met the man and could not judge if he looked worse than usual, but his exhaustion was obvious. His face was drawn, his eyes were dull and vacant, and his light blue pajamas had seen enough washing that the cuffs and sleeves were threadbare. Barney looked equally frayed. "Barney, my name is Anna Owen," she whispered. "You work with my niece, Nic." Barney gave her a slight, but encouraging nod. "She's worried about you. Can we talk for a few minutes?" His eyes drifted to the door and back. "Don't worry. Mary Rose is keeping the officer occupied."

Anna told Barney she hoped he was feeling a little better, and that his co-workers missed him, but knowing they didn't have much time, she abandoned the small talk and got down to business. He listened quietly as she explained how once the motel owner confirmed Nora's alibi, O'Brian shifted his focus to him. At first, he responded with one or two word answers to only a few of her questions. Eventually, Anna proved Mary Rose right. Barney talked. He told her what he could remember about coming to the hospital, which was little. He also told her what he was doing on the night of Carolyn's murder. Those memories, although clear, were much more difficult to share. The one thing he knew without a doubt was that he had not killed Carolyn Park.

When it was time to leave, Anna put the key under the bible as Mary Rose had instructed and told Barney with a grin that she wasn't worried about O'Brian finding it there. She also told him to keep his chin up because they were doing everything they could to find the killer, and he needed to do everything he could to get well.

Anna pushed the door open an inch and peeked out, then hurried through as it closed noiselessly. She heard Mary Rose talking to the officer. "I'm sorry to be troubling you. Do you want me to hand you the screwdriver?"

Hugging the wall, Anna worked her way down the corridor, but froze in place when someone pounded on the front door. She leaned over and saw the reflections of Mary Rose and the officer in the glass, and O'Brian and Jones on the other side. When Mary Rose went to the door to let them in, Anna ran to the closet. She could hear O'Brian yelling at the officer. Then he made the mistake of raising his voice at Mary Rose.

"Mr. O'Brian."

"It's Detective."

"Mr. O'Brian. It would make no difference if you were the Chief of the entire Chicago Police, which you are not. You don't come into this ward screaming at the top of your voice. These men have come home from terrible places and they don't need to hear you yelling. I'm sure that if you served, you understand."

Anna held the closet door open a crack to hear the conversation. She chuckled when her friend rendered 'Mr. O'Brian' silent.

*

"You were where, Aunt Anna?"

"Nicole, there's no reason to be upset. It went well. Nothing terrible happened and the important thing is I talked to Barney."

What surprised Nic was not so much Anna's news, but her own surprise at hearing it. "How did you do it? It was Mary Rose, of course. She helped. How did you sneak past the policeman into Barney's room? I don't want to know, do I, Aunt Anna?"

"There was only one little snag." Anna hesitated and that hesitation sent a chill down Nic's spine.

"What was that?"

"When I left Barney's room, I was sneaking down the hallway to go out the back door, but O'Brian showed up and I had to run back to the closet until he left."

"O'Brian showed up?" Nic gulped and decided to ask only questions whose answers she could handle. "He didn't see you? How long were you in the closet?" Before Anna said a word, Nic decided she was not prepared to handle any answers. "Never mind. I don't want to know."

Anna patted the sofa and Nic sat. "Let me tell you about Barney. He isn't great, but he's not as bad as he wants the police to believe. He told me he has some memory loss from the shock treatments, but he is confident those will return after a while."

"Was that why he didn't remember where he was the night Carolyn died?"

"He does remember where he was that night. He just isn't proud of it. He met a woman at one of the restaurants in the Mart. She was young and attractive, and started running into him when he was leaving work. She told him she found him interesting. Barney said he should have known she was lying, but it made him feel good, and he continued to meet her for coffee. The last time they met, she asked if he'd like to go to a bar and have a few drinks. That was the night of the shooting. Barney thought he could miss his meeting at the hospital and that way his wife wouldn't wonder where he was. After they'd had several drinks, she told him she was an actress and wanted him to help her get a job at the radio station. He thought she was kidding and explained that he was a sound effects man and couldn't do a thing for her career."

"What did she say?"

"She picked up her belongings and stormed out of the bar. It didn't take him long to realize he'd been duped."

"Why didn't he tell the police?"

"He was sure that even if he could find the woman, she wouldn't come forward to be his alibi, and he wasn't anxious for his wife to find out. They hadn't done anything more than talk, but Barney felt guilty about not telling his wife where he was."

"Aunt Anna, I didn't think Barney was that upset when Carolyn died. I mean, he was upset that she died, but he didn't seem more troubled than anyone else at the studio."

"Barney felt stable when he heard the news about Carolyn. After his experience in the war, he learned to check his moods when emotional situations occurred. As you said, it saddened him because he considered Carolyn a friend, but he didn't feel a problem with his nerves. O'Brian's badgering raised a few doubts. The detective knew about his breakdown and used it to upset him. He told Barney that he was dangerous and that he probably killed Carolyn and couldn't remember. O'Brian told him if he confessed, he'd help get him a lighter sentence by telling the court he wasn't right in the head. The incident with the woman added to his confusion, as did the guilt he felt for deceiving his wife. Thursday morning, Barney was digging around in the sound box and felt a shape he didn't recognize. It was the gun. After that, he wasn't sure what happened, but he left the building and at some point checked himself into the VA Hospital."

"The gun was in the box the entire time? How did the police miss it, and how did Barney and George not find it for almost a month? They were constantly in that box."

"I'm not sure the police missed it, Nicole. I have a hunch it landed in that box shortly before the police received their anonymous tip. The person who put it there and phoned in the tip is probably the murderer."

"None of this makes sense, Aunt Anna. Who would frame Barney? Do you think the woman who wanted a job might have done it?"

"I suppose that's possible. What do you think?"

"If she wanted a job badly enough, she might have killed Carolyn. And that would explain why I became a target."

"You might be right. You're also right how little sense this case makes, and that is interesting. Someone kills Carolyn, but the police don't know why. You're a suspect, then Nora, and now Barney, yet they harassed all three of you from the beginning. The gun that killed her suddenly shows up weeks later, and since the only prints on it are Barney's, someone had to have wiped it clean before depositing it in the sound effects box. It's as though the killer doesn't know who to frame."

After a quick and energetic knock, the front door opened and their pleased-looking neighbor stepped in. "Ask me how my first day went. Go ahead, ask." In unison, Nic and Anna invited Millie to enlighten them. "Wonderful. I was made for this job—born to talk. If you two want to know how good I am, next time I go to work, dial zero until you hear me say 'operator.'"

Chapter 20

As Nic entered the lounge, she exchanged greetings with Belia and one of the other band members who were on their way out. Their departure left Nic alone, but before she reached the sink, Nora arrived.

She wore a wide-brimmed black hat draped across her head at an angle and an unnecessarily slimming red jacket and black slacks. The jacket had black yokes, padded shoulders, and a thick black belt. The slacks hung straight to a pair of matching three-inch heels.

"You look nice. What's the occasion?"

"Nothing. I just decided to put an effort into dressing this morning rather than throwing on an outfit without looking. I haven't cared how I looked for a while." Nora sat and placed her hat on a neighboring chair. "What's new at the Owen Detective Agency?"

Remembering the outfits Nora wore over the last few weeks, Nic decided that if she had thrown them on, it might be wise to enlist her help in fashion decisions. That discussion would have to wait. "I do have interesting news. Of course, now that you've met Aunt Anna, you won't be as surprised when I tell you what she did."

"What did she do?"

"She visited Barney at the Veteran's Hospital yesterday."

"You mean the police let her talk to him? How did she swing that? The last I heard, they weren't allowing anyone in."

Nora had not understood, so Nic provided another detail. "She didn't have permission to visit." The additional clue failed to bring enlightenment, and for several minutes, the woman who made her living with words sat quietly considering them, her dark eyebrows joined at the narrow space above her nose and her red lips pursed. The sudden rise of her eyebrows signaled understanding. "Wait a minute. Anna snuck in to see Barney?" Nic confirmed with a nod. "Then, no, you're wrong."

"Wrong about what?"

"I don't know Anna well enough not to be surprised. She visited Barney and the policeman happened to be away from the door?"

"She was lucky she wasn't caught." Nic told her about O'Brian's arrival.

"You do know that your aunt is a remarkable woman."

Nic pictured Anna and Mary Rose plotting against the Chicago Police Department and her heart rate increased. "I know. I just wish she'd stopped doing dangerous things."

"You wouldn't have done it if you had the chance, Nic? You've already taken risks asking questions that seem to be upsetting someone. And that someone could be a murderer."

"That's different. Of course I'd have done it if I could, but I'm not sixty-two years old."

"From what I've seen, she puts most of us youngsters to shame. And her friend, Mary Rose, is equally amazing."

"She is. Aunt Anna said she told O'Brian off for yelling in the hospital and left him speechless. What's more amazing is that she risked her job."

"It sounds as though she and Anna knew what they were doing. I know you don't want to think about it, but I'd love to see O'Brian's face if he discovers what they did. More than that, I'd love to have seen Mary Rose telling him off."

"You don't plan to take my side in this argument, do you, Nora?"

"I'm afraid not. Your aunt is too good to be true."

"She is, and I am constantly learning new things about her. Last week I found out that she and Allen Reed have known each other for years."

Nora listened to Anna and Allen's adventure with a growing smile. "Our Allen Reed? She fixed his Bearcat?"

"Aunt Anna raised me after my mom died. I feel closer to her than anyone." Nic explained the tragedies her aunt endured, including the death of her brother, Johnny. "It was because of the article about you in the newspaper that Aunt Anna and I discussed homosexuality."

"I did wonder why you were more at ease with things than most people. You and your aunt should be proud of overcoming those tragedies, and grateful for each other."

"I don't know if our lives were more or less difficult than anyone else's, but Aunt Anna sure made mine easier. What about your family, Nora?"

Nora focused on the cigarette she'd pulled from her purse for a few seconds before lighting it. Only after exhaling did she speak, her face and words devoid of passion or pain. "My father had a farm in Michigan. It wasn't large, but he had set his mind on making it work and on my brother taking over when he retired."

"Oh, you have a brother." Nic saw something flicker and die in Nora before she continued.

"Had. His name was Dan, and he was a great guy. We did everything together. He introduced me to these." She waved her cigarette. "It's amazing we didn't burn down the barn. He told me more than once that he'd never be a farmer. He wanted to go to college and become a writer, to live in Chicago, not the middle of a cornfield. My father overheard us talking one day and was furious. He took Dan out of school and made him work in the fields. That lasted only a few months, until I found him hanging from a beam in the barn."

The picture Nic imagined of a young Nora and Dan plotting their futures amid straw bales and clouds of smoke burst with the final remark. She threw a hand to her throat. "*You* found him hanging?"

Nora focused on the cigarette. "My father didn't blame me but his plans were for his son, not his daughter. We rarely spoke after that, which was one of the reasons I knew I had to leave. I decided to live the life that Dan couldn't. After the University of Chicago accepted my application, I moved to the city where I eventually met Carolyn. I still thank Dan for that."

"Did your parents know about Carolyn?"

"I went home to see my mother every so often. The last time was right after Carolyn and I met. I never considered taking her to meet them, but one of the members of the church my father belonged to had a daughter at U of C. She heard about our relationship and told him. Apparently, he felt obligated to share the news with my parents. Maybe he wanted to save my hell-bound soul, I don't know. I think he was just a hateful, spiteful man. After that, my father couldn't look at me. The few times he did, I saw his disgust. When I went for what we all knew was the last time, my mother tried to hug me, but he ordered her to the kitchen. I heard she died shortly after. My father blamed me and barred me from the funeral. I never saw him again." Nora extinguished her cigarette and looked at Nic. "I don't have many tears left to cry over that, but it still hurts like hell." She tossed a tissue to the trash and leaned forward. "So, tell me what Barney said."

The years might have helped Nora exhaust her tears, but Nic questioned whether she could stifle the flood behind her eyes. She took a shuddering breath and told Nora about the twenty minutes Anna spent with Barney, explaining his recovery and how finding the gun led to his checking into the hospital. "She promised Barney we'd find the killer."

Nora stood. "And find him we shall. The killer doesn't know he's up against Anna Owen and her band of merry women." Nic whimpered as Nora recovered her purse and hat. "Did you ask Anna what I should bring tomorrow?"

"She said that if you absolutely have to bring a dish, dessert would be nice. We'll eat around three, but you may want to come earlier."

"I'll be there at seven in the morning if you want. My only suggestion is you don't have me help with cooking." They left the lounge and parted at the stairway that took Nora to the twentieth floor.

The studio was quiet when Nic entered. She saw Frank on stage and George warming his spot on the back wall. Although she said good morning as she passed, George seemed not to hear.

"Hi, Frank."

He turned. "Hi, Nic."

Convinced that Frank had not killed Carolyn, and that he was a good person to have in her corner, Nic decided to share Anna's recent encounter and see if Frank had any ideas about how they could help Barney. She stretched her entwined fingers toward the ceiling, releasing them as she sat. "Frank, there's something I want to tell you, but it you have to keep it quiet."

He laughed. "Keeping things quiet is my most important job around here."

"My aunt talked to Barney at the hospital yesterday."

Frank didn't speak.

"Frank?"

He shook his head. "I'm sorry, Nic. Did you say your aunt went to visit Barney?"

"Yes, I did."

"He's under a police guard, isn't he? They wouldn't let me in."

"Yes, he is."

Frank took another short pause and made another quick shake of his head before responding. "Your aunt really is Miss Marple, isn't she?"

Nic agreed and related the conversation between Anna and Barney. "Frank, we have to find out who killed Carolyn so Barney can recover." She lowered her volume. "Did George have an alibi?"

"He helped his buddy move furniture."

"His buddy confirmed that?"

"According to O'Brian, George is in the clear."

Nic saw George drop his head as soon as she turned in his direction. "What's his buddy's name?"

"George said his name is Ray and that he started working as a janitor for the Mart about the same time he started at the station. I don't know if I heard his last name, but I'll see what I can find out."

"What about Jimmy's alibi? He won't talk to me." Nic saw no reason to mention why.

"Jimmy doesn't talk much to anyone. He did tell me that he spent the night at his mother's house. I'm guessing she confirmed that because the police haven't shown an interest in him."

It occurred to Nic that she would not mind terribly if the police discovered Jimmy was the killer. It also occurred to her that she disliked him because he had not been friendly, and that seemed a tad weak to accuse him of murder. She felt a twinge of guilt, but before she could indulge in additional self-recrimination, the back door flew open.

All eyes turned to the doorway where Nora and fellow writer, Cliff, hobbled in. Her shoes and purse hung from one hand and her hat dangled from the fingers of the other, which she had wrapped around his waist. Nic hurried over and saw Nora favoring her right foot and a bruise on her left cheek. "What happened?"

Cliff eased her into a chair. "I'll call the police."

"Don't bother." Nora told him. "If they send O'Brian, he'll say I was trying to kill myself and arrest me."

"Nora, whoever did this needs be caught. He could have killed you."

She patted his hand. "Cliff, you know what would be great? If you could find ice for my ankle." He hesitated but left on his mission.

Nic had gone to the lounge and soaked a towel in cold water to put on the darkening bruise. "What happened?"

"I'm not sure. When I got to my office I discovered I'd left my cigarettes in the lounge and came back down. I was about to open the door from the stairwell when I heard footsteps behind me. The next thing I knew, someone wrapped an arm around my neck, and grabbed my hair. I couldn't turn my head, but I did hear him make a comment in perfect B-Movie fashion." Nora lowered her voice for a thug imitation. "He said 'You're supposed to be dead', and dragged me to the stairs and pushed, but I grabbed the railing and held on. When I saw his foot over my head, I held my breath and waited. That was when Cliff opened the door on twenty and the creep took off."

"How did you hurt your ankle?"

Nora pointed to her heels and frowned as Cliff returned with his hands full of an ice-laden towel and dressing tape. He knelt in front of her swelling ankle. "I'm sorry it took so long. I had to go to a restaurant for the ice. Are you sure you don't want the police?"

"No police, Cliff."

After laying the lumpy towel over her ankle, he explained to Nic how he happened on the scene. "I came from twenty and heard a noise, but she didn't scream or anything. I didn't know she'd been hurt until I saw her sprawled on the stairs."

"That conjures up a delightful image."

If Cliff heard Nora's comment, he ignored it. "By then, I heard him running down the stairs. I couldn't go after him and leave her lying there."

Frank joined them. "Do you want to go to the hospital, Nora?"

"No. I'm going to the lounge and lie down. Nic, would you give me a hand?" She added to Frank, "Could you pinch some aspirin from Marcy's secret stash?"

"No problem. I'll grab a couple."

When Nora reached for her things, her overprotective associate intervened. "I'll carry your stuff. Nic can come out for it."

Nic helped her stand, gathered the ice, and wrapped her arm around Nora while Cliff managed the door. When Nora sat comfortably on the couch, Nic put the ice on her ankle and brought her another wet cloth for her face. "Did you recognize the guy?"

"No. I didn't see much of him. We were on the landing when he put his arm around my neck. When I tried to turn my head, I caught a glimpse and saw he had short hair, almost a military cut, but it was too dark in the stairway to tell what color it was other than not black. All I can accurately describe is the hair on the arm wrapped around my neck. It was blonde, but I'm guessing that's not enough to talk O'Brian into a lineup."

"Nora, you might want to take this seriously. Cliff was right. He could have killed you. What if he had kicked you and you fell down those concrete stairs?"

"I know. I know. I'm just tired of people messing with me."

Nic stood. "Let me see if Frank found the aspirin." She stepped from the lounge and saw Cliff and Frank leaning on the wall. Cliff held the hat, purse, and shoes, while Frank had two white packets. "Why didn't you knock on the door?" The men looked at each other and shrugged.

Nic shook her head while gathering up Nora's belongings and the aspirin. She put the hat, purse, and shoes in a chair and gave Nora the aspirin powder and a cup of water.

After taking the aspirin, Nora looked thoughtful. "You know, Jimmy has short light-colored hair, and he's a strange guy."

"I agree with you on that, Nora, but Frank told me he was at his mother's house the night Carolyn was killed. I was glad Frank knew his alibi, because he won't tell me much."

"Why not?"

"Because I asked him if he killed her."

"You asked him if he killed Carolyn."

"That was the morning I talked to Marcy. Then George almost knocked me down trying to leave. When Jimmy wouldn't talk, I ran out of patience and blurted it out." Nic shrugged.

"What did he say?"

"No, and that I should back off."

"Nic, I would never presume to tell you how to run your investigation, but you might want to try a little more subtle approach." Nora put the empty Dixie cup on the table and slid down on the couch.

"That's what Aunt Anna said."

"Thanks for the help, hon. I'm worried about you, too. We know these aren't nice people, and I'd hate to see my new friend hurt."

Hearing that Nora considered her a friend pleased Nic. She stood. "I feel the same way. Why don't you rest for a bit? I'll check on you later. Do you need anything else?"

"Nope. Just a short break. Thanks."

Nora closed her eyes, and Nic went to the mirror to check her hair. She glanced at her reflection and then at Nora. The bruise was darker, but her hair was perfect. Maybe after they solved the murder, and the killer was behind bars, she would start an investigation for a new hairstyle.

Chapter 21

Nic left the lounge and found Frank on stage. "Nora is resting. She's sore, but otherwise in good shape. I'm not an expert, but I'd say her ankle isn't sprained, but it is twisted."

Frank did not look pleased. "Nic, do you think Nora was hurt by the person who killed Carolyn?"

"I don't know. I suppose it's possible."

"Maybe we should report her attack to the police."

"I don't think she'd like that. Besides, you've seen how Detective O'Brian runs an investigation. Our writers are better detectives than he and Jones are."

"That's probably true, but I'm concerned about you and Nora, and anyone else involved. I can't tell you to stop, but please promise you'll be careful."

Nic found his concern touching and she had no problem vowing to be careful as she had repeatedly over the last few days, but she was not going to stop her search for Carolyn's killer. "I will, Frank. I promise, but we will keep investigating. By the way, where is George?"

"He went to borrow an extra microphone from one of the other studios, but he should be back by now. What's this sudden interest in George? Is he a suspect?"

"He's on the list. Did you ever find out how he knew about Barney's discharge?"

"He said Barney told him. I know Barney is open about his recovery, so that could be true. While I'm checking on this Ray person, I'll see if I can find anything else about George. One of the owners recommended him for the job. He can probably help."

As people filled the studio, Nic was sure the conversations were about the attack on Nora. If Marcy knew what happened, the entire station knew.

She turned when someone tapped her arm. It was Belia, and she looked worried. "Is she hurt badly? Miss Hahn, is she all right?"

"She'll be okay. She was more startled than hurt. Nora has had a rough go of it lately, but she's hanging in there."

"Nic, I…I. I had better go to set up." Belia ran from the stage. Nic wanted to follow and see what she had to say, but Frank called the cast for rehearsal.

With Thanksgiving the following day, they worked into the evening. When Frank felt they were ready for the final rehearsal on Friday, he wished everyone a Happy Thanksgiving and joined Alice in the engineer's booth.

Nic saw Belia hurrying out and stopped her. "Belia, dinner will be at three o'clock. My aunt was hoping you'd bring your violin."

"You still would like me to come?"

"I'd very much like you to come. Will you bring your violin?"

"Yes." Again Belia seemed about to speak. Instead, she said goodbye and left.

"What is going on with her?"

"Hey, Nic." Greg called. "Have a great Thanksgiving."

"You too. Do you have plans?"

"I'm having dinner with my family, but then the band is hooking up at Sammy's on Wells to lay down some riffs. Do you want to boogie-woogie?"

"You're going to a club and you want me to come and listen to you play music?"

"You're translation is on the money, but doesn't it sound more fun the way I say it?"

"It does, as a matter of fact, but I'm afraid I can't boogie-woogie tomorrow. My aunt is making dinner."

"That's cool. Tell her I said gobble, gobble." Greg gripped his bass and boogied out.

"Good night and Happy Thanksgiving." Frank called as he left. Before the door swung shut, Cliff came in.

"Nic, I took Nora home a little earlier and she's doing fine. She asked me to tell you that she'll be at your place around two. Nothing as trifling as a twisted ankle and banged-up face would keep her from a home-cooked meal."

"Thanks, Cliff." Nic noticed they stood in a now-empty studio. "Cliff, would you mind if I grabbed my coat and rode the elevator with you?"

"I'd be delighted. With all that's been going on, I should've thought of it myself. Hey, why don't you let me take you home? It'll be a short walk to my car, but I live on Orleans off of Armitage and Nora said you live by Wrigley, a hop, skip, and a few traffic lights."

When she and Cliff walked through the empty reception area to the elevator, Nic was grateful he offered to take her home. As they boarded the elevator, she heard a noise in one of the empty offices. She was not aware of the shadow that fell across the doors as they closed.

"Thanks for the ride, Cliff." Nic waved, and as she opened the front door, smelled baking bread. She inhaled deeply, leaning on the heavy outside door to push it closed. With her fingers crossed that the aroma came from her apartment, she opened the inside door and smiled. She had arrived at the source.

Anna and Millie sat on the sofa examining a list of dishes for Thanksgiving dinner. Anna put a check next to the word 'bread' and welcomed her niece. "You worked late. Is everyone ready for Friday?"

"Yes, Frank thought we were, but he was in a hurry to go home. His wife is making dinner for the entire family tomorrow, and it's the first time they're coming to his house for a holiday meal. She's a nervous wreck, which makes him a nervous wreck."

"From the way you've described him, I can't picture Frank Myers a nervous wreck about anything," Anna said.

"He is today, but before I tell you why, I have to tell you that Cliff, one of the writers, drove me home. What a treat that was. I think I'll buy a car." She smiled at Anna, "and you can do the repairs. Which reminds me, Aunt Anna, where did you learn to fix cars?"

"Your dad loved to tinker with the different engines the auto makers were developing. When I was in college, he had an Oldsmobile that he worked on constantly, and I loved to watch. He taught me how to do a few repairs and how to drive. It was fun."

Millie joined the conversation. "I didn't know you drove, Anna. Joe and I are buying a car when he comes home, and I plan to drive."

"It's easy, Millie. You'll do fine and don't let anyone tell you a woman shouldn't drive. We drive better than most men." Anna turned to Nic. "That goes for you, too."

"Goodness, you mean men have allowed us to drive, too?"

"You plan to let that fester for a while, don't you? There were never restrictions on women driving in this country, although men did tend to scoff and growl as they do when women do anything over which they claim dominion. A few men tried to limit women to driving only electric cars because they were slower."

"Well, I'm sure those big powerful gasoline engines were too much for us fragile little things." Nic stopped her tirade and gave Anna a grin. "I'm sure my frustration will subside sooner or later, Aunt Anna. I just don't understand why a woman would think she needed a man's permission to do something, or why a man would think a woman needed his consent."

"Things are changing every day, Nicole. Maybe now that there's no war, we can think about things that matter and there won't be such nonsense. So, what happened that made Frank Myers a nervous wreck?"

Nic fell into the chair and temporarily tabled her personal women's rights campaign. "A guy attacked Nora in the stairwell this morning and tried to push her down the stairs."

"How is she?"

"Surprised, but okay. She hit her face on the railing. That left a bruise, and she twisted her ankle. You've seen those skinny high heels she wears. Cliff, the person that gave me a ride home, is one of her co-writers. He came down the stairs and found her. Whoever did it, took off."

"Did she see him?" Anna threw her list to the table and leaned into the sofa.

"No, but he knew who Nora was." Nic deepened her voice and repeated the threat. "Her tough guy imitation is much better than mine because her voice is so low. Nora won't stop investigating, and she's even more adamant now. She said since she's enduring the pain, she wants some of the glory."

Anna laughed. "She's absolutely right. The more people we have asking questions and making the perpetrators nervous, the more likely it is they'll make a mistake. That doesn't mean you should relax your guard, Nicole. Keep your eyes open."

"I'm glad you said that, Anna." Millie said. "I was going to, but thought maybe Nic was tired of hearing it from me."

"I'll keep my eyes open, I promise. The other thing I wanted to share is also about Nora. Before the incident on the stairs, she told me a little about herself." The sadness Nic felt earlier returned as repeated the conversation.

"Nicole, even though you're not my daughter by birth, I couldn't imagine anything anyone could say that would make me push you away." Her head shook as she added, "I worry about these people who blame their fears and judgments on their God. It's sad, immoral, and extremely dangerous."

"It is sad, and hard to imagine someone behaving that way with their child." Nic reflected for a moment, and remembered another conversation she'd had. "Speaking of unusual behavior, Belia was acting strange. Twice she started to say something and stopped. I never did have a chance to talk to her, except to confirm that she'll be here tomorrow with her violin."

"Maybe she'll be more comfortable talking after we've eaten. Did Nora say she'd bring dessert?"

Nic spent the last of her energy telling Anna that she did.

*

"Should I start the potatoes, Anna?" Millie stood at the partially open back door.

"Yes, dear, and thanks for offering to boil them. I'm out of room." Four burners were enough for most meals, but Thanksgiving dinner required additional help. Millie volunteered the use of her otherwise idle stove for the potatoes. Anna would finish boiling them right before dinner. "What time are you going to your mom's house?"

"Anthony is coming by around ten so we can help with the food. We'll walk over. Is Mrs. Murphy joining you?"

"No. I talked to her last week. She's spending the day with a member of her church. She seemed quite pleased. Don't forget to give your parents my love, Millie."

Nic pulled a half-chewed carrot from her mouth. "Mine too."

"Nicole, peel the carrots, don't eat them."

"Oops. Millie, be sure to stop by if you're home early. I want you to meet Belia."

"I will. Nic, I want to take the potatoes up. Go ahead of me and open my door."

When Millie hoisted the pot to her stove, Nic returned to the kitchen, where she finished peeling carrots, chopped celery, and cut bread for the stuffing, while Anna mixed the remaining ingredients in a bowl. With the bird in the oven, Anna cut yams, and Nic sat at the table lost in thought. "Aunt Anna, what if we aren't able to find the killer? Do you think O'Brian will be able to pin it on Barney?"

"We can't think about that possibility, Nicole. We'll keep searching until we figure things out."

"I tried to imagine how it was for Barney. For the soldiers and the people who lived there. I mean with bombs exploding all the time, being afraid every waking minute of every day. I wonder if that's how it was for Belia. She always looks afraid. How do you forget that?" Nic returned to her thoughts, not expecting an answer. Seconds later, Millie opened the back door and Anthony carried in the partially boiled potatoes.

"They only need another few minutes, Anna," Millie announced. "We're going to Momma and Pops'. Is there anything you need? I mean, since we have this big strong hulking guy for lifting and carrying and other forms of manual labor." Millie gave her barrel-chested brother Anthony a punch in his muscular arm.

"Ow. Don't hurt me."

"You two have fun with your family."

Millie led her brother out, fingers waving.

All items on the dinner list had a check, and the smells from the kitchen filled every inch of the apartment. The morning of cooking had fogged the windows requiring Anna to open the back door to cool down the kitchen. While she was on the porch, she checked items relocated there from the overstuffed refrigerator. The cream had separated and pushed through the paper seal on top of the milk bottle. To keep it from running down the side, Anna spooned it into a small dish and squeezed it into the icebox.

A few minutes after two, the front door buzzed and Nic stopped setting the table to watch Nora limp into the living room. She had covered the bruise on her face with makeup, but it looked painful. Nic narrowed her brows. "That's pretty nasty looking."

"I hope you mean the bruise and not the face." Nora put a gloved hand to the darkened spot. "It feels better, although it does look worse. The bruise on your eye did that too. You haven't forgotten, have you?"

Instinctively, Nic touched the spot where her own cut had healed almost completely. The number of assaults between them was noteworthy, but she wanted to enjoy the holiday and not think about the case. "We're a pair."

"I'll say." Nora seemed equally eager to keep the mood festive. "Boy, it smells unbelievable in here. Here's dessert."

Nearly a dozen beautiful pastries filled the dish Nic took from Nora. "Did you make these?"

The tone of her question suggested shock or disbelief and amused Nora. She pointed to the offering with a grin. "No, no. My kitchen skills are quite limited. I did relocate the delicacies from the box to this serving dish. That struck me as rather domestic." She removed her gloves and slid them into a pocket, then swept the long black cape-like wrap from her shoulders. "I learned to cook on the farm, but once I moved to the city, I forced every bit of that knowledge out of my brain."

Nora wisely chose not to wear her three-inch heels, but that did not detract from her outfit. She wore a royal blue silk blouse with puffed sleeves and wide cuffs closed with brushed gold cufflinks. Her black trousers had two pleats in front, slant pockets, and a sharp seam running down the front and back of the wide comfortably fitting legs. Barely visible were a pair of black shoes with a low heel. Her hair held its pageboy to above her shoulders, and brushed gold earrings matched the cufflinks and a piece of jewelry that hung from a chain around her neck. She wore a moderate amount of carefully applied makeup, and subdued red lipstick that matched her long fingernails.

Nic looked at the plain gray trousers and rust colored blouse she wore. She had never taken much of an interest in fashion, and realized that was something else in her life that was changing. She was pleased, and glad that her new interest came when there was someone around who might be able to offer guidance.

She set the pastries on the coffee table, and was hanging Nora's wrap by the door when Anna joined them. "It's good to see you, Nora."

"Ah, the great detective." Nora smiled.

"I'm pleased you've joined the Owen gang."

Nora grasped Anna's offered hand warmly. "They seem to have the most fun."

Her duties in the kitchen allowed Anna only a brief visit. When she went to check on dinner's progress, Nic and Nora sat in the living room. Nora lit a cigarette with the gold lighter she often carried. "That's a nice-looking lighter." Nic took it and read the inscription: 'Thank you for being my light. Love CM.' "What does CM stand for?"

"Carolyn Morris. I never could say Carolyn Park without cringing."

"It's nice." Nic said softly as she laid the lighter on the cigarette case. "Nora, can I ask you a question, and if I'm out of line, please tell me."

"You don't want a cigarette, do you?"

Chapter 22

"No, I don't want a cigarette." The question amused and embarrassed Nic, but she appreciated that Nora had a good sense of humor. "I don't know what came over me the other morning. I want to ask you a more personal question, if it's okay?" Nora consented. "How did you know you were a lesbian? I mean, when you and Carolyn met, you were young. Did you become lesbians then or were you lesbians before? I'm doing a bad job asking this, aren't I?"

"Yes." Nora tried not to smile, but the awkward rambling and embarrassed look Nic wore made it impossible. "But I know what you're asking. When I met Carolyn, I fell instantly and completely in love. Until then, I never thought about relationships. I was fresh from the farm, where, besides my brother, my best and only friends were female, but they were cows. I was oblivious and didn't know it was love. I had no idea what the feeling was that consumed me. I just knew I wanted to be near her.

"I'd been in Chicago three years but didn't know many people. I worked at the library and spent my free time studying there. One day Carolyn sat with me at the table where I was doing a paper. When I looked at her, my brain stopped. I couldn't concentrate and decided it would be best to study in my room. When I stood to leave, she asked if she could join me. I said yes. I bumbled and stuttered for weeks after that. I think she enjoyed stringing me along because I was so pathetic. In a short time, I knew she loved me, and I knew I loved her. I never doubted for a minute that we'd be together."

Nic sat quietly and Nora spoke again. "That didn't answer your question though, did it? The answer is, I don't know. Seriously, Nic, I don't know if I was a lesbian before I met her. I suppose I must have been to be attracted in the first place, but in my sheltered world, I knew little about homosexuals."

Nic laughed, "I can relate to that."

"Carolyn had a relationship with a woman before we met. She said she always knew she was 'queer', and I cringed when she used the word because I'd only heard people use it as an insult. She laughed and told me if I intended to be with her, I'd better learn to ignore the insults. I was completely naive, but what I felt for Carolyn had nothing to do with whether she was a man or a woman. I felt as if I'd found the other half of my soul."

A few minutes before three, the buzzer sounded again. This time it was Belia, violin in hand. Nic ushered her in and took her coat, while Anna and Nora greeted her from the sofa they shared. At the sight of Nora's bruise, Belia covered her mouth and approached her with a strained smile. "Miss Hahn, I am very sorry about what has happened to you in the stairway."

Her excessive concern puzzled Nora. "Thank you, Belia, but I feel fine. Please call me Nora."

Anna didn't wait for an introduction. She stood and shook the new arrival's hand. "Belia, I'm Anna. Nicole told me you are being considered for a chair with the Chicago Symphony.

Such an honor, and that means you're a talented violinist. I hope we'll have a chance to hear you play."

Too embarrassed by the praise to face her directly, Belia spoke to her violin. "Thank you, Miss—I mean, Anna. It would be my pleasure."

Anna sniffed the air. "Right now there's a turkey calling my name. Why don't you all take a seat at the table, and I'll bring the food."

"I'll help, Aunt Anna. Nora, Belia, sit anywhere you like." Nic watched Nora grimace as she stood. "As slow as you're moving, the food might need reheating."

Nora assumed a mock frown as she extinguished her cigarette and squared her shoulders. "You won't be so smart when I'm back to my fighting weight." She and Nic laughed, but Belia remained grim.

In every corner of the world, the number of hours required to prepare a holiday meal far outweighs the hours spent indulging. It was no different at the Owen residence. The four average-to-thin women had reduced the turkey by half and emptied the bowl of mashed potatoes and a neighboring gravy boat. Nic slid the last yam to her plate and extended her lower lip when her fingertips found only the wicker bottom of the breadbasket. Belia took another spoonful of carrots and Nora dragged a final piece of turkey to her plate. When they could no longer raise a fork, the women leaned back in their chairs in satisfied silence.

Anna, like any cook, was pleased to see the food enjoyed and her guests happy. After Nicole carried in the coffee pot, Anna poured and expressed her relief that dairy rationing had ended. "I like milk in my coffee."

Nora agreed. "It is nice that most things are available again. I have to admit, making the coffee last was a challenge in our house. Carolyn was an avid imbiber. Growing up on the farm, I was used to making do. Carolyn had never experienced that, but she was determined not to take more than her share and to give back as much as she could. Do you know where I spent last Thanksgiving?" Nora glanced at the expectant faces. "Serving food at the Clark Street soup kitchen. Picture me in three-inch heels and a gravy-covered apron." No one missed the sadness that escaped with Nora's sigh. "Whenever Carolyn dragged me into one of her projects, I felt better about other people, and, believe it or not, myself." She added quietly, "I'll miss that, too."

Nic thought it might be helpful for Nora to talk about Carolyn. "I wish I'd had a chance to know her better."

"You would have liked her, Nic, and she you. She was tough, hard, gentle, and kind. She loved literature and art, boating, and the Cubs. Her sense of humor was wonderful, but if you crossed her she could cut you in half with words before you knew it." Nora looked at Anna. "I'd love to have seen the two of you go toe-to-toe, but you'd have agreed on most subjects, I think." Nora folded her hands on the table. "You wouldn't have learned anything about Carolyn at the station, not anything good anyway. She didn't hide who she was, but she didn't explain. Her theory was that once people decided on something, even if it was a judgment based on no evidence, they were unlikely to change their minds. To her, the irony was that if people realized that homosexuals' lives were as ordinary as their own, they wouldn't hate them nearly as much. She liked people, and though she never said, it hurt her when they were cruel. Because of that, she kept to herself and people called her a snob." Nora pushed her chair back to stand.

"What do you need, Nora?" Nic sat up.

"My cigarettes."

"I will get them for you." Belia almost ran to the living room, setting the cigarettes and ashtray next to Nora when she returned.

"Thank you, Belia."

This time, Nora wasn't the only one puzzled by Belia's behavior. Nic studied Belia for a moment and wondered what was on her mind, but instead of asking in front of the group, she decided to talk to her in private. She turned to Nora. "You and Carolyn lived comfortably. Why did you both work?"

"Even though we came from different worlds, we both felt we had to. Not for the money, at least it wasn't for Carolyn. If you live on a farm, you have chores. I grew up working, and as I said, I worked while I was in college. I was used to it, and never considered not working."

The conversation about money reminded Anna of a question that had been bothering her. "Nora, did Carolyn have a will?"

"Yes, she did. We didn't talk about it much, but I know she's made changes and updates over the years."

"Why haven't we heard anything about it? With the charities she funded, you'd think it would be all over the papers."

Nora shrugged. "That makes sense. I hadn't given it much thought. I'm afraid I haven't thought about much of anything."

"Do you know who drew up the will?"

"Jack Sutherland prepared her original will. I don't think she changed it since he died, but if she did, I suppose there is a chance that Cecil would have been involved."

"What kind of relationship did he and Carolyn have? Their marriage was a business arrangement, and it doesn't seem that he had much to do with Carolyn's foundation, but the papers portrayed him as an outstanding member of society."

In her desire to gather information, Anna missed the change on Nora's face. The bruise grew more apparent as she paled, and when she spoke, it was with a clenched jaw. "Cecil Park is a beast. He'd agreed to play the fine upstanding husband as long as Carolyn kept him funded. She married him because she thought it was the safest thing to do. She wouldn't risk her charities."

"Aunt Anna and I talked about that before, Nora. How could her charities have been hurt?"

"Cecil convinced Carolyn that some of her important donors had found out about our relationship. He told her they were planning to stop their contributions and talk their friends into doing the same. I never believed it, but Carolyn wouldn't risk the chance he was right."

"What made her decide to divorce Cecil?" Nic asked.

"He's broke. He's lost clients and gambled away most of his money. He borrowed five thousand dollars in the last six months, but apparently, that wasn't enough. The last time he asked, she turned him down. She decided that his behavior had become more of a threat than if people knew she was a lesbian. She knew his gambling would only get worse, and was determined that her money would not go to his debts." Nora became more emotional with each word. "Now, he'll take it all. Carolyn is gone, her foundation will be gone, Barney may go to prison, and that pig will walk away with everything. Everything."

She laid her arms on the table and as her head dropped, Belia, leapt to her feet, her eyes filled with terror, and screamed, "No!"

Nic and Anna were staring at Nora when the shriek from Belia sent Alley flying from Anna's lap. Nic bolted from her chair. Even Nora lifted her head to listen. "I see the man kill her. I see him shoot Mrs. Park. I come back and I see them in the studio. She stood on the stage. I see him." Her knees suddenly failed to support her and Belia collapsed to the floor.

"Happy Thanksgiving," Millie shouted as she leaned around the front door.

Chapter 23

Belia weighed almost nothing. Millie and Nic carried her to the sofa where Anna covered her with a blanket, but her eyes remained closed and her skin was deathly pale.

"Aunt Anna, should we take her to the hospital? She looks terrible."

During the war, large cities like Chicago ran practice drills to prepare citizens for enemy air attacks. When the Civil Defense siren wailed, people evacuated streets and turned off lights or pulled heavy curtains over windows to eliminate targets for incoming aircraft. Officials made an effort to announce the drills, but at times, people without access to a news source found the sudden noise and blackout terrifying. One of the duties Anna performed as a Civilian Defense Force volunteer was to assist people who panicked during those drills. "I don't know yet, Nicole. If she awoke alone in the hospital, she'd be terrified. Look in the medical kit for one of the smelling salt capsules, and Millie, bring a wet cloth and a glass of water."

Millie set the water on the table and laid the cloth on Belia's forehead. When Nic returned with the smelling salts, Anna broke the capsule and waved it briefly under Belia's nose. The young woman's eyes opened filled with fear.

"Belia, do you know who I am?" Anna patted her shoulder and kept her voice soft. Belia tried to speak. "Don't say anything, just nod."

After helping Belia slide up on the sofa enough to drink, Anna retrieved the water glass. "Take a few sips and a deep breath." Belia took the glass in her trembling fingers and Anna patted her shoulder once more. "You're all right, dear. Stay quiet and I'll be right back."

Anna joined Millie and Nic in the hallway. "She doesn't need to go to the hospital. It's a mild case of hysteria. She'll be fine if we keep her calm. She's been living in terror for weeks with no one to talk to about what she saw. I don't want to leave her alone for too long." Anna returned to the living room.

Millie had no idea what had happened and wanted answers. "Nora is sitting at the table crying, and I'd guess by the bruise that someone hit her. There's another woman almost unconscious on the sofa, but Anna says she only has a mild case of hysteria." Millie shook her head. "And you two say my family's dinners are crazy. Did you hit Nora to calm her down? Or did she and the other woman have a fight?"

"She's crying because Belia told us she saw someone shoot Carolyn, and that bruise is from when she was attacked in the stairway yesterday. Come on. Let's make sure she's okay."

Nic dragged Millie to the dining room and they joined Nora at the table. After Nora confirmed she was all right, Nic filled Millie in on the little they knew about what Belia saw.

They talked softly until Nic saw Anna help Belia sit up. She joined them in the living room. "How are you, Belia?"

"Better, Nic. Thank you." She turned to Anna. "Thank you also, Anna. You are kind. You will like me to tell you what I see?"

Nic leaned forward. "Belia, would it be okay if Millie and Nora join us?"

Belia looked to Nora in the dining room and her eyes grew moist. "Yes. I would like to tell Nora." While Nora joined Belia and Anna on the sofa, Millie brought in one of the dining room chairs and sat.

With her hands clenched in her lap, Belia took a deep breath and began. "I stay late to practice my violin at the studio because in my apartment I could not do this in the evening. Mr. Reed say it will be all right to practice there. On Friday when Mrs. Park is shot, I finish the practice and leave the studio to go home."

"What time did you leave, Belia?" Anna spoke in soft, soothing tones.

"It was eight or soon after. That was the truth, and I did not see anyone else in the studio. When I am at my apartment door, I see I do not have my keys and have to come back. I take the elevator and think maybe that I drop them when I put on my coat in the lounge. I go there first and that is where they are. When I walk past the studio door, I hear a noise. I pull it open to peek inside and see the man point a gun at Mrs. Park. She is faced to the back of the stage when he yell. When she turn, he shoot her." Her eyes filled with tears and terror as she turned to Nora. "I am sorry you lost the person you love. That is a hard thing."

Belia put her face in her hands and Nora held her to whisper, "Thank you." When she let her go, Nora leaned back in the sofa and wrapped her arms around herself.

Nic hoped Nora wasn't replaying the scene in her mind, but they had to know what happened. She asked Belia to continue.

"When he shoot, it scare me and I drop the keys. I don't know if he hear or not. I leave the door close and grab my keys, but instead of going to the elevator, I run down the stairs."

"You ran down nineteen floors?" Millie looked and sounded stunned.

Belia nodded. "I could not think. I take my shoes off and I run. I want to tell, but I am afraid. When I talk to the Detective O'Brian and he is mean, I am sure they will arrest me and put me in jail or send me back to Czechoslovakia. I saw people shot so much there. I do not think I will see it here." She lowered her head again. "I should go to jail because I did not tell what I see." Pain filled the eyes she directed at Nic and Nora. "That is why you were hurt, because I did not tell about the man that kill Mrs. Park."

"Who was the man, Belia?" Nic asked.

Seemingly afraid to say, Belia wrung her hands. When she looked at Nora, her courage returned. "It was the men who make the sounds."

The women inhaled and Nic cried out, "Not Barney."

"No." Belia shook her head. "Not him. The one with the fuzzy hair."

A name slid from Nic's tight lips. "George."

The room was silent until Anna stood. "Belia, Nora, why don't you rest while we clean off the table and put on coffee? Then we'll enjoy the wonderful desserts Nora brought and consider our options."

"You do not call the police?" Belia asked.

"No, dear. Just relax."

Millie pulled Nic aside and whispered, "Doesn't she know that no one in this house goes to the police unless they're invited?"

Nic frowned at the comment, but didn't argue as she watched Anna offer Belia additional advice. "You relax and don't worry. We're your friends."

"All of us," Nora added.

After thanking Nora, Belia turned to Anna. "You will like music with which to work? I will play."

The offer was one Anna couldn't refuse. "Belia, I'd love it. Are you sure you're up to playing?"

"Nothing make me more relaxed than playing my violin." Belia went to the hall where she had left her violin. She took it from its case and returned, holding the instrument in front of Anna. "Nic say you know of Amati the violinmaker. This is one he made."

Anna lifted the instrument from Belia's fingers and stroked the flamed one-piece back. The stretch of velvety maple exploded in rich shades of gold and red and glistened from layers of hand-rubbed varnish oil. She turned it to admire the fine grain of the spruce front graced with silky f-holes carved on either side of the bridge. Her finger traced the ebony fingerboard along the neck to a carved scroll and four wooden pegs. She sensed the memory of Belia's family alive in the wood and varnish of the exquisite instrument and returned it to the violinist. "It is beautiful, my dear. Please play."

While Nic, Millie, and Anna readied things for dessert, Nora stretched on the sofa with her eyes closed and rolled an earring on her stomach. Belia played.

The haunting piece she selected fit the mood and calmed both the performer and her audience. As the melody flowed through the apartment, it told a story of first caution, and then courage, a mix reflected in Belia's impassioned eyes.

Nic returned and leaned on the wall to listen and study the women in the living room. Both appeared fragile, but she doubted she knew two stronger people. At the song's conclusion, Nic entered the room and touched Belia's shoulder. "That was beautiful."

"Thank you, Nic. Is there something you would like me to play?"

"I hope you'll play again later, but we should sit down for dessert."

Anna returned as Belia put the violin in its case. "Your playing is absolutely brilliant. The symphony will be lucky to have you. She pulled the young woman into her arms. "My dear, if you don't win that chair, I will be amazed. I have no doubt that your family is very proud."

Nora saw that Belia was ready to cry again and hobbled over to take her arm. "Will you help me to the dining room, Belia?"

Nic watched curiously, and Nora, who had walked without assistance all evening, responded to her inquisitive look with a wink.

In her self-appointed position as "chairperson", Millie, brought the dining room chair back from the living room and retrieved a chair from the kitchen to place at the table. The five women sat, and with varying degrees of grace and poise, demolished the desserts Nora supplied.

"These are sinful." Anna raised the remainder of a flakey cream-filled pastry. "Where did you find them?"

Nora had a mouth full of cinnamon bun when Anna inquired about the deserts. She took a sip of coffee and cleared the remainder before answering. "There's a new Swedish restaurant on Belmont owned by a woman named Ann Sather. It opened this year and Carolyn discovered it...." Nora took a breath. "She discovered it last month. Everything they make is wonderful, and," she added, "sinful."

Eventually, the conversation returned to Carolyn's death and addressed the problem at hand—how could they share the information about George with the police without Belia having to come forward.

"Aunt Anna, I don't understand why George would put the gun in the sound effects box when it could throw suspicion on him. Then there's the question of why the police didn't find it when they searched the studio?"

Nora put her earring on the table and lit a cigarette. "What I don't understand is why George would have killed Carolyn in the first place. She didn't know him. I mean, she knew him less than she knew anyone at the show. I remember her making mention of him only once when he first started at the station. She was surprised that Frank hired a sound man without experience."

Nic remembered her conversation with Frank. "He told me one of the station owners recommended George. That probably translated as an order to hire him."

"And, there's the gun." Nora said. "I've seen that gun only once when we were having a fundraiser at the house in Evanston. Carolyn came across it when we were searching a closet for extra candles before the guests arrived. She had completely forgotten it was there, and I know for a fact that she never carried it in her purse, or anywhere else."

Millie remembered the article in Saturday's paper. "Cecil told the police she bought the gun to protect herself."

"He's a damn liar." Nora looked furious. "He bought her that gun. Imagine giving someone a gun as a gift. She kidded about it later. She said maybe he bought it expecting her to use it on herself."

Anna looked up. "You told the police?"

"Yes, I did." Nora rubbed out her cigarette. "Would you like to know O'Brian's theory? The detective said she bought the gun to protect herself from me, knowing she planned to end our relationship in the future."

"What a small man." Anna stood. "Ladies, it has been a long day, and we won't accomplish much more this evening. Why don't we stop?" She turned to Belia. "Don't think about anything except preparing for your audition. You have my word you will not go to jail." Anna held the young woman's face between her hands. "I have season tickets for the symphony, my dear, and I cannot wait to hear you in the string section."

"Can I help clean up before I go?" Nora looked at Nic. "I don't cook, but I've swung a mean dish towel or two in my day."

"We'll be fine, Nora. Thanks. You should take it easy on that ankle."

"I'll do that, doc." Nora turned to Belia, "I couldn't drive because of my ankle and I'm calling a cab. Would you like a ride?" She clipped on her earring.

"You are kind."

"Why did you send Nora and Belia home, Anna?" Millie stood on her toes to put a dried dish in the cabinet as Nic set a clean one on the counter.

"It isn't necessary for them to sit through more talk about the murder." Anna sat at the table and slid off her glasses to squeeze the bridge of her nose. "Belia is a masterful violinist and she needs to stay focused on her audition next week. And no matter how strong the woman is, Nora is running out of energy. She lost the woman she loved, was almost killed, arrested for her murder, pushed down the stairs, and scorned and ridiculed at a time when she needed support." Anna shook her head, slipping her glasses on to look at her notes.

"What about Barney, Aunt Anna? Unless the police know it was George, they'll take Barney to jail."

"Mary Rose told me his doctors have refused to release him to O'Brian." Anna shook her head. "Detective O'Brian has a way of endearing himself to people. Barney is where he needs to be, and he told me he's glad to have the private room. That's a luxury at the VA Hospital."

"What do we do now?" Millie asked.

"I think our goal is still the same. To see that Carolyn's murderer goes to jail. Don't you agree, Aunt Anna?"

"I do, and now we know who the murderer is. That should make things a little easier. It's important that Belia stay uninvolved. At least until we're sure George is in jail. Let's look at the things we haven't worked out yet. A big one is how George wound up with her gun."

The dishwashing continued as Nic answered over her shoulder. "Maybe Carolyn took it out to protect herself and he grabbed it."

"Or maybe he took it from her purse earlier in the day," Millie suggested.

Anna pressed her lips in a frown as she considered both possibilities. "Nora said she didn't carry the gun, and Belia said he had it before Carolyn turned around. I suppose it is possible that Nora is wrong, and George did take it from her purse. Okay, let's assume he took the gun earlier in the day."

"So he uses it to shoot Carolyn, but why would he have thrown it in the sound effects box? Unless he was scared." Nic stopped her comment and after gloomily assessing the mountain of dishes left to wash, she sighed and continued. "Belia dropped her keys. Maybe he heard them fall, and in a hurry to leave, threw the gun in the box without thinking. George doesn't strike me as extremely quick-witted."

"That may be true, Nicole, but the police didn't find it when they searched after the murder. No matter what they thought about her relationship with Nora, Carolyn Park was well known, and Cecil Park was her husband. I can't believe they didn't make a thorough search. Even if it was there and they didn't find it, George had plenty of time to take it out later. I'm convinced that George left with the gun."

Millie put another dish in the cabinet before offering a possible explanation. "Could he have put it in the box after the police searched?"

Anna nodded. "He could have, just as easily as he could have taken it out, but why? Unless he wiped it off and put it in hoping Barney would pick it up. Nicole, you said George knew about Barney's discharge, right?"

"You think he framed Barney?"

Anna shrugged. "He killed Carolyn. Framing another person for the murder wouldn't be much of a burden on his principles."

"Aunt Anna, do you remember what Gerald told me? He said he saw Carolyn climb into her limo outside the Mart. Maybe we could talk to the driver and see what he knows."

"Good thinking. We should also talk to the elevator operators that were on duty that night. Belia said she didn't recognize the operator that was working when she returned for her keys. Maybe you can find out who it was and talk to him, Nicole."

"I'll do that tomorrow if there's time."

"I'm still curious why no one has discussed the will. A large number of charities depend on her support and they would certainly be curious whether that support was going to continue. If Cecil isn't the beneficiary, and I'm certain by what Nora said, he isn't, it would be in his best interest if the will never appears. Even if he didn't kill her, he won't let her money slip away." Anna sat quietly for a few minutes, and then made an announcement. "I think it's time for action. Tomorrow, Nicole, I want you to ask Nora if Carolyn's things are still at their apartment. If they are, we're going to plan a party."

Millie rested her hands on her hips and looked as stern as she could with a dishtowel. "Judging by what I saw tonight, if you two are planning a party, you'll need my help."

Chapter 24

The next morning, Nic surprised Sam by requesting he take her to the twentieth floor. When they arrived, she wished him a good day and stepped into a smaller version of the floor below. A version without a reception area and Marcy. She followed the sound of voices down a hall and looked into a large office with four wooden desks sharing the floor space. She saw Cliff preparing to toss a paper airplane at Nora who sat across the aisle putting on makeup, unaware of the launch.

"Good morning. You two look busy."

Nora turned from her compact with a smile. "Why, Miss Owen, we're honored. Aren't we, Cliff?"

Cliff slipped the airplane into a desk drawer and bowed his head. "And delighted. We are busy, of course, but happy to take a short break for our company. What brings you to our humble surroundings, Miss Owen? I'm guessing that it is not, alas, to see me." With a hand over his heart, he released a dramatic sigh.

Nora approached Nic, tilting her head at her fellow writer. "Cliff also does dramatic writing for local theater groups."

He sniffed and stood. "While it is true that I've written a mournful line or two, my most important work is the prose penned for our damsel detective, Inez Ingalls."

"He means that's the job that pays." Nora laughed.

Hiding his own laughter, Cliff bowed again. "I've grown quite accustomed to the lack of appreciation for my genius. Now, since I can see your visit is neither to bury nor praise *moi*, I'm off to find a soothing cup of black coffee in which to wallow." He sulked from the office, head bent in overdone but humorous distress.

"He's great, Nora. I laughed the entire ride when he drove me home Wednesday."

"He is funny, and a talented writer. He makes you sound good every week. He's been a real support to me, too."

"I'm glad to hear that, Nora. I wondered if you had anyone to talk to."

"Thanks, and thanks again for inviting me to dinner yesterday. It was one of my more interesting Thanksgivings."

Nic appreciated her unembellished summary of the previous day's events. "That's a good description."

"What's up, Nic? I'm guessing you didn't drop by for the latest gossip."

"Aunt Anna wants to know if Carolyn's belongings are still at your apartment." Nic had not considered the effect of her question, and felt bad when Nora returned to her desk and stared out the window that framed downtown Chicago. Her smile disappeared.

"I keep meaning to pack her things, but whatever I pick up reminds me of her and I have to stop. Why do you want to know about Carolyn's belongings, Nic?"

"Aunt Anna has a plan, and she said if they were there, we're ready to take action. I don't know what she has in mind, but she's been in touch with a number of her old students. That usually means she's discovered information not everyone could access."

"Whatever her plan is, I suspect it will make more sense than anything O'Brian and Jones have done."

"That's probably true, but I don't have much information. Why don't we find out? Do you mind if I use your phone?"

Nora turned the phone on her desk and handed Nic the handset, pointing to her chair while she moved to Cliff's desk.

"Hello, Aunt Anna? I'm with Nora. She says everything is at the apartment."

Nic listened for a minute, and then relayed the information to Nora. "She wants to use your apartment tonight and tomorrow night." Nora looked curious, but nodded. "She said yes, Aunt Anna."

With the phone pressed to her ear, Nic stayed quiet for a few minutes. At an apparent lull, she passed on additional information. "Tonight, Aunt Anna, Millie, and I will visit if that's okay."

Nora leaned back, crossed her arms, and stretched her legs under the desk. "Sure, but don't expect much. My housekeeping skills are on a par with my cooking."

Nic interpreted her response for Anna. "She said we can come over."

More information flowed, and again Nic stopped to inform Nora. "On Saturday, we'll be at the apartment, along with George and Cecil." After repeating Anna's message, Nic took the handset from her ear and gave it a confused stare before resuming her conversation. "Aunt Anna, what do you have planned?" She edged forward on the chair and pressed a hand to her lowered forehead. "Okay. I'll see you tonight."

Nic sat motionless, holding the phone in the air until Nora rose, took it from her fingers, and dropped it in the cradle. She sat on the edge of the desk and looked at her stunned friend. "What's the plan?"

"I don't know. She said we'll discuss it tonight, but judging by her guest list, it should be another interesting event."

*

"Seeing you this often, my dear, makes me dizzy." Anna had opened the door and found Allen bowing at the waist. When she spotted the light from Mrs. Murphy's slightly open door, she grabbed his lapel and pulled him into the living room. "Come in and sit down, Allen. I just made a fresh pot of coffee. Have you eaten? Would you like a snack?"

"Not necessary. Your beauty is sustenance enough."

"Fine then," she shook her head. "I'll bring the coffee and you can look at me. When you're full, we'll work."

Anna returned with the tray and filled their cups. "I heard Belia play yesterday, and saw her remarkable violin. She is truly gifted."

Allen had just taken a sip of his coffee, but set the cup down with a sigh. "She is, and it is a wretched, wretched world."

"Why, for heaven's sakes?"

"Because shortly, my dear Anna, I will lose her to the Chicago Symphony."

"You think they'll give her a chair?"

Allen pushed the fingers of his right hand through his ample white hair. "I'm positive. After I heard her practicing one night, I asked Désiré Defauw to drop by and listen. You know he's the music director of the Chicago Symphony Orchestra. We stayed out of sight, and he was as stunned as I was when he heard her play. I knew at that moment, he was determined to have her in his symphony. If it had been up to him, he'd have snatched her away from me right on the spot, but there is protocol. She must audition. I think the only thing that would keep her from winning a chair would be if she didn't show. From Defauw's reaction, he'd seek her out. She mustn't know Anna. It wouldn't be fair."

Anna put her cup down and put her hand on Allen's knee. "Allen, Belia saw George Sokal kill Carolyn."

Allen kept his startled eyes on Anna as he spoke. "What do you mean she saw George kill Carolyn?"

"Exactly what I said. Belia saw George shoot her. What we need to do is find a way to inform the police without involving her. She would be in trouble for not reporting it and O'Brian won't be sympathetic to how terrified she is of uniforms and the people who wear them."

"I'm sure you're right. How do you plan to implicate George without reporting what Belia saw?"

"If I knew that, Allen, my sweet, would I be sitting here waiting for you to give me the information you've gathered? Now would be a good time to share what you learned."

Dipping two long fingers into his front pocket, Allen retrieved a folded paper. "I hope it helps. That woman should be performing with the symphony, not dealing with the likes of O'Brian." He opened the document and smoothed it on his leg. "I couldn't locate the limo driver who worked for Carolyn. I spoke with other drivers at the City Theater and no one has seen him or her car since she was killed, but this," he removed a photograph from the same pocket and handed it over. "is the kind of limousine he drove.

"Your student, Thomas, was right about ⸳' met Cecil Park on the night of the murd Sandburg. Mr. Sandburg was more th⸳ of complaints about Mr. Park's be Cecil looked and behaved disgu⸳

She Overheard Murder

but he couldn't figure out why. He only saw him order two drinks. He thought Cecil might have had a flask tucked away, but since prohibition ended a number of years ago, he couldn't understand the need."

"I talked to Robert this morning. He was one of my students when I taught at the university and is now with the police department. He located Cecil's bookie and it turns out that Cecil had a runner, but he is presently otherwise engaged. The bookie didn't know the reason for his occupation, but because of it, Cecil has been contacting him in person. Apparently Park owes this procurer of wagers a great deal of money, but he hasn't tried to collect because Cecil assured him that once the police solved the murder, he'd have a fortune and could pay off the debt."

"So Cecil wants this solved as badly as you do, Anna. Of course, he has a very different motive."

"That's true. Were you able to talk to any of the clients that quit Cecil Park and went to other attorneys?"

"I talked to four of the people on your list." Allen pointed to the paper on his leg. "Since they all said the same thing, I didn't see a reason to contact the others. According to those I spoke to, over the last six months, Cecil stopped caring about his business. He was almost impossible to reach and when they did reach him, he offered little or no help or information. Not the attorney you want in your corner, I'd say."

"I'd say you're right. His obsession with gambling has become the driving force in his life."

"So, tell me, Anna. How did I do on my first outing as a ʼ˸ctive?"

˸e from the sofa, sat on the arm of the chair, and ˄f his head. "You did terrific."

Jean Sheldon

Delighted by the kiss, the new detective took her hand. "My dear, once you've solved this case and the murderer is apprehended, will you do me the honor of joining me for dinner?"

"I'd love to, but let's not drive."

*

Nic caught up with Greg as he was leaving after rehearsal. "Greg, the other day, you said that you only heard the rumor about Carolyn and Nora breaking up a few weeks before Carolyn died. Do you remember who told you?"

"George. That in itself was weird, because he never talked to me."

"What did he say?"

"Something like 'I heard the queers are having a lover's quarrel and the blonde is gonna dump her girlfriend.' I said 'uh-huh' and he left."

"Thanks, Greg. Are you and the band playing this weekend?"

"We're working on some new tunes at an after-hours jam session. It's at the Sunset if you want to drop by."

"I can't this weekend, but I promise I will soon. Are you heading to the El?"

At his nod, Nic grabbed her coat and purse to join him. Traffic was light on the elevator and people on the sidewalk made room for the duo and the bass. Watching him maneuver it over the turnstile and drag it through the train doors, Nic decided that if anyone needed a car, it was Greg.

Anna was in the living room finishing a phone call when Nic arrived. "Thank you. I hope I'll see you then and we can wrap this. Hello, Nicole. How was your day?"

"My day was fine, Aunt Anna, but it's time you tell me what you have planned."

"I intend to do just that, dear. Did you ask Greg who told him the rumor? It was George wasn't it?"

"Yes, it was George. Why do you suppose he did that?"

"I'm guessing he was following orders. We can also surmise that because Nora described the person who attacked her in the stairway as having very short hair, George has an assistant. You don't seem to think that George is very capable, and luckily for us, his assistant hasn't proved to be much better. I think they are working for someone else, someone who is calling the shots. Someone who had a reason to want Carolyn dead."

"Aunt Anna, do you think that someone is Cecil Park?"

"I do. What do you think?"

"I agree."

Anna shared with Nic the information Allen and Robert gathered. "Now we have almost everything we need to expose George and with any luck, he'll reveal the other players in this sordid plot."

Anna exuded confidence, but Nic had questions. She started with what, to her, was the most obvious. "We do?"

*

Nora left work early to clean the apartment. There had been no one but her to see it in the last few weeks, and she had given little thought to housekeeping. Her neglect showed. With Anna, Nic, and Millie due in a few hours, she decided to make an effort.

She and Carolyn normally had a live-in housekeeper and cook. The woman that worked for them for four years quit in June when her husband returned from France. She was sorry to go, but ready to start a family. The woman that replaced her came from an agency and quit after hearing about Carolyn's murder. The agency offered a replacement, but Nora declined. She was not ready to share the space with a stranger.

After collecting strewn articles of clothing and depositing them in the laundry room next to the vacant housekeeper's quarters, Nora went to the foyer to put away discarded shoes and coats. The marble-top entry table held a large red porcelain urn and weeks of mail that she had deposited there without opening.

She gathered the envelopes and took them to Carolyn's office. As she tossed the correspondence to the desk, one of the envelopes slipped to the floor. It was addressed to Carolyn Morris, and the return address said Hines and Stanford, Attorneys at Law. Nora retrieved it, puzzled, but unable to bring herself to open it. She put it with the others and made a silent promise to sort through the piles in the near future.

The phone rang while Nora was straightening pillows on the sofa. It was Nic. "Aunt Anna wondered if you have the necessary items to make coffee."

"There's a coffee pot, but I'd have to check for coffee. If there were any, it would be a few weeks old. I've been drinking mine at the restaurant downstairs. Oh, and Anna said she likes milk. If there is any here, it's probably spoiled. I can run out for supplies if you like."

"No. We'll bring everything but the pot. See you in a few hours."

Nora hung up and slumped in the nearby chair, wondering why not knowing if there was coffee made her sad.

Chapter 25

After ushering Anna, Nic, and Millie into the apartment, Nora deposited their coats and purses on her bed and offered to show them around the large space. Nic followed the group until she spotted a row of windows where she could just make out a view of the moon over Lake Michigan, enticement enough to leave the others for a better look.

Heavy blue floor-to-ceiling drapes framed a moonlit lake and sky. It was the most extraordinary view of Lake Michigan Nic had ever seen. Only days earlier, a brash full moon tested the strength of her first-floor apartment's bay window. Even without the lake as a velvety backdrop, her heart quickened. From the sixteenth floor, the waning orb left her speechless, and rewarded her awe by recklessly shedding its halo on the choppy waters below. Nic was reluctant to leave the scene, but anxious to see the rest of the apartment. She took one last look before rejoining the others.

The residence warranted a tour. Rooms flowed from one to another each more beautifully furnished and decorated than the one before. Paintings and drawings filled the walls, lit by small lights in the ceiling whose sole purpose was to show off the art. With all its beauty, in every room, Nic felt a sadness as dark as she imagined the view at the end of the hallway on a moonless night.

When the tour brought them back to the living room, Nora sat on the arm of the sofa as the others found seats. "Anna, I have complete faith in your plan, whatever it is. Where do we start?"

Anna responded without hesitation. "Carolyn made a new will, and I believe she left it here. Before we do anything else, we should find that."

"Oh." Nora looked startled. She slid down the sofa arm to the cushion. "Why do you think she wrote a new will, and why do you think it's here?"

"In answer to your first question, what you said about Carolyn not wanting her money to go to Cecil made me think she would have been certain to protect the foundation, her beloved charities, and you. I talked to an ex-student of mine who's an estate attorney. He works at Hines and Stanford, the same firm that employs the attorney Carolyn used to file for divorce."

"Divorce? Hines and Stanford? Wait a minute. I'll be right back." Nora returned with the sealed envelope she had found earlier. "This is addressed to Carolyn Morris, her maiden name."

"Have you read the contents?" Anna asked.

"No. I wasn't sure…." Nora ran her thumbnail under the flap and removed the letter. "She did file for divorce. This says it will be final in January 1946." Nora appeared not to know whether to laugh or cry.

Anna continued. "Yes, she did. She filed on the Thursday you were in Michigan, the same day she had a new will made. This," Anna pointed at the letter, "was mailed that Friday, to confirm the divorce agreement. My student couldn't tell me the contents of the will, but he said if I asked, he could tell me that it existed." She grinned. "I asked. In answer to your second question, Nora, you said in the last six months Cecil's gambling was totally out of control, and Carolyn knew it, right?"

"Yes."

"Carolyn also knew that if anything was to happen to her and Cecil accidentally misplaced her existing will, he would inherit her estate. She knew that if he'd found out about the new one, there was no bank, vault, or safety deposit box that her husband couldn't legally access. She went to a new attorney for the will and put it where he didn't have access. Do you have a safe?"

"Yes, behind that picture." Nora stood and removed a painting, revealing the safe. After rotating the dial a few times, she opened the door and removed a small stack of papers. She started to look through them but changed her mind and handed everything to Anna. The elder detective Owen quickly found the will.

Anna had limited legal knowledge but found the papers straightforward. Carolyn left everything to Nora—not just her personal property, but also the foundation and the responsibility of serving as director, or, if she chose, overseeing its dissolution.

Nora sat in silence until Anna finished. "Anna, I can't tell you how much it means to know her work will continue. An important part of Carolyn is alive because of you. Because of all of you." Her eyes watered. "I don't know what else to say, except thank you. You're wonderful."

Anna stood, straightened the pages of the will, and handed it to Nora. "Carolyn certainly thought the same of you to put this in your hands."

"Why didn't she tell me she was planning to go through with the divorce?" Nora asked looking at the letter.

"Carolyn may have considered how difficult the trip to Michigan would be and that you'd need cheering up after taking care of your father's affairs. She might have thought it would be the perfect time to tell you about the divorce to lift your undoubtedly poor spirits."

Nora stared at the document, but her eyes watered until it became impossible to focus. When Anna clapped, it scared her back to consciousness and brought the rest of the gang to attention. "It's time to prepare for our party. Nora, first thing tomorrow call Cecil and tell him you discovered the will. Tell him he needs to come by to discuss it, but don't tell him the contents."

"What if he refuses?"

"I don't think he will. Would he have a key to your apartment?"

"Carolyn had one on her keychain and the police gave him what they didn't consider evidence."

"Tell him to be here at seven tomorrow evening. Tell him that you have an appointment and won't be back until then. My guess is he'll show up early to search on his own. Tell the doorman to stay out of sight until Cecil and George have come up."

Nora looked about to ask a question, but Anna continued.

"Cecil will arrive first. You and Nicole will come next, and George should be right behind you. Millie and I will follow soon after." She pointed to the will Nora held. "Put that away. Does Cecil know about the safe?"

"No. The apartment is in my name. He doesn't know anything, except where it is." Stunned by the revelations, Nora took the papers to the safe, hung the painting, and returned to the sofa. Anna continued.

"Nicole, did you talk to George this afternoon?"

"Yes. I told him I overhead Cecil tell Nora he knew who killed Carolyn and wanted to meet at her apartment tomorrow at around 6:30 to tell her who it was. I also told him that when I left the building for lunch, Cecil was outside talking to a guy with short blonde hair and I heard him say 'I'm taking care of George.'"

"Do you think he believed you?"

Nic laughed. "I'm sure he did. He muttered some extremely unkind words about Cecil and stormed away."

Anna looked over her glasses at Nic, Millie, and Nora. "I have a plan, which I explained to Robert earlier. He is trying to collect a group of officers he can trust to help. Since Cecil Park and O'Brian have connections inside the department, he has to be careful. If he can get assistance, a few members of the police department will be joining us. The plan is to get everyone here and convince George to confess and tell the police he was working for Cecil."

"Well, that's a nice plan, Aunt Anna, but do you really think George will confess just because we ask?"

"Hopefully, after what you told him, he'll believe that Park is planning to stab him in the back. His anger could work to our advantage." She studied her three co-detectives. "I can see you're not convinced. I understand. It is certainly not a foolproof plan, and there is a chance it could be dangerous. If any of you think we shouldn't give it a try, we won't."

Millie shrugged. "I say we go for it."

Nora agreed with a nod.

Nic rolled her eyes. "I must be getting used to danger. I agree. Let's do it."

"Then," Anna rubbed her hands together. "After I look into a few other details, we should be ready for tomorrow. Millie, will you help me make a pot of coffee?"

When Anna and Millie went to the kitchen, Nic asked Nora if she would mind if she went back to look at the lake. "No, I don't mind. In fact, I'll join you if that's okay."

They settled in on the couch and sat in comfortable silence for a few minutes before Nic spoke. "How are you doing?"

"Okay. Why do you ask, Nic?"

"I thought it might be hard to have us here. Aunt Anna has only the best intentions, but I don't know if she considered how this might affect you."

The moon, having moved along on its journey, was no longer visible through the window, but the Milky Way shimmered across the heavens with equal grandeur. Nic watched the spectacle quietly, waiting several minutes for Nora to respond. "We weren't big entertainers, but people dropped in now and then. It's good to hear voices other than my own, and even better to hear how confident Anna is that we'll solve this. I've been thinking that maybe when it's over, I'll sell this place. Find something smaller with less…well, less memories."

"You should wait to make that decision, Nora. Maybe when the pain lessens, you'll want the memories."

As Nora turned to comment, Millie called from down the hall that the coffee was ready. Her response dissolved, but as she stood, Nora wiped a tear from her cheek and squeezed Nic's hand. "Thank you."

Chapter 26

At twenty minutes after six the next evening, Nora unlocked the door and she and Nic entered the apartment. They put their purses next to the urn on the hall table and walked through the foyer into the living room as Cecil Park stepped from the bedroom. He stopped, startled by the company. "What are you doing here?"

"No," Nora glared. "What are you doing here? I said seven o'clock and I didn't say that you should let yourself in. How did you avoid the doorman?"

"The guy must have been on his break. Look, Nora, give me the will and I'll be on my way."

"Why would I do that, Cecil?"

"Because if you don't, I'll see to it you spend the rest of your pathetic life in jail for Carolyn's murder. You know I can do it."

"You tried that without success. Were you the one responsible for Barney's arrest?"

"Well, ain't this a pretty picture? Members of the upper crust talking nasty to each other." George stood in the foyer holding a gun. Jimmy stood behind him. "Hey, fat boy. You were gonna send me up the river, weren't you? You were gonna let me take the fall for your so-called wife's murder. Like it wasn't your idea. I ought to waste your fat ass right here."

Cecil rushed toward George, hands aimed at his throat. "If you hadn't been such an idiot, this would have been finished long ago."

"Shut up, old man. Did you not see what I'm holding here?" George waved the gun. "Sit down before I lose my temper." He tapped the gun on the sofa arm and Cecil sat. His face grew red and his eyes bulged.

The gun stayed on Cecil as George looked around the room. He went to the windows and ripped the cords off the drapes. He threw them at Nic. "You. Tie him up like a big stuffed bird."

Jimmy stood behind George. "What's going on? You said we were going to a party."

"It is a party, Jimmy." George turned and slammed the gun against the side of Jimmy's head. He crashed to the floor. "And you're gonna be the sucker of honor."

Nic tied the stout wrists and ankles of Cecil Park and stood.

"Tie Jimmy. Although it don't look like he's going nowhere for a while." George was right. Jimmy didn't move while Nic tied his hands and feet. When she finished, George pointed the gun at Nora."

"Now, you. Tie your girlfriend."

"No."

George shrugged. "If you don't, I have to shoot her."

It amazed Nic how much tougher George thought he was with a gun in his hand.

Nora took the cord and waited for Nic to sit. She tied it loosely around her ankles, but George bent to check her work, and as he stood, gave Nora a shove. "Don't mess around with me, girly. Tie her up, and make sure she can't get out. Got it?" Nora said nothing but crouched next to Nic.

George was savoring his growing sense of power. He leaned next to Nora and pushed the side of her pageboy back with

Jean Sheldon

the gun barrel. "Maybe when she's tied nice and tight, you and me can use that big bed I see in there."

Nic raised her hand, but George grabbed it. "Sit still and be a good girl. Who's in charge now, Inez?" He grinned and put the gun to her shoulder to push her back in the seat. "Your friend here is gonna tie you properly." George poked Nic's shoulder again. "You, Inez, are one lucky broad. My pal was not happy when he almost fell in front of that train instead of you. Of course, he ain't my pal no more since he planned to make a deal with the fat boy and let me go down for the murder."

"What are you talking about?" Cecil yelled.

"You know what I'm talking about. You think you can buy anybody."

"I don't know...."

"Shut up." George yelled loud enough to stop Cecil's reply and Nora's tying efforts.

She refocused and finished tying Nic's ankles and was about to start on her wrists when a loud crash and a thump brought her to her feet. George lay face down on the floor surrounded by pieces of the red vase. Anna and Millie stood over his body. "Sorry about the vase, Nora," Anna told her. Park had tried to stand, but Millie grabbed his collar and yanked him back to the sofa.

The gun George held had flown from his hand after Millie conked him. When the dust settled, Nora retrieved it from the floor and held it in Cecil's face. "Few things would give me greater pleasure than to pull this trigger. You had her killed. She gave you more than you ever deserved and you had her killed." Her hands shook. "You shouldn't be breathing this air, you bastard. Carolyn should be breathing this air."

At that moment, no one was breathing the air. Several seconds of silence passed before Nora shook her shoulders and let them drop. She observed the broken pieces of vase as she handed Anna the gun. "I don't ever want you mad at me."

"It was Millie who bopped him, but I could say the same about you." Anna took the weapon, supplying the cue Nic needed to breathe. She untied her ankles and joined Millie and Nora in moving George to a chair, where they tied him securely.

Anna disappeared into the kitchen and returned with a rag soaked in ammonia. She placed it in Georges face and held it there until he coughed and opened his red, watery eyes. Cecil was no longer red. His skin color nearly matched the light gray of his suit.

George was twenty-eight and had the resilience of youth on his side. He recovered quickly from the blow and the ammonia, and glared at Cecil. "This was your stupid plan, old man. I'm not going down for it alone. I'm telling the cops everything."

Cecil rallied to his own defense. "Will you shut your mouth. Do you think the police are going to listen to a loser like you instead of me? You're dumber than I thought."

Anna placed the rag under Jimmy's nose until he woke. When his eyes focused, he glared at George. "What are you doing?"

Nora stood over Jimmy. "Is he a friend of yours?"

"He's no friend of mine. He said he was bringing me to a party."

"Aunt Anna," Nic whispered. "Could I see you in the kitchen, please?"

As the door closed behind them, Nic asked Anna what time Robert was supposed to arrive. "Actually, we are running a little ahead of schedule, but I'm sure it'll be fine." She patted Nic's hand and as she pushed the door into the living room, heard George shout.

"You bitch."

Anna and Nic returned to find Millie holding Cecil's collar and George with a bright red mark on his face. They watched Nora run to the bedroom.

Anna turned to Millie. "What's going on?"

"She punched me in the face." George stopped struggling against the ropes when Anna crossed the room to examine his recently added bruise.

"Why do I have the feeling you deserved it? Sit quietly." He eyed the gun and settled down.

"What happened, Millie?" Nic stood in front of the sofa, directly across from her, with an uncomfortable Cecil between them.

"He told Nora she should untie him and he'd teach her how to be a real woman." Millie tipped her head toward George. "Nora told him to shut up but he kept going. He said he'd wished he'd had a chance to straighten Carolyn out, because Cecil certainly couldn't. That was when she socked him. I was surprised she stopped after one punch."

George opened his mouth, but saw Anna glaring. If he had anything to say, he changed his mind.

Nic found Nora in the bedroom lying amid the coats. "Are you okay?"

"I wanted to kill him. If I'd had the gun, I could have killed him. I could have killed them both." Her entire body shook.

Spotting a box of tissue, Nic grabbed it and sat on the bed. "I don't think so, Nora. You had a chance to shoot Cecil but you didn't. Hold on a little longer, hon. I'm sure Robert will be here soon, and this will be over. Those creeps will be punished for what they did to Carolyn, and her good work will continue."

Nic's words had the desired effect. Nora sat up and used a tissue to wipe her face, and then crawled from the bed to follow Nic back to the living room. It was still a shambles, but quiet because Anna had asked everyone to remain silent for a few minutes.

Nic took a seat while Nora leaned on a wall. It was easy to guess what she was thinking as her dark eyes darted between Cecil and George.

George continued to squirm against the ropes without success and that increased his frustration. Despite Anna's request, he could no longer keep quiet. "Hey, what are you broads gonna do? Are you one of them Amazon cults that kidnap and torture men? I read about dames like you."

Instead of upsetting Anna, his remark brought a smile to her face. She leaned forward and patted his knee. "You do read, dear. That's nice."

Cecil hadn't tried to wiggle out of his ropes. There was far too much of him to maneuver, but when George broke the silence, he joined the conversation. He issued a threat. "Go ahead and enjoy yourselves. You'll all be in jail for a very long time. Do you know who I am? There isn't a cop or a judge in this city that would take the word of any of you over me."

Anna eyed both men before responding to Cecil. "Mr. Park, if you believe that to be the case, we may have to resolve this differently than I'd hoped."

She had meant it to sound like a threat, and accomplished her goal. George believed he'd been right about his captors. "I told you, they're a bunch of crazy man haters. They're gonna kill us."

"Shut up, you idiot. I'll handle this." The reddish glow returned as Cecil believed he was in charge.

Even Jimmy, who was still on the floor and secured in ropes recognized who was really in charge. He shouted at Anna. "I didn't come with him to hurt anyone. He told me there was a party." He jerked his head at George.

"You'll stay right where you are for now, Jimmy. For your own sake, just keep quiet."

As Anna spoke to Jimmy, she noticed movement in the foyer. She straightened in her chair and with a calm, impassive face, addressed her three accomplices and their unhappy prisoners. "I think it's time we wrap things up. Mr. Park, Mr. Sokal, I want you to tell me about Carolyn's murder." Anna tapped the barrel of the gun. "You would have no way of knowing this, of course, but I am quite a mystery fan. Over the years, solving puzzles has become almost an obsession with me. I want to see if I figured it out."

Cecil gave her a doubtful look. "You want to see if you figured what out?"

"I want to see if I guessed how and why you murdered Carolyn."

"You're nuts," he barked.

"Well, you may be right. As I said, I can be a little obsessive about solving puzzles. So, tell me about Carolyn's murder."

Cecil was not convinced. "And what if we don't?"

"I'm an old lady and have nothing to lose by shooting you, just as George followed your orders and shot Carolyn. He already told us that. Now you tell us the rest of the details, and if it turns out that I figured it out correctly, I'll let you go."

"You'll let us go?" George looked stunned.

"Yes, I'll let you go." Anna offered a polite smile. "What's your decision, George?"

"Yeah. If you mean it about letting me go. I'll tell you. I ain't going to jail for that jerk."

"What about you, Mr. Park?" Anna asked.

"Why would I tell you anything?"

"As I said, I want to know if I guessed correctly." Anna picked up the gun and looked down the barrel at Cecil. "Keep in mind that I don't need you both alive. I'm sure if I shoot one, the other will see that I'm quite serious." Anna looked at her watch. "You have five minutes to decide Mr. Park."

Chapter 27

Cecil might have concluded that the woman with the gun really was crazy, and that she meant what she said. Whatever his thoughts, he agreed to Anna's request and began telling his version of events.

Carolyn had announced that she planned to divorce him and file a new will. In his arrogance, he believed she would have him draw it up, proving to the women listening that George was not the only dumb criminal in the room.

"I wasn't going to let her divorce me. I have a reputation to protect. On top of that, she stopped giving me money."

"So you decided to shoot her and destroy her will." Anna suspected that once Park started talking, he would enjoy the sound of his own voice too much to stop.

"Don't be stupid. People of my status don't kill. We pay some dumb schmuck to do it. I found the gun I gave her at the house."

"You told the police she bought it."

"Oh, did I? I must have forgotten." He smirked. "I knew about the history of depression and suicides in her family. I thought it might be a good idea to give her a gun, so if she ever had the urge, she'd have something handy."

Anna bit the inside of her mouth to control her disgust. "So you didn't shoot her. You had George do it."

"It is amazing that one person can screw up as much as he did."

George was ready to respond to Cecil's remark but Anna waved the gun to suggest he didn't.

Park continued. "I called her and said I wanted to talk about the divorce. She agreed to meet me at the studio around ten o'clock. It was a perfect plan." He glared at his assistant across the room.

Cecil had been planning to get rid of Carolyn for a while, but when she announced her intention to divorce him and shut off his cash flow, he realized he had to move quickly. George was already in place. Cecil used his influence with one of the station's owners to have him hired to do sound effects. As it turned out, George was no better at sound effects than he was at murder. "He went to the studio and shot her, but he was supposed to make it look like suicide. Instead, the jackass took the gun and forgot to leave the note."

"I told you I heard a noise. I had to get out of there." The look George gave Cecil was pure hate. "You weren't the one taking chances, old man. I was the one the cops were gonna nail."

"You still are, you fool."

George and Cecil yelled until Millie pulled Cecil back in his seat and Anna convinced George to quiet down.

Nic had been watching Nora, and saw her growing increasingly tense. She leaned against the wall next to her and gave her hand a squeeze. "Hold on, Nora. It will be over soon."

Cecil explained that he had given George Carolyn's gun and a suicide note that he had written. 'I cannot live with what I am. Cecil, please forgive me. Carolyn.' In his mind, it was believable that Carolyn would kill herself on the stage where she was a star, a dramatic ending.

After George heard Belia drop her keys, he forgot to leave the note or the gun. Instead, he used the freight elevator to avoid the operator, ran out, and found her car. When the driver rolled down the window, George pounded him with the gun, pushed him to the passenger's side, and drove away. He took him a wooded area southwest of the city, emptied his pockets, and tossed his body.

The plan had not been for George to pick Cecil up at the Palmer House, but George panicked. He knew Cecil planned to establish his alibi there and waited for Park's regular driver to show up. When he arrived at around 12:30, George told him that Cecil was meeting with Carolyn and he was there to pick him up. He gave him ten dollars and told him to take the night off.

"I couldn't believe the idiot showed up in her car." Cecil shook his head. "The concierge thought he was helping me into my car and I couldn't let on anything was wrong. I was supposed to be drunk. When this idiot told me what happened, I took the gun and had him drive me home and park her car in the garage."

"Yeah," George yelled. "I parked the car and you told me to take off without even offering me cab fare, and after I gave my last sawbuck to your driver. How was I supposed get home from Evanston?"

Anna shushed George. She had a few more questions for Cecil. "You might have to help me on this part, Mr. Park, but I think I know what happened. When it became clear that they would not be able to charge Nora with murder, you decided to frame George. You wouldn't actually be framing him since he shot her, but you planned to let him 'take the fall,' as he said."

Park had George start rumors that Carolyn planned to end her relationship with Nora a few weeks before her death.

She Overheard Murder

His plan all along had been to frame Nora, but when Carolyn announced the divorce, he had to act quickly and went for the suicide angle. That was the plan until George screwed up. He switched back to Nora. It surprised him that she managed to beat the murder charge. He had given O'Brian and Jones five thousand dollars and they guaranteed they would successfully arrest the person he wanted charged. Cecil wanted his wife's girlfriend, if not executed, at least in jail. When they failed at that, and Nora survived her 'suicide', his plan to frame George sounded better and better.

His confession to paying off O'Brian and Jones delighted Nic, but it disgusted her that Cecil had probably paid with Carolyn's money. "Aunt Anna, how did the gun end up in the sound effects box?"

"I'd be willing to bet that you saw it being put there, Nicole, the day Mr. Park stormed into the studio." Anna turned to Cecil. "I'm guessing that on your way out, when you pretended to run into the box, you deposited the gun. You had handled it only with a gloved hand, and planned to set up George. You figured with his criminal record it would be easy, but Barney touched the gun before the police retrieved it. Were you the one who sent the anonymous note?" Anna asked.

"I sent the note, but I thought they would pin it on him." Cecil swung his round head in George's direction. "When they found that other sound guy's prints and discovered he was a nutcase from the war, it was perfect. Not even O'Brian could mess it up."

"What did you do with the original will that Carolyn filed?"

"She didn't have one."

Anna marveled at the ease with which he lied. "It doesn't matter, Mr. Park, because the new one was in effect at the time of her death. Even if you walk out of here in one piece, you will be penniless, worse than penniless, because of your gambling debts." His face darkened. "Mr. Park, I appreciate your honesty. I have one last question for George. "Is Jimmy your assistant?"

George shook his head. "I brought him to take the fall. The cops were supposed to think he killed you guys and then killed himself."

Anna thought they had heard enough. "Well, I promised that if I had correctly figured out the puzzle I would let you go, and I did, so I will. You may, however, need to make a deal with these gentlemen." Anna looked toward the foyer where the front door had been open since Nic and Nora arrived. Four smiling police officers introduced themselves to Cecil and George.

When another officer joined Anna, Nic squeezed past Nora and dashed to her aunt's side. Millie and Nora followed close behind.

"We heard every word." The young officer smiled at Anna, and then nodded at the bits of red china scattered around the room. "Who hefted the vase?" Anna pointed to Millie. "And who gave George the face decoration?" She pointed to Nora.

"I feel terrible that we broke your beautiful vase." Anna told Nora. "Do you feel bad about what you did to George?" Nora could only smile and shake her head. Anna turned to the officer. "You're quite welcome, Robert. You won't have trouble with O'Brian, will you?"

"No, Ma'am. Those statements Mr. Park made will have him and Jones off the force and behind bars. Oh, and about your friend, Belia, I can't see any reason to mention her in the report." He turned to leave but stopped to retrieve a small object from his pocket and hand it to Anna. "I almost forgot."

Nic watched Anna close her hand around the object, and was about to ask what it was when she saw an officer cuffing

She Overheard Murder   261

Jimmy. "Wait, he wasn't involved in this. George brought him to set him up for our deaths."

"I heard that." Robert turned to the officer. "Let him go, Skip. See if he needs a ride to the hospital to check that cut on his head."

To Nic's surprise, Jimmy smiled and thanked her.

Robert returned from the foyer with another man in handcuffs. "Miss Owen, we found this guy downstairs poking around in George's car. He said he followed him here because he stole his gun. Do you know him?"

Nora ran to the door. "That's the guy that pushed me down the stairs. I'm sure of it."

Nic stood behind her. "And he's the guy who tried to push me into the lake." She remembered where she'd seen the blonde at the coffee shop. She'd caught a glimpse of him before he pushed her. "Ask him to say 'She's dead. The hard part's over.'"

An officer convinced him to repeat the sentence and Nic knew she'd been right about something else. "That's the guy I heard on the phone. He was in on the murder too, and I'll bet his name is Ray, isn't it? Frank told me George's friend Ray was a janitor at the Mart. I'll bet Cecil helped him get his job too."

When the police cleared the apartment, Nic returned to where Anna sat. "So that's Robert."

Anna stood next to her niece and stretched her arms skyward. "Yes. I should have introduced everyone, but there was so much going on. Well, I don't know about the rest of you, but I'm ready to call it a night. Nicole, Millie, let's go home." She turned to Nora, "would you like help cleaning before we leave?"

"No, you don't." The other three women encircled Anna and eased her back into her seat. "We aren't going anywhere until you fill in all the blanks."

Anna succeeded in looking innocent, but not in wriggling out of an explanation. She agreed to supply the missing details of their successful sting operation under one condition. She wanted a cup of coffee. Nic and Millie did the honors, and when they arrived back in the living room with cups and a pot of coffee, Anna began.

"Thomas, you remember Thomas from the Palmer House?" The other women remembered. "Thomas called yesterday and told me he talked to the other doorman that worked the Friday Carolyn was killed. His friend didn't see the driver close up, but did see that he had curly red hair. Thomas's friend only noticed the hair because he didn't wear a cap. Cecil's earlier driver wore a cap." Anna looked at Nora. "Did you know Carolyn's driver?"

"Yes, Rocky. I can't believe George killed him too."

"Thomas's friend provided us with another clue that will help convict Mr. Park. He described the car that picked Cecil up that night and Robert found that there were only six of that model in the city. One of them belonged to Carolyn. They discovered it in the garage behind the Evanston house where Cecil put it. It had Rocky's blood on the seat. Robert released a bulletin with the chauffeur's description and the county sheriff called to report a body found in the woods. It was Rocky." Nora released a soft groan and sank into a chair.

Anna rose and stood in front of Nora, taking her hands. "You are welcome in our home. No, let me restate that. You are expected in our home."

Nora stood to hug Anna, who after returning the embrace placed an object in her hand. "This is my earring," she told Anna. "Where'd you find it?"

"That's the piece of jewelry the police found in Carolyn's pocket. Robert brought it since it is no longer needed as evidence."

Nora looked at the earring. "It's from the pair I wore when we had dinner on Wednesday. I have a habit of pulling an earring off and playing with it. I'm always leaving them somewhere. She must have picked it up and kept it with her." After weeks on an emotion roller coaster, the ride for Nora was ending. She hugged Anna again, and repeated the action with Nic and Millie as tears streamed down her face. "You are extraordinary people. I promise I'll be in your home, often."

Nic looked past Nora and pictured the blonde waiting on the lounge. She wished she could have known Carolyn Park and wondered if, as Millie believed, spirits stayed around those they loved. If that were true, she hoped Carolyn knew that she didn't have to worry, because the Owen women would take care of Nora.

*

Nic sat on her bed thinking about events of the last few weeks and wavered between tears of sadness and joy. She had gone with Millie to her parent's house the day after they solved the case and her mom brought out a Tarot deck. According to Momma, a spirit followed Nic and assisted her. Nic didn't think it meant much since Millie knew what was going on in her life. Then Momma turned the card that represented the spirit and Nic shivered. It was a female figure in a navy blue cloak with wavy blonde hair. She stood with crossed swords in front of her body and piles of gold at her feet.

"Nicole."

"Yes?"

"Millie called. She wants us to come upstairs."

"She called?"

Anna opened the front door and Alley jumped off the sofa and darted up the stairs. "What was that about? Running isn't her style."

When they reached the second floor landing, the door opened. "Here come the second and third most beautiful women in the world." Joe walked out holding Alley.

"Joe, you're home." Nic shouted as she and Anna wrapped him in their arms and forced Alley to seek a safer spot. Millie stepped from the apartment, grinning through her tears.

"Millie, why didn't you tell us?" Nic asked.

"I didn't know. The big galoot showed up a few hours ago." Millie winked and went inside. In seconds, a hand grabbed Joe's shirttail and dragged him in.

"Welcome home." Nic and Anna called as the door closed and the lock turned. Anna recovered Alley and descended the stairs, but before going in, stopped at Mrs. Murphy's door. "Joe's home."

"I know. I gave him a big hug when he came in, before he even went upstairs." Mrs. Murphy shared a smile through the slight opening and Anna saw her tears before she disappeared behind the door.

Chapter 28

Seven months passed before Cecil Park went to jail. George and Ray never left their cells after the initial arrest, but Park still had a few connections. Unfortunately, for him, not enough to keep him from facing a murder charge. The police dropped all charges against Barney, which was a considerable boost to his recovery. He returned to work only a month later and found the station had hired an experienced sound effects man to work as his assistant. Belia Malecek won her chair on the Chicago Symphony, and Nic, Nora, Anna, Allen, Millie, and Joe had perfect seats for her first performance.

By mid-July 1946, Nic felt generally pleased with her life. The only areas of discontent were the sweltering temperatures in the apartment and the fact that Nora had been in a strange mood for the last few weeks. She thought they had become friends, but recently, Nora pulled away. She had been to their apartment for dinner a few times, and they'd gone to an occasional movie, but those visits and outings suddenly stopped.

Nic sat in the living room as Anna came in the front door, looking as wet and uncomfortable as she felt. The wilted senior fell into the chair and waved the newspaper she held to move the stagnant air. "They sentenced Cecil Park to twenty years to life."

"I read the paper, and although they didn't ask my opinion, it wasn't enough. He'll be eligible for parole in twenty years." Nic told her. "Nothing would be punishment enough for that man."

"At least he didn't get away with murder. He really believed he would. Where are the flowers from?" Anna asked.

Nic sat up and looked at the bouquet. "I forgot about them. Nora brought me home from the studio a little earlier. She bought them at the Mart after she heard about Cecil's sentence. She said the same thing you did. At least he didn't get away with murder. The flowers were to thank us again."

Nic wondered if Anna had noticed that Nora was behaving oddly. "Do you think Nora has been strange lately? Of course, you don't see her everyday, and it might not be obvious." Anna shook her head and Nic saw her amused grin. "Why are you smiling?"

"Nicole, you are a bright and intelligent woman and you've accomplished a great deal in your life, but there are times when you can be a bit thick headed."

"I don't suppose you'd care to give me a hint about what you mean by that. Like maybe what I'm being thick about."

Anna rose, smelled the flowers, and headed toward the back of the apartment. "No."

The next morning, Nic ran into Nora on her way into the Mart and talked her into stopping for a cup of coffee. Since her acceptance was not enthusiastic, Nic wasted no time starting the conversation. "The flowers were sweet, Nora. Aunt Anna loves fresh flowers in the house. I never think about buying them. Have you ever heard of putting aspirin powder in the water? Why aren't you answering my questions?"

Nora waited for the waitress to refill their cups before she spoke. "If you would take a breath once in a while, I might answer one, or who knows, maybe all of your questions." She stirred her coffee.

"Have I upset you, Nora? If I did, I hope you know I didn't mean to. You do, don't you? I haven't taken a breath again, have I?" Nic watched her closely but could not read her face.

Nora took another swallow, sighed, and responded with a completely unrelated comment. "It's going to be another hot one."

Of all the possible responses Nic thought Nora might give, a weather prediction had not entered her mind. She took a drink before offering her exasperated reply. "Yep. Sure is."

The short discussion about weather ended and the women took the elevator to their respective floors. Nic spent the rest of the day trying not to think about Nora or her strange behavior. She focused on her work, and although the rehearsal went an hour over, they were ready for the live broadcast on Monday.

When they finished, Nic found her purse, left the studio, and went to see Nora in her office. "Are you going home?" Nic thought Nora stiffened when she heard her voice. "Sorry, I didn't mean to startle you."

"You didn't. I have to stay and finish this. I might be another hour or so. Are you done for the day?"

"Yes. Well." Nic did not want another conversation about the weather, but had no idea what else to say. "Have a good weekend, Nora."

*

There were few people on the beach when Nora arrived. She couldn't bring herself to go home after work, and sitting in a restaurant filled with people celebrating Friday and the coming weekend, a long lonely weekend, was equally depressing. She found a quiet place on the sand and enjoyed the clear, star-filled sky.

When Anna discovered the will after Carolyn died, Nora believed she could carry on the work. Spurred by her anger, shock, and loneliness, she felt a determination that she hoped would carry her beyond her own insecurities. The determination was waning, and she was not sure how to stop it, or how to recover her momentum.

With a sigh, she fell back on the sand and put her hands behind her head. She made a feeble attempt to count stars, then to count only a section of stars. Failing that, she counted the stars in the Big Dipper. Maybe believing she could continue the work for Carolyn was as foolish as trying to count stars. Surprised to feel tears stream down her face, Nora dug her handkerchief from her purse and stood. After wiping her face and brushing the sand from her clothes, she reluctantly went home.

Inside the apartment, Nora's mood did not improve. She curled on the sofa and felt the tears return. "So what," she said to the empty room. "You're lonely. Get over it." She banished thoughts she could not allow to slip through and cried herself to a restless sleep.

*

By noon on Saturday, the apartment felt steamy enough to open a spa. Nic and Anna had gone to the A&P for groceries earlier and after putting things away, sat in the living room, exhausted by the oppressive heat. "How's Nora?" Anna asked casually.

Nic stared through the front window. "She was quiet again yesterday. I saw her come down from her office once, but she didn't talk. She dropped off papers and left. I thought she looked tired and maybe a little sad. We were right in the middle of rehearsal and I couldn't stop to talk. When we finished, I went to her office and she said she had to work late. I haven't seen her this way since we first met, Aunt Anna."

Nic looked through the bay window at two girls jumping rope. That was how her brain felt, as if it were jumping rope. Thoughts spun around inside and she kept jumping to avoid them. Nic hated feeling so confused, and thought it might be time to face whatever it was she seemed determined to avoid. "Aunt Anna, when you said I was being thick about something, did you mean feelings?"

"Yes, dear."

"Mine or other peoples?"

"Maybe a little of both, Nicole, but don't be too hard on yourself. Understanding an emotion is more difficult than learning a new job, or how to drive a car. Is there something on your mind?"

"Yes, but I'm not completely sure what." Nic stood and picked up her purse. "I'm going for a walk, and that walk might take me to see Nora."

"Good for you, Nicole. Give her my love."

Nora answered the phone in the foyer on the second ring. "Yes, send her up." She opened the front door and waited for the elevator and its passenger to arrive.

"At least you stay in air-conditioning all day, Eddie." The conversation Nic was having spilled into the hallway before she stepped from the car. She waved at Nora.

"This is a nice surprise. Were you and Eddie involved in a deep, philosophical conversation?"

"When you know me better, you'll know that I don't have many philosophical conversations. Eddie was taking a package up to one of your neighbors when I arrived. I rode with him. The discussion started by my saying 'is it hot enough for you.' I'm glad it's a nice surprise, Nora, since I showed up unannounced." Nic stood in the hall and waited for a few seconds. "Are you going to ask me in or should I see if I can catch Eddie on his way down?"

"Oh. I'm sorry, come in. You see why I don't entertain. Do you want a drink or something to eat? Forget that, there isn't anything to eat. I do have wine. Would you like a glass of wine?"

"Wine would be good." She followed Nora to the bar and watched her pour two glasses of a deep red liquid. Nic threw her purse on a stuffed chair and sat on the arm quietly until Nora handed her a glass. She held it in a toast. "Thanks, Nora. So, what's going on in your life?"

"Nothing." Nora tilted her head. "Is that why you came by, to find out what's going on in my life?" Nora stopped. "I'll bet you walked here didn't you? In this heat. You and Anna do still have a telephone, don't you?"

Nic sipped her wine and gazed around the large apartment. "Now who's asking questions without taking a breath?" She watched Nora, hoping to find the right words. The words she found were not profound. "It's nice and cool in here."

"Yes the apartment is cool, I'm fine, and there is nothing new in my life." Nora spoke sharply and looked immediately apologetic. "Nic, I'm sorry. I haven't been feeling that great lately."

"You looked sad at work. It worried me. What's going on?"

If asked, Nora would have said she was an expert at hiding her feelings. Nic's observation surprised her. "It's nothing. I'm, I don't know. It's nothing."

"Are you worried about the foundation?"

Nora shrugged. "That's part of it, I guess. I don't want to talk about that right now."

"Sure. That's not what I came to talk to you about anyway."

"What did you come to talk about?"

Nic nodded at the windows at the end of the hall. "Let's go look at the lake."

They settled on the small couch and Nora removed an earring. She waited quietly for Nic to speak. When she didn't, Nora's curiosity won out. "So, what did you want to talk about?" She turned, dropping the earring and nearly the wine glass when Nic kissed her gently on the mouth and leaned back smiling.

"Nic, do you know what you're doing?"

"No, I don't. Am I that bad?"

"Bad? No, that's not what I meant. You're not…I mean…is this my fault?"

"Fault?"

"No. That was dumb. I'm sorry."

Nic looked at the dark eyes that she had first seen months ago, filled with anger and sadness. "Are you repulsed?"

"Oh god, no, Nic. No." Nora shook her head rapidly.

"The way you've been behaving toward me lately I thought maybe you were mad at me, but on the way here, I had another idea. I wondered if maybe you liked me more than you let on. As Aunt Anna pointed out, I'm not good at understanding emotions, but I'm gambling on it being that you like me. Do you?"

Nora looked at her wine and inhaled deeply. "Yes, I do like you. More than I ever intended. What about you? You never said anything. All these months I've known you, you never hinted you were a lesbian, and you knew about me."

"I didn't know for most of the months in question. In fact, not for sure until about a half hour ago. You do remember how naïve I was when I found out about you and Carolyn?" The memory prompted a smile on both faces. "I started thinking about my own life. Why I was twenty-seven and not interested in marriage or the usual things women my age are supposed to want. I dated a few guys in high school, and a few guys at the USO, but never felt connected to that life. I never felt an attraction for a man as strong as the desire I feel for you. I didn't take the thoughts further. There was no reason to. Then I realized how often I found myself thinking about you, or I'd find myself looking at you and hoping you didn't notice. I thought I saw you looking at me, too."

"You…yes." Nora lowered her head and brought it up with a sigh. "I mean, I did."

"At first I didn't know what to think, I wasn't sure what I wanted, and how could I know what you wanted. You weren't talking. All I knew was that you and Carolyn were together for a long time." Nic took a sip of wine. "Then, when I realized how much I liked you looking at me, you started acting strange and distant. I didn't know what to think. What was that about?"

Nora took a breath and allowed every thought she had forbidden over the last few weeks to enter. "When I realized I had feelings for you I thought, well, that you'd be offended and I'd lose you and Anna as friends. I couldn't imagine that." Her eyes didn't move from the emerald pair in front of her.

"What about Anna? What will she think?"

"What Aunt Anna thinks is that I'm not always quick. She's been dropping hints about how I felt for a while, but I wasn't listening to her or my heart. She also seemed to know that you liked me. Aunt Anna cares about you, Nora, and me, but what she cares about most is that we're happy." Nic looked out at the lake.

"Nic, I'm eight years older than you."

"Uh huh."

"What about your friends? Some will drop you like a hot potato. What about Millie?"

"Some will, but they wouldn't be worth having as friends." She leaned closer to Nora and ran a finger over her smooth cheek. "Millie loves me, and you. I only have one concern." Nora didn't move. "Is there room in your heart for both Carolyn and me? I know I'll never replace her, but you have to be sure you want to let me in."

"Yes," she said without hesitation, and watched Nic through moist eyes. "I'm sure there's room. There's a great deal of room."

Nora stood to retrieve a tissue, and returned with more arguments. "What about the radio station?"

"What about it? Do you think Frank will fire me if I'm involved with you?"

"What about Marcy?"

That brought a chuckle from Nic. "It's funny. When I talked to her, I implied I was a lesbian. I might not have to tell Marcy anything."

"I'm running out of arguments."

"Thank god." Nic put her glass down and her arms around Nora. "Should we try again? If I don't know what I'm doing, maybe you can help."

"Yes. I can do that."

Coming soon...the next Nic and Nora Mystery

Puzzled by the Clues

The second story in the Nic and Nora Mystery series, *Puzzled by the Clues*, follows not only the blossoming relationship between Nic and Nora, but also that of Anna and Allen. Of course, their lives would not be complete, or nearly as much fun, without a mystery to solve.

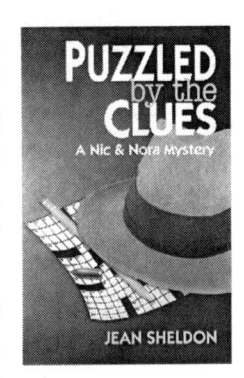

When an old friend of Anna's is found dead, supposedly by his own hand, the women suspect foul play and begin a case that involves everyone from local hoods to city and state officials. The investigation takes a few of our heroines undercover where they discover that efforts to create a superior race did not end in a bunker in Berlin with Hitler's suicide.

Other Books by Jean Sheldon

An Uncluttered Palette

"If your palette is cluttered, your painting will reflect that clutter." Rayna Hunt introduces her students to the world of oil painting with these words, but they apply to more than her art. After an accident destroyed her hand and she began the long journey to recover her skill, she avoided clutter in her paintings and her life. Her quiet, safe world is disrupted when an anonymous call to the police draws her into a case of forgery and art theft. Her students, a diverse group of ages and personalities, take more than a casual interest in the investigation. They, along with museum director and previous romantic interest, Paul Lingstrum, and a Chicago police detective recovering from her own loss, work to prove Rayna's innocence and solve the crime.

Flowers for Her Grave
Snuggle up in your favorite chair with an old fashioned 'whodunit'. An article appearing in the Raccoon Grove Gazette about a 20-year-old unsolved murder and kidnapping, rekindles interest in the tragedy. Growing curiosity makes someone in town nervous, and when local gossip columnist, Tracy Kendall, and gardener, Kate Chandler, team up to solve the decades old case, accidents threaten to stop the investigation. Their narrow escape from a blazing building, car windows shattered by a wayward bullet, and confrontations with unhappy neighbors prompt the women to hold a garden party to discover what really happened. No one could have guessed the truth. Can you?

The Woman in the Wing
A historical mystery that takes place in a defense plant. This well-researched book offers a glimpse into the lives of women who served at home during World War II, and sheds some light on the seldom told stories of the women who ferried military planes from plants to air bases around the country.

More information at:
www.jeansheldon.com